Whistl

MW00533449

Whistling Pines book 4

Dean L. Hovey

Print ISBNs
Amazon Print 9780228613169
LSI Print 9780228613176
B&N Print 9780228613183

BWL Publishing Inc.

Books we love to write ...
Authors around the world.
http://bwlpublishing.ca

Dedication

To Brian Johnson, tuba player extraordinaire

Acknowledgements

As with all books, there are a bevy of people who help me through the process. Julie puts up with my endless hours on the computer, proofs the very first draft of each book, corrects the medical details and terminology, and makes sure I'm humble. Mike Westfall asked the quintessential question: "What are in all those wedding gifts you mention at the end of Whistling Wings?" beginning the consideration of this book. Brian Johnson is my reference person for all things related to Two Harbors, bands, the band shell, tuba playing, tuba jokes, and is my muse when I find that the characters have led me down a blind alley. Brian suggested the time capsule idea when the actual Two Harbors band shell demolition was being considered. Frannie Brozo critiques, eggs me on, offers support, and throws even more chaos into my twisted plot ideas and crazy characters. Fran grew up in an old haunted farmhouse and had many ghostly suggestions. Natalie Lund and Annie Flagge proofread this manuscript and provided invaluable suggestions and corrections. Dan Fouts helped with a veteran's perspective of life after the Navy and PTSD.

Thanks to Jude Pittman of BWL for your support.

Chapter 1

The departure from our wedding reception was a blur. Jenny and I thanked our guests, danced to "If You Said I Had A Beautiful Body," then slipped out the back door of the church while the reception wound down. Despite having my car keys in my pocket the entire day, someone had moved my Toyota to the front of the church, painted "Just Married" on the windows and tied cans to the rear bumper.

I'd told everyone, including my mother, Jenny, and her parents, we were planning to spend the night in Duluth, south of Two Harbors. Being under the influence of pain killers to deaden the pain of broken ribs (due to a painful incident on the eve of the wedding involving a bull moose, a broom, and my elderly neighbor), I handed Jenny the keys. At the highway I told her to turn north.

"We're not going to Duluth?" Jenny asked.

"I'm sure some smart person will try to call our Duluth hotel room at 2 A.M. We're going to Lutsen."

Jenny, the Whistling Pines director of nursing, reached across and put her hand on my leg. "I didn't expect the Whistling Pines recreation director to be so sneaky."

The Lutsen parking lots were nearly filled with early-season skiers there for the pre-Christmas cold weather that provided enough man-made snow for the opening of a few ski runs. We pulled under the portico and let a bellman take our bags out of the trunk. Seeing the wedding greetings marked on out car, he grinned and congratulated us. We checked into a suite in a new condo complex, carefully avoiding the wedding suite just in case someone started looking for us beyond Duluth. Due to the lingering pain from my moose incident, I let the valet park my car and a bellman carried our bags to the room. The view of Lake Superior was probably stupendous, but it was hard to discern in the starlight. We ordered dinner from room service, ate a little of it, then climbed into the giant hot tub in the corner of the room.

"Can we stay here forever?" Jenny asked, her head resting on my shoulder while gazing out the window at the dark expanse of Lake Superior.

"Probably not. Your parents expect us to be at their house to open presents at noon. More importantly, there's an eight-year-old who'll probably be sitting by the window, waiting for us."

"I suppose," Jenny said with a sigh.

After an addition of more hot water and another half hour we got out. Jenny quickly wrapped herself in a towel as if I'd never seen her naked. She rummaged through her suitcase, pulled out a plastic shopping bag and dashed into the bathroom. I climbed into bed.

The next thing I knew, the sun was shining in my eyes and my left arm was numb. Jenny's head was in the crook of my elbow, my broken ribs hurt with each breath, and my bruised face ached. As my head cleared, I realized that I'd committed one of the most heinous wedding crimes—I'd fallen asleep on my wedding night while my new wife was changing into something sexy in the bathroom. I closed my eyes, tipped my head back and felt like an idiot.

"You're awake," Jenny said, sleepily.

I kissed the top of her head. "I'm sorry."

"You're forgiven."

"But our wedding night . . ."

Jenny pushed herself up, revealing a diaphanous nightgown that left nothing to my imagination. My eyes drifted to the soft curves of her body. When our eyes met, she was smiling.

"I take it you approve of my nightie."

"I'd approve if you'd worn flannel."

"Don't worry, I'll be back in flannel as soon as we're in our drafty bedroom." She reached up and ran her hand over the unbruised side of my face. "I had low expectations about your ability to perform your husbandly duties last night. Between your broken ribs and the pain pills, I'm surprised you didn't drown in the hot tub."

"I feel like . . ."

She put her fingers to my lips. "Remember, the ER doctor told us to skip the post-wedding gymnastics. We're going to get out of bed, take showers, eat breakfast and drive back home. Our parents are waiting for us to open wedding presents."

I reached for her, but she deftly slipped away and ran to the bathroom. I heard the bathroom door lock, a definite sign there wasn't going to be a shared shower that might lead to something amorous.

Chapter 2

Since I'd taken a Percocet with breakfast, Jenny drove back to Two Harbors with snowflakes swirling in the air. We wove through town on the way to her parent's house.

I noticed one of the neighbors was hanging Christmas lights on the pine tree in his yard. "Wow, with all the wedding stuff going on I'd forgotten Christmas is only a week away."

We pulled into my new in-laws' driveway. Decorative icicle lights twinkled from the eaves and a garland was draped from the porch railing. A wreath encircled the brass door knocker. Barbara, Jenny's mother, met us at the door with a hug that involved briefly touching our shoulders and cheeks while making a kissing sound.

Jenny's son, Jeremy, stood back, waiting for us to enter. I'd hired a lawyer to formally adopt Jeremy and we were awaiting finalization of the process. Despite the promise of having a *real dad,* Jeremy was skeptical, and I sensed he was afraid of losing his mom instead of gaining a dad.

I kicked off my shoes and knelt down in front of him. "How was the night with Grandma and Grandpa?"

"Okay."

"Were you the last people to leave the wedding reception?"

"Yeah."

"Did they make you carry presents?"

"Yeah."

"Can you answer with more than one word?"

He took a deep breath and thought. "I guess so."

I smiled. "You know I married more than your mom yesterday."

Jeremy shook his head.

I pulled him into a hug and felt the tension in his body. "I married a family, including you."

Jeremy didn't relax.

"I'd like it if you called me dad."

"Instead of calling you Peter?"

"Yeah," I whispered. "Peter is what everyone else calls me. You're the only one who can call me dad."

I felt him relax and I released my hug.

"The kids say I'm the only one in my class who doesn't have a dad."

"Tell them you have a dad who loves you very much. Okay?"

Jeremy nodded, then dashed to Jenny. He hugged her waist and whispered something I couldn't hear.

She looked at me, then tilted her head down and whispered something back.

I was still kneeling, at Jeremy's eye level, when he turned and stared at me. He held on to Jenny's waist but nodded to me.

Barbara watched the exchange, unsure of what had transpired. Jenny's father, Howard, put his hand on Jeremy's head and mussed his hair. "Give me a hand in the kitchen, Bud."

The wedding presents were neatly stacked in front of the fireplace. I stood at the living room threshold unable to bring myself to step on the snow-white carpeting that appeared to have been carefully fluffed for the occasion. I'd never set foot in the room before. I was pretty sure that no one, with the exception of the carpet layers, had ever stepped on the carpeting. I knew that wasn't true. The presents were sitting on the hearthstone, so someone must've walked on the carpeting.

I was silently theorizing that the presents might have been placed there by a drone or remote-control helicopter.

Barbara scared me half to death by whispering in my ear, "It's okay to step on the carpet...today."

Her eyes sparkled and the slightest hint of a smile curled the corners of her mouth. It was the closest she'd ever come to a smile that would've creased her carefully applied makeup.

I nodded and took a tentative step forward in my stocking feet. The carpet was plush and felt like I was stepping into shallow mud. I looked back and saw that my feet had indeed left footprints in the carefully fluffed pile. I had no idea how Barbara had managed to raise the pile so uniformly after placing the presents on the hearth without the tracks of a vacuum cleaner or other tool.

"You and Jenny should sit on the couch," Howard said, motioning us towards a sofa as white as the carpeting and apparently woven from silk. I made an involuntary glance at my khaki slacks, hoping I hadn't spilled bacon grease, eggs, or even crumbs on them while eating breakfast at the hotel before our departure.

Jeremy raced into the living room, fell to his knees, and skidded to a stop just before hitting the pile of presents. It was a move equal to those performed by stunt drivers. With hands extended he considered which package to deliver to us first. He selected a large box, picked it up, and immediately tripped. Barbara's eyes went wide, and her hand flew to her mouth as she watched the present flying through the air. It landed on the carpeting with a thud, rolled a quarter turn before landing at Jenny's feet.

"It'll be okay," said Howard, patting Barbara's knee gently. He looked sternly at Jenny's son. "Jeremy, getting the presents to them undamaged is more important than delivering them fast."

Jeremy, not particularly distressed by the flying present, listened to Howard, thought for a second, then nodded agreement.

"We are expecting your mother?" Barbara made it a question as much as a comment.

"As far as I know, she's planning to be here. She's not always punctual."

"Did you read the newspaper this morning?" Howard asked, trying to defuse Barbara's rising frustration with my mother's delayed arrival.

"I didn't have time. Did we miss something big?"

"The workers tearing down the old band shell in Owens Park found a time capsule. It was on the news last night and both the Duluth and Minneapolis newspapers picked up on the story."

Jenny picked up the present at her feet. "What did it contain?"

"They're going to open it tonight. The local stations are going to cover the ceremony live on their five o'clock broadcasts. It seems that no one remembers a time capsule being put into the foundation, so it was a surprise when it fell out when the workmen knocked down a chunk of wall."

Jeremy considered the pile of presents, trying to decide which to deliver next. "I told them it probably contained gold. But Grandpa said the bandshell was built during the depression and there wasn't any gold around."

Howard nodded. "The historical society chair, the mayor, the band shell fundraising committee chair, and the chamber of commerce chair are all going to be there for the opening. I talked with Molly Schroeder from the historical society, and she's speculating the capsule contains the names of the workers who built the structure."

The doorbell rang and Barbara sprang to her feet. The door opened. The clanging of bangles preceded my mother's voice. "How nice to see you Barbara!"

Mother didn't wipe or remove her shoes before walking across the carpet and taking a seat in a white chair next to the fireplace. "I see I didn't miss any of the presents."

Jenny opened the first present, a cut glass serving bowl from her aunt and uncle. It was carefully packed and hadn't been damaged in the tumble across the floor. Barbara picked up a notebook with a white silk cover and carefully noted who'd given the present, wrote a description, and looked up, apparently surprised to see us all staring at her.

"What? You'll have to write thank you notes and this way you'll have a record of who gave you which present." She paused, apparently thinking we were unappreciative of her effort. "You might lose the tags in the hubbub." She glanced at Jeremy who was removing the bowl from Jenny's lap and throwing the card, wrapping paper, and box aside. We now understood.

Jenny tapped Jeremy on the shoulder. "Put it gently back into the box with the card."

Jeremy rolled his eyes but did as requested.

Jenny opened the gifts as Jeremy delivered them, alternately oohing and aahing over some expensive and beautiful items, then stifling laughs as we opened gifts from the senior citizens residing at the Whistling Pines care center. Among the more interesting gifts were the hand-crocheted beer can cozies...at least that's the description Barbara wrote in the book although that wasn't the consensus of their function.

Jenny opened a large, heavy box and pulled out crumpled newspaper. "We got stoneware from Alice Krauss." Jenny took out five cups and set them on the hearth. "It appears to be a place setting for five. Wait, there are eight dinner plates, six bowls, seven saucers, and four salad plates."

Barbara poised her pen over the book. "So, an incomplete set of used stoneware. Do the pieces all match?"

Jenny laughed as she replaced the pieces in the box. "Yes, mom, the pieces all match."

Howard was grinning like he knew something that had escaped the rest of us. "Audrey and Barbara, don't you recognize the pattern?"

Barbara shook her head, but Audrey studied them, then threw up her hands. "Why would I recognize that?"

"Jenny, flip over a plate and read the bottom."

Jenny picked up a plate, read the bottom, then cocked her head. "Thanks for patronizing your local Citgo gas station?"

Mom started laughing. "Of course! When we were children the gas stations used to give away a piece every time you filled up with gas."

Barbara made her note of the gift and associated name. "An incomplete set of second-hand stoneware from a gas station."

My mother looked at me. "I assume that's from one of the old people where you work."

I nodded. "We call them residents, Mother."

Jeremy gave Jenny a flat box. Jenny opened the attached envelope. "It's from the Whistling Pines Ladies Club." She opened the box, lifted the tissue paper, and grimaced.

Barbara had her pen poised. "What is it, Jenny?"

"I'm not sure." Jenny lifted the corner of a piece of white fabric. Handprints and signatures emerged as more and more fabric came out. Jenny had to stand to extend it.

I picked up a note that fluttered to the floor. "We don't want you to spend a night without thinking of us."

Jenny took a deep breath. "It's a bedsheet with a handprint and signature of every ladies club member."

Howard was covering his smile with his hand. "Isn't that special."

Barbara glared at him. "I'll call it a sheet with... I can't even come up with an adjective."

Mother shook her head. "Tacky comes to mind."

The discussion went over Jeremy's head and he delivered a flat box as Jenny folded the sheet and put it back into the just opened package.

I peeled off the card as Jenny opened the box. "This is from Janet Shallbetter."

Jenny lifted the lid and looked at me, shaking her head. She lifted out a "paint by numbers" landscape I recognized from one of our art classes, carefully mounted in a chipped wooden frame.

Barbara drew a breath and held her pen over the book. "I don't need to write that one down. She signed it."

Jenny put the painting aside and picked up a smaller, white chipboard box. "This is from Herbert Walker, one of our other residents."

She lifted the lid and pulled back white tissue paper, then stopped, looked at me, then gently lifted out a cut glass vase. She turned it over to read a tiny label on the bottom, then looked at me again. "It's Waterford crystal."

Mother huffed. "Well at least one of your *residents* has good taste."

Jenny set the chipboard box aside and Jeremy handed her a present as large as the box of stoneware. "The card says this is from Cashmans."

She tore open the wrapping paper, exposing a cardboard box that had originally contained a punchbowl. She frowned, then pulled off the tape. She reached into the box and lifted out a pressed-glass cup.

Howard smiled. "It appears to be as advertised. I'll expect punch at our next family celebration."

Mother shook her head as Jenny pulled out more cups, leaving them in their newspaper wrapping. "I haven't seen anyone use a punchbowl since the '60s."

Jenny reached deeper into the box and pulled out an envelope. "There's another card inside." She unsealed the envelope, read the card, and started laughing.

She handed me the card. "It says, 'Happy 25th anniversary Rona and Charlie."

Barbara frowned. "Rona and Charlie Cashman regifted their punchbowl?"

Jenny composed herself and wiped her eyes. Still smiling she said, "The gift is from Paul and Annette Cashman. I have no idea who Rona and Charlie are."

Howard threw his head back and laughed.

Mother looked angry. "I suppose it's something Cashmans bought at a thrift shop."

Jenny repacked the punch cups, shaking her head. "It doesn't matter. I'm sure they knew cut-glass punchbowls were in vogue when they were young and thought we should have one."

Barbara diligently made notes in the book. "It's not like you'll get two of them."

The next box was smaller. "This is from Jennette Van Allen." Jenny unwrapped it and cut the tape. She pulled out a blue velvet pouch and something metallic clunked inside it.

"My word," Mother said. "That's a Tiffany's bag."

Jenny loosened the drawstring and pulled out a black gravy ladle. She set it on the hearth and pulled the bag off a tooled, albeit tarnished, gravy boat.

She shook her head. "Peter, have you ever used silver polish?"

Mother's mouth was agape. "It's sterling silver."

I put up my hand. "I've never polished silver and I don't plan to start now."

Jenny flipped it over and read the bottom. "You're right, Audrey, it's from Tiffany and Company. It's sterling."

Barbara made her notes. "That's lovely, but as useless as the punchbowl."

Jenny packed the gravy boat away and opened the next card. "This is from Brian Johnson." She frowned and looked to her mother, who shrugged.

I put up a finger. "Um, that would be the tuba player."

Jenny hefted the package, which was the size of a shoebox. "It's light. Do you think it's something with a band theme?"

19

"Who knows. Brian never ceases to amaze me."

Jenny unwrapped the package and lifted the box lid. She stared for a second, as if she was hesitant to put her hand into the box. She twisted the box around a couple times as our curiosity mounted.

Barbara couldn't stand the suspense. "What is it, Jenny?"

"I'm not sure."

Jenny finally found the orientation she wanted and gingerly slipped her fingers into the box. She lifted the item halfway out, then tilted it and brought it out completely. We stared at it in stunned silence.

Howard finally had an opinion. "I think it's a fish made from two cow horns."

Mother frowned and leaned away while Jenny twisted the "sculpture" around.

Jenny got it oriented and set it on the hearthstone. "Yup. It's a fish. See how the tip of one horn turns up and there are eyes and a mouth cut into it like it's rising up to eat something. Then the artist, and I use that term loosely, cut lower fins from another horn and attached them so they are legs supporting it. Then he made the dorsal and tail fins."

Jeremy stopped his present delivery and studied the sculpture, his tongue sticking out of the corner of his mouth. "That's supposed to be a fish?"

Barbara was shaking her head. "I think we should take a break and have a cup of coffee." She set the book aside and got up.

Howard looked at me. "After that, I need something stronger. How about you, Peter?"

I got up and followed Howard to the bar in the dining room while Jeremy went into the kitchen with the women. Howard took out two lowball glasses and poured an inch of Scotch into each of them.

He swirled the liquor in his glass while staring at the sculpture. "It may take more than one of these before I see the cow horns as a fish." He took a sip of whiskey and continued to stare at the fish.

"I suspect Brian searched a long time for that gift."

Howard drained his Scotch, poured another, then topped off mine. "I have friends like that." He touched his glass to mine, then leaned close, making sure no one could hear him. "They're very special people. Barbara sometimes cringes at the things they say or do, but I know that any one of them would give me the shirt off his back if he thought I needed it, and I'd do the same for them."

We continued to stare at the fish and talk about old friends. Howard, who I'd never seen consume more than one drink, was pouring his third, and topping off mine. He was feeling the alcohol, but both of us were relieved the wedding was behind us.

Howard waved me into the living room. "We're going to ignore the rule barring food and drink from the white room." We sat in adjoining chairs, staring at the sculpture.

Howard twisted his head and frowned, tilting his glass toward the fish. "You know, the top of the fish is open. I think it's meant to be a candy dish."

I started to laugh and couldn't stop. It was contagious, and Howard was laughing alongside me, trying not to spill his Scotch and wiping tears from his eyes.

Barbara and Jenny peeked around the doorframe. Barbara saw the glasses of Scotch and was about to comment when Jenny asked. "What's so funny?"

I wiped my eyes and caught my breath. "The fish is a candy dish!" That brought another round of laughter.

Jenny smiled, but Barbara marched past and snatched the drink from my hand. She was reaching for Howard's glass, but he anticipated the move and drained it, then handed the empty glass to her.

His eyes sparkled. "Ha! Beat you to it!"

Barbara shook her head. "You're in your cups."

When she turned away, he leaned close to me and whispered. "And I might have ideas about what might happen after everyone leaves."

"I heard that," Barbara said as she rounded the corner.

Howard wiggled his eyebrows and we started laughing again.

* * *

It was well past noon when we got through the gift pile. There were a number of beautiful, thoughtful gifts. Then there were others, like the set of unmatched coffee mugs, some leaning and two with handles too small to accommodate an adult finger, made in our pottery class by Jerry "Sarge" Sargent. When we were done, there was a mound of boxes and a box of cards with monetary gifts. Barbara closed the book and stood.

"I'll pull the ham out of the oven. Howard, will you pour wine?"

We walked to the dining room and Mother, who'd been mostly bored by the presents, started a monologue about her latest charity project. She took the chair at the head of the table, one usually occupied by Jenny's father, and continued her monologue about the difficulty of finding able and willing volunteers to do tasks as simple as folding flyers and stuffing them correctly into envelopes.

I sat next to Jenny. Jeremy pulled up a chair next to me. He studied my bruised face. "Did it hurt when you kissed mom?"

I was caught off guard by his question. "What do you mean?"

"At the end of the wedding the minister said you could kiss her. Did it hurt?"

I shook my head. "It didn't hurt at all."

He nodded as Barbara walked in with a platter of sliced ham surrounded by yams and garnished with whipped potatoes, piped onto the edges of the tray with a pastry bag. Barbara was ready to hand it to Howard, at the head of the table, when she realized Mother had usurped his position. Mother grabbed the platter and helped herself.

Jeremy looked at Howard. "Grandpa, I thought you were going to say a prayer before we ate."

Mother was undeterred. "Certainly. Howard, why don't you pray while we pass the platter."

Jenny took the platter and set in on the table. "We hold hands when we pray."

Mother wiped some of the potatoes off her hand onto a linen napkin and took Jenny and Barbara's hands. "This is just like they do at those Pentecostal churches, isn't it?"

Howard smiled politely, bowed his head, then asked for the Lord's blessing of the meal and the newlyweds.

Mother dove into her food and started a new monologue about the inspired young Democratic candidates who were going to set the City of Duluth, the county, the legislature, Congress, and the entire United State on a "proper" course, overcoming the middle-of-the-road mediocrity that had overtaken the party.

I looked at Howard, knowing he was biting his tongue and politely enduring the diatribe. When Mother paused to take a bite, I jumped in. "Howard, tell us more about the band shell demolition and the time capsule."

"It's a total mystery. No one knew the time capsule was there, so no one has any idea what it contains. Even the old-timers, who were children when the band shell went up, haven't a clue. The shell has been remodeled and repaired a few times over the years and there's some speculation that the metal box might've been slipped in during remodeling."

Jeremy had been quiet through all the discussion, and I'd assumed he was thinking about texting his friends, doing homework, or playing an electronic game. He blew me away when he looked at Mother. "Mrs. Rogers, since Peter is going to adopt me, should I call you grandma?"

Mother's eyes went wide, and she choked on a piece of ham. Howard and I jumped up, ready to do a Heimlich maneuver, but she waved us off.

She wiped her mouth, avoiding Jeremy's stare. Mother had told us she was too young to be a grandmother, and before the wedding she'd told Jenny to wait before giving her any grandchildren. She gave Jenny and me pleading looks. Jenny was going to comment, but I put my hand on her leg to stop her, instead letting the silence hang in the air. I knew Mother couldn't stand silence, but I also knew she didn't want to answer Jeremy because deep down I knew she didn't consider him her grandchild. Jeremy had been born long before I'd met Jenny. Jeremy's father was never a part of her life after the conception.

"Jeremy, I haven't given it much thought..."

Before she could go on, Jeremy jumped in. "I've been living with grandma and grandpa for my whole life and that's what I call them, but Peter's going to be my dad, so I guess that makes you my other grandma. Is that what I should call you?"

Mother's eyes darted to Barbara who was always soft-spoken and rarely offered a controversial comment. Barbara folded her napkin and took Mother's hand. "Most all of Jeremy's friends have two sets of grandparents. He'd like you to be his second grandma."

I got up and walked behind mother and leaned close to her ear. "Every decision you've made since Dad died has been about you or some vague charity. This is a chance for you to make a personal connection with a child who is asking you to be a part of his life. He's my son, Mom. Do the right thing."

She wiped her lips with the napkin while she framed her answer. I expected her to stand up and walk away, but she stayed seated. I wasn't sure if she was trying to decide how to say, no, or if she was choosing her words carefully.

"I'll make you a deal, Jeremy. If you let me hug you every time I see you, I'll let you call me grandma." Mom got up and walked around the table to Jeremy and she knelt down. "Do we have a deal?"

They were eye to eye and Jeremy stared at her for a second, then he put out his arms. "Deal."

Mom glanced at Jenny and me with tears in her eyes, tears I hadn't seen since my father's funeral. Barbara got up quickly, holding her napkin to her face, trying to keep her own tears from ruining her perfect makeup.

Howard reached out and squeezed Mother's hand. "I never thought I'd see the day I accepted a Democrat into the family."

Mother glanced up. "You're a Republican?"

Barbara had composed herself in the kitchen and walked in carrying a plate with a tier of the wedding cake. "I didn't see any point making dessert when there was enough leftover wedding cake to feed the whole neighborhood."

Howard got up and dug into the cupboard beside the dining room table. I thought he was getting plates, but he came back with champagne flutes. He set them on the counter, then popped the cork on a bottle of sparkling wine. Barbara looked unhappy but didn't say anything until he set a flute with a teaspoon of wine in front of Jeremy.

"Howard…"

He dismissed her and held up his glass. "To Jeremy getting a second grandma."

Jeremy glanced at Jenny, who nodded her okay. He lifted his glass like everyone else, then drank his sip of wine. He grimaced and swallowed. "Do you guys actually like this? It's sour."

Chapter 3

Mom prepared to leave immediately after lunch, giving everyone a hug. Jeremy's hug was extra long, and he was squirming by the time Mom let go. I walked with her to the car.

She punched the remote to unlock it, then stood with the door open, staring into the distance. "You had me over the barrel with Jeremy."

"You could've said no or walked away."

She turned her head and met my eyes. "Why are you adopting Jeremy?"

"He's my son. The adoption is just a formality."

"You didn't even know Jenny when she got pregnant. You're not that boy's father."

"I couldn't love him more if we shared blood."

"He's had a family with Barbara and Howard."

"He needs a father."

Mother looked at me. "Is that why you married Jenny, to give Jeremy a father?"

"Mom, I love Jenny and Jeremy. They're a package." I tried to come up with something else to say, but I knew she was stubborn and hadn't been interested in my opinion or issues since my father died.

"I'm not ready to be a grandmother."

"You spend thousands of dollars and endless hours organizing charity work, but you never touch the recipients. You want to look like you're a great contributor, but you don't want to actually contact the unwashed masses. Don't you think it's about time to get committed instead of being involved?"

"I don't think there's a difference."

"It's like a bacon and eggs breakfast. The chicken is involved. The pig is committed."

Mother opened her mouth, but nothing came out.

The front door opened behind me. Barbara wrapped herself in a sweater as she walked down the steps. We watched her in silence as she approached the car.

"Audrey, I sensed hesitation when you offered to be Jeremy's other grandma." Barbara paused, composing her thoughts. "I don't want to seem uncharitable, but if you're not going to take that role seriously, I'd rather not raise Jeremy's hopes and have him disappointed. We've tried to fill the hole in his life left when that pilot flew out of Jenny's life, but it hasn't been easy or complete. Peter has stepped up and…Jeremy's a different person. He's confident and energized. In short, he loves Peter and we see that Peter loves him.

Barbara looked at her shoes. "If you're going to let him down, I'd prefer that you just walk away now rather than dragging Jeremy, and us, through the disappointment." She walked into the house without looking back.

Mother's face turned red. "I'm not accustomed to being spoken to like that."

"That's because you swoop in, drop money and promises with your charities, then you swoop out. You don't know what people say behind your back when you're gone and all they've got is a check with no action to back it up."

"I've donated thousands of dollars to hundreds of charities!"

"This is your chance to help Jeremy become a responsible, loving adult. To do that, you're going to have to get your hands dirty."

"I will. He'll get wonderful presents every birthday and at Christmas."

"No, mother. You'll attend baseball games and school concerts. You'll volunteer at the school carnival and you'll show him, and me, that you care by your actions, not by your checkbook."

"I live in Duluth. I can't be buzzing up here for school events."

I leaned on the top of her car door. "Sitting in a lawn chair for a baseball game means more than whatever present you'll give him. He'll remember that you were there for him long after any toy is broken, outgrown, or discarded."

"This is about you, isn't it? You're telling me I let you down."

"You didn't show up at the school when my Eagle Scout badge was presented, much less participating in the mother/son camping trips, spaghetti dinners, or courts of honor. You didn't come to baseball or football games. You didn't know who my friends were. You sent me a card instead of attending my basic training graduation. You weren't at the airport when I flew home from Iraq."

"I was...busy."

"You weren't engaged. You stopped being a mother when Dad died."

Mom's eyes teared up and she dug in her purse for a tissue. She blew her nose, and glared at me, expecting an apology.

I reached out and held her hand. We'd hugged a thousand times, but we'd never held hands. "Mom, stop mailing in your proxy and show up."

"I'm very charitable."

I tried to think of something that would crack her veneer of self-righteousness.

"When I was deployed with the Marines there was a saying that some sergeants wore their stripes. They strutted around reminding people they were important. There were others who everyone knew were sergeants because they looked and acted with military bearing. They could walk into a room without their

32

uniforms and people would look at them and say, 'He's a sergeant.'"

"I don't understand what that has to do with me."

"Mom, you wear your stripes. You strut around bragging about your charity work and political connections. Maybe it's time to let your actions speak for you."

She stared at our hands while she digested my words. "My therapist asked if I was sublimating through my charity work. Maybe it's because I wasn't much of a mother."

"You've got a chance to make a little boy's life more complete, but you have to get engaged and it'll take a real effort. Jeremy's hurting, Mom, and he's willing to let you hug him. That's a big concession for him."

Mom looked up at the house. "He's staring out the window at us."

"Here's your opening. Get in the car, drive away, and don't look back. Or, come in the house. There's a card table set up in the basement with a half-completed jigsaw puzzle. The whole family has been working on it since before the wedding."

Mother looked at her watch. "What time is it?"

I put my hand on top of the watch. "Mom, it's time to make a real difference."

She dropped her keys in her purse and closed the car door. We walked to the house holding hands and Jeremy met us at the door.

Mom handed me her purse. "Jeremy, I heard there's a jigsaw puzzle in the basement. I can't remember the last time I worked a puzzle."

"It's really hard, grandma" Jeremy said as Mother took off her coat. "It's all red licorice and the pieces look the same."

Mom handed me her coat, then reached down and took Jeremy's hand. "Why don't you show me."

Jeremy was chattering about school. His voice faded as they went downstairs.

Jenny came out of the kitchen with a towel in her hand. "I thought Audrey was leaving."

"She decided it was time to be a grandma."

Jenny cocked her head. "What does that mean?"

I told Jenny about our driveway discussion and Mother's decision to come back inside.

"Do you think she'll really engage with Jeremy?"

"I don't know how long her attention span is, but she listened to me for the first time in many years. I think her heart melted when she saw Jeremy watching us from the living room."

Jenny and I walked to the top of the basement stairs and listened to the conversation. "It's like the Grinch changed at Christmas."

Howard was reading the Sunday newspaper in his recliner, half listening to us. He folded the section he'd been reading and set it next to the chair, then waggled his finger at us.

"Barbara and I were thrown into being grandparents and grew into the role over the years. It's going to take Audrey time to find her footing. Give her a chance and a little guidance."

Jenny sat on his lap, nearly tipping the recliner. "You're so wise."

Chapter 4

Mom and Jeremy worked on the jigsaw puzzle for an hour. They wandered up when Jeremy was reminded to do his homework. She looked a little shell-shocked.

Mom sat in an overstuffed chair. "He has so much energy."

I looked up from a crossword puzzle. "Yes, and it seems endless."

Jenny and Jeremy were discussing a book report Jeremy was typing into a laptop computer in the dining room. Mother looked at me. "Does he have homework every weekend?"

Howard smiled. "Audrey, he has homework every night."

"And he needs help every night?"

I shook my head. "Mostly, he just needs a reminder. He's easily distracted from it."

Jenny came in from the dining room and sat on the arm of my chair. "It's our usual report negotiation. He needs a two-page report and we had to discuss font size, double-spacing, and narrow margins versus content."

Mother shook her head. "How do you keep up with him?"

"We tag-team the effort. I hand off to Peter or my parents when I wear out or lose my patience."

Mom looked concerned. "How do single parents deal with it?"

Jenny shook her head. "I don't know. It's draining and, if you're sick or overwhelmed it's easy to give up."

"I've been donating to a shelter for women and families in conflict. I hope they provide backup for the mothers."

I looked at Mother. "Have you ever considered volunteering to read for the children or to give the mothers a break?"

Mother looked uncomfortable. "No. I think they hire people to do that."

Jenny got up to check on Jeremy. "There's a place like that in Two Harbors and they're always looking for volunteers to help. They need people who can do anything from changing diapers and cooking, to reading for children and helping with homework."

Barbara walked out of the kitchen. "I go to the library on Tuesdays and help with the children's reading hour."

Mother nodded. "That's very thoughtful. I donate to the library."

Barbara, who can smile without wrinkling her face, smiled. "We donate too, but they seem to appreciate my presence almost more than the cash contributions."

I could see Mother digesting that information when Jeremy yelled in the dining room, "I need someone to see if I have enough pages…I mean content."

Jenny stood up, but Mother struggled from her chair and held up her hand. "I'll look at it, Jenny."

Mother walked to the dining room with her bangles jangling. There was a muffled discussion, and I caught part of Jeremy's explanation of the book. We all sat quietly listening as Mother responded by telling Jeremy that she had never heard of the book he'd read. I expected her to gloss over her lack of understanding and pat him on the head. Instead, she offered constructive criticism.

"I think you need a little more meat in your plot explanation. You wrote about the characters, but I don't know the plot and you haven't told me enough to understand it."

I was surprised by Jeremy's response. "Mom's read it and she knows how it goes."

"You need to tell it in a way that explains it to someone who's never read it."

Jeremy sighed. "Okay, Grandma. Let me add a couple more sentences. But that'll be more than two pages."

Mother walked back into the living room looking apprehensive. "Did I do okay?" she whispered.

Jenny gave her a thumbs up gesture and a smile. "That was perfect. You were constructive in a way that gave him direction. And it was good for him to hear that from someone other than me."

Mother returned to her chair and looked at Barbara. "What else do you folks do in the community?"

I saw a look pass between Barbara and Howard. He cleared his throat. "We really aren't looking for accolades or recognition."

Mother nodded, although I could see she wasn't satisfied with his answer. I put three fingers on my upper sleeve to remind her about my sergeant comments, but it went over her head.

"But you are active in community things."

Howard stared at her for a second, then decided she wasn't going to let the topic pass. "I'm a member of the Kiwanis and we do fundraising for community projects. I'm also a deacon at our church. Barbara is a member of the library board."

Barbara smiled. "I still chuckle when I remember you coming home from the Kiwanis pancake breakfast spattered with grease. I threw away your shirt and pants."

"Howard was the cook?"

Barbara shook her head. "No, he cleaned the griddles. They had so much burned-on grease he used a wire brush attached to his drill, and it sprayed brown grease all over his face and clothes. He wore goggles so he looked like a raccoon."

Mother looked like she'd been gobsmacked. She'd been so busy trying to impress them with her check-writing philanthropy, it had never occurred to her that Barbara and Howard were financially and physically engaged in their community. More than that, Howard had literally gotten his hands dirty.

Jeremy's voice interrupted Mom's thoughts. "Okay, Grandma, see if this is better."

Barbara got up, immediately responding to Grandma. Mother put up her hand and got up from her chair. There was a pause as she read.

"This is much better, Jeremy. Now I know why the people were on the island and what they were struggling with."

Mother walked back, smiling and I heard the printer start up in the den. She looked at me. "Did you ever read *The Swiss Family Robinson*?"

"I suppose I did when I was Jeremy's age."

The grandfather clock chimed, and Howard reached for the television remote. "Let's watch the news and see what's in the time capsule."

The local news opened with a teaser about the time capsule, then they went into the international and national news, followed by the weather and sports. The last five minutes of the broadcast featured the train museum while the mayor, president of the historical society, band shell reconstruction committee, and chairman of the chamber of commerce stood in ranks behind a table with a rusty metal box resting on top of butcher paper. A brass quintet played in the background. I recognized all the musicians from my stint as the fill-in Two Harbors band director. The sight of Brian, the tuba player, brought a smile to my face. He'd been a pain in my butt, interrupting my days with silly tuba jokes, but he'd always made me smile. He'd shown up, unannounced, with a polka band at our wedding reception. Brian's band brought life to a quiet church-basement reception, bringing even my reserved in-laws to their feet, clapping and dancing.

Mayor Quincy Parker, dressed in a suit, stepped to the microphone. "This time capsule presents our community a great opportunity to link Two Harbors' history with its future. It was found unexpectedly, bringing another chance for us to remind the city that we're still raising funds to complete the reconstruction. I will personally challenge our residents..."

Molly Schroeder, president of the historical society, politely cleared her throat.

The mayor gave her an annoyed look, then realized the television cameras were broadcasting. He smiled. "Since there isn't a key, the president of the historical society is going to pry the lid open."

Molly was wearing an apron over her blouse and white work gloves. She placed a small crowbar under the lid and gently pried.

The metal groaned, but the lid gave way. She gently lifted the lid, then looked inside. She had a concerned look on her face when she looked at the mayor.

Parker looked in the box, then reached in and lifted out a rusty pistol. He set it on the butcher paper and reached in again, this time lifting out a newspaper and two other sheets of paper. He held out the yellowed newspaper to Molly. She put on her reading glasses and gently accepted it.

"It's a copy of *The Duluth News*. The date says August fourteenth, nineteen fifty-one. The headline is about a setback in Korea." She turned the paper over and read silently, then glanced at the television camera, which she seemed to have forgotten about. "There's another story, circled in pencil. That headline says, 'Two Harbors man found dead in his basement.'"

The mayor leaned forward with the other two sheets of paper. "And someone put two poems in the box."

Ken Hawthorne, a senile member of the band shell reconstruction committee, leaned forward. "What the hell. You mean all that's inside is a..."

Luckily, someone at the station had time-delayed the broadcast and had a finger on the censoring button. Hawthorne's voice was bleeped out, but it didn't take a lip reader to

42

discern the "F" adjective that was being repeatedly bleeped.

The camera cut away to a cute, blonde broadcaster, who might've graduated from high school a few months earlier. Her mouth was agape, the voice in her earbud had apparently been screaming at her to say something. The situation rattled her, and she dropped the microphone which rolled under the table supporting the time capsule. The camera followed her as she crawled after the mic, but the cameraman quickly cut away when he realized they were broadcasting a tear in her distressed jeans providing a glimpse of her bare behind and lacy red underwear.

The camera moved back to the city fathers, who were wrestling with Hawthorne, trying to squelch his profane tirade. The cameraman cut to the band, all laughing but looking more professional than anyone else within sight. Several seconds of dead air were interrupted by bleeps as the band shell fundraisers tried to shuffle Hawthorne and his profane tirade farther from the live microphone.

The young reporter thumped and scraped the mic a couple times as she crawled from under the table. Looking at the camera uncertainly, she lifted the microphone to her mouth and swept hair out of her face once she realized she was still on the air. She pressed the earbud, then struggled to find words, "Yes, we are all...surprised...by the...unexpected contents of the time capsule."

The station censor was torn between continued broadcast of the young announcer's comments and bleeping out the string of expletives being spouted by Hawthorne.

Band conductor, John Carr caught onto the situation and started waving his baton. The musicians slowly joined the trombone player in "The Agate March." Brian struggled to play his tuba while laughing.

The station cut away to a commercial.

Jenny, Mother, and I were laughing, and Barbara was holding a tissue over her mouth, looking more horrified than amused. She got up and peeked into the dining room to see how much of the broadcast Jeremy had seen or understood. Luckily, he'd been retrieving his paper from the printer in the office.

Howard, who was chuckling, clicked off the television. "Do you think any of your senior citizens will know anything about this?"

I shook my head. "Even if they don't know anything, I'm sure it'll be the only topic of discussion the rest of the week."

Jenny looked at me, wiping her eyes. "Please don't get dragged into this. We've got a move ahead of us and a house to fix up."

"How could I get mixed up in it? I wasn't even born when the time capsule was put in the band shell."

Barbara's eyes went wide, and she put her hand to her mouth. We looked at her as she shook her head. "I was a kid and I remember my

44

parents talking about Mr. Lundquist being found dead in his basement. It was a big deal, because no one knew anything about it and the police didn't have any clues."

Howard smiled. "I guess they've got a clue now."

Chapter 5

Whistling Pines

Bingle, the maintenance man, and Holly, the receptionist, were hanging a pine garland decorated with frosted pinecones and red bows around the reception desk. A moose head, rescued from a long defunct bar, supposedly to add the feel of a lodge to the entryway, had red balls hanging from his antlers. A large Christmas tree in the reception area was adorned with mismatched ornaments, one from each resident. I waved to Holly and walked down the hallway.

I hung my coat behind the door in my tiny office and checked my email, mostly wedding congratulatory notes, spam and ads. I walked to the dining room to get a cup of coffee and to take the pulse of the residence. It was still before breakfast, but there were a few people sipping coffee and chatting. I drew a cup of coffee from an urn and was going to join a group of men at the nearest table when Wendy waved at me from the back corner.

Wendy is the assistant director of the Whistling Pines Senior Residence. Her title hardly reflected her duties which included helping me set up programs, being my duet partner when we play music (she has a voice like an angel and a three octave vocal range), maintaining the staff computers, and pretty much anything else that needs coverage when someone needs a break or calls in sick. As near as I could tell, she has no written job description but takes it upon herself to fill in as she sees appropriate. One of her duties seems to be doing the *New York Times* crossword puzzle every morning. Another of her self-appointed duties was annoying me.

I was tempted to ignore her, but experience told me that not responding to her waves usually meant I'd be put in some embarrassing situation, she'd walk away, and I'd be left cleaning up whatever hubbub was created. I took a chair across from her.

She looked up while tapping her pencil on the crossword. "I'm stuck."

"Crepuscular," I said.

"I didn't even tell you the clue."

"See if crepuscular fits."

"Why would I do that without giving you the clue?"

I tapped the crossword puzzle. "Try it."

"Spell it for me."

She touched the squares as I spelled the word. "Does it fit?"

She frowned but wrote in the letters. She set down the pencil and stared at me. "Have you taken up mind reading?"

I stood up. "The clue is, 'Hunts at twilight.'"

She picked up her pencil and tapped the eraser on the puzzle. "Sometimes you're really irritating."

I sat at a table with Howard Johnson and Lee Westfall. Howard smiled and shook his head. "I assume you did that crossword and guessed she'd get stuck on that word."

I smiled and sipped my coffee.

Lee looked over his shoulder at Wendy, who was studying another clue. "You know she'll get even."

"Ah, but I'm one ahead for now."

Howard had a folded newspaper under his elbow. He opened it up and spread the front page of the second section before me. The headline was, "Time Capsule Mystery."

I nodded and turned it back to him. "We watched it live on the news last night."

"You know what's going to happen today, don't you?"

I nodded. "The rumor mill will be grinding away on that at full speed."

He glanced at a table with three women who were huddled close and whispering. "It's already started."

"Do you remember that murder?"

"I was in Korea. My wife sent a letter that mentioned it, but I wasn't around for any of the investigation or the rumors that must've been flying."

Lee pulled the paper over and read the opening paragraph. "I was in North English, Iowa, but we had an incident like this. A guy shot himself in his basement, then set the house on fire."

"That's a suicide, not a murder, Lee."

"The local coroner called it a suicide, but it's hard to see how it wasn't a murder because the guy was shot in the back of his head, the gun was leaning against a basement wall, and the guy had his shoes on. We talked a lot about how a person could only reach the trigger of a 30-30 with their toes and it'd be even harder to shoot yourself in the back of the head and lean the gun against the wall after the shot."

I thought about it for a second. "So, what was the answer?"

"They left it a suicide, but we assume the sheriff's ne'er-do-well cousin shot him over a gambling debt and paid off the coroner."

Howard frowned. "So, the cousin got away with it?"

Lee laughed. "Oh, hell no. He was digging a well the next week and it collapsed on him."

"That might be divine justice, but hardly legal justice," I said.

"You might think so, but the well collapsed when a tractor, driven by the dead man's brother, got too close to the well pit. It all got sorted out. Justice was served."

People started seating themselves at the tables so I got up and topped off my coffee before returning to my office. I smelled pipe tobacco smoke as I turned into my office. Len Rentz, the Two Harbors police chief, was sitting in my guest chair with his eyes closed, puffing on his pipe.

His eyes popped open when he heard me walk in.

"You know…"

He waved off my comment. "Yes, I know it's illegal to smoke inside. I wasn't smoking. I was pondering."

He reached for my wastebasket and I pulled it away. "The last time you dumped your pipe into my wastebasket the ashes set it on fire and my office smelled like burned paper and tobacco for a week."

Len chuckled. "Almost as long as the smell lingered on you after the unfortunate incident."

"Did you want something, or are you being uncharacteristically social?"

"I'm thinking the people here know more about the 1951 murder than nearly everyone else in town."

I swept my hand toward the door. "Why don't you ask them?"

"As soon as I start asking questions there'll be a different lead from everyone in the place. If *you* ask the questions, you can sort the cockamamie wild geese from the stories that might actually have merit."

"Len, I have a new wife, a new son, a new house, and a job. I can't help with your investigation."

Len edged the door shut with his toe and leaned close to me. "I talked to Nancy Helmbrecht last night and she said I could have whatever of your time I needed."

"Why would the Whistling Pines director say something like that?"

"Because she knows this will be the only topic of discussion here for at least the next week, and the sooner we solve this or determine that the killer is dead, the sooner things will get back to normal."

There was a dainty rap on my door and Len pulled it open. Dolores, my eccentric former neighbor, who'd given us her house as a wedding gift was standing at the door. She smiled when she saw Len in my chair.

"Well, this makes it easier. I'll only have to tell this story once." She looked at me earnestly and leaned on her cane. "The man who was killed was a Swedish plumber. He was blond, blue-eyed, very handsome and very busy. Somehow, he always found time to fix a leak for one of the stay-at-home moms or war widows.

There were many rumors about his philandering, but I happen to know some of the stories were true."

I was stunned. "You and the plumber…?"

Dolores sighed. "Oh, Peter. Of course not. I've stayed faithful to my husband to this day. The plumber got my friend, Patty, pregnant."

Len watched our exchange quietly, the unlit pipe jammed between his teeth. "Dolores, was that a rumor or a fact?"

Dolores looked around me and glared at Len. "I don't engage in rumormongering. Patty was a devout Catholic woman who raised that child with her six other children. The others all had dark hair and brown eyes. Richard was a blue-eyed blonde who was the ugly duckling. He endured all kinds of bullying by his siblings and schoolmates."

Len nodded and pointed the pipe stem at Dolores. "Ricky Mathis."

Dolores nodded, turned, and then paused. "I don't suppose you know this, Len, but as I recall, Lundquist's house burned down in the '80s. It was one of those meth houses. If there was any evidence there, it's gone now."

I closed the door as Dolores walked away and turned around as Len dumped his pipe into my wastebasket. I sat down and pulled the wastebasket out of his reach. "That was an interesting conversation."

Len pulled out a tobacco pouch and went through his pipe filling ritual while he thought.

"Let's assume Dolores is right. It's plausible that some jealous husband found out the plumber was engaging in an affair with his wife. Why wouldn't he drop the gun in Lake Superior? It'd never be found."

"I don't know, Len. Suppose he wanted it to be found at some later time for his own reasons. He shoots the plumber, then puts the murder weapon in a box with the newspaper article. How would he get it into the wall of the band shell?"

"I've always thought the band shell had been expanded and repaired a few times based on the changing texture of the walls. Maybe the killer was a carpenter who was working on the bandshell during one of the construction jobs."

"I suppose the newspaper would have an article about construction if that's when the band shell was remodeled. They might even list who was working on the project, or at least who the contractor was."

I expected Len to get up and pursue that inquiry. Instead, he leaned back and put the tobacco pouch away. "The killer was an adult in 1951, sixty years ago. Even if the killer was only twenty-one at the time of the murder, that means he's over eighty years old now, if he's still alive."

Len shook his head. "Jobs back then were hard work. Men were working in the mines, on the railroad, and on the ore boats. Lots of those guys died young or soon after they retired. My gut says whoever killed the plumber is dead."

"So, you're not going to pursue the case?"

Len stood up. "I've got an obligation to try and solve it, but I can't justify throwing my few resources into an investigation that leads to a dead end."

"What are you going to do?"

Len put the pipe between his teeth and took out a lighter. "You and I are going to stir this up and see if anything floats to the surface."

I stood up. "Len, I told you I'm up to my eyeballs here and at home. I don't have the time or energy to 'stir' this."

Len smiled. "I don't think you'll have to stir. All you'll have to do is listen. I suspect that your residents will be more than stirring. They'll whip this into a frenzy."

Len opened the door and I watched the pipe smoke start to trail him as he walked out the back door.

Len was right about the churning. Every time I started something there was a knock on my door and a resident had a story about Ole Lundquist. When I walked to the dining room for coffee I was accosted by half a dozen people who either had an opinion about the murder or were looking for inside information they thought I'd have through my contact with Len. By the end of the day my head was buzzing with two dozen different stories, rumors, and accusations, most of them obvious fabrications. Some were told so earnestly I thought they might be true. Others were so twisted it was hard to say if they were true, lies, or the product of a feeble mind.

There was a break in the line at my door when the dining room opened, so I grabbed my coat and snuck out the back door.

Chapter 6

I picked Jeremy up from school and drove home. "We're eating supper at the new house tonight. Is there something special you'd like?"

Jeremy looked at me and thought. "Is this like a celebration?"

"Sure, let's make this our new house celebration."

Jeremy cocked his head. "Let's have pizza."

I'd been thinking about steak, crab legs, lobster, or something exotic. Then I realized this was more than a new house for Jeremy, this was the beginning of a new life, away from his grandparents, and with me, his new father. The special dinner should be something of his choosing, not mine. "Sure. We can order pizza when we get home."

"No, let's make pizza like Mom and Grandma. We only have that when it's a special occasion."

I pulled into the grocery store and we grabbed a cart. Jeremy found big rounds of prebaked pizza crust. We found pizza sauce and shredded mozzarella cheese.

"What other toppings do you like on your pizza?"

Jeremy thought for a second. "Pepperoni and green olives are okay, but I don't want the green peppers and onions that Grandpa likes."

I found a jar of green olives and Jeremy raced to the meat department and came back with a package of sliced pepperoni. I was ready to check out when I thought about breakfast. My history with breakfast items was poor, running toward moldy bread and questionable milk, often well beyond its expiration and not passing the sniff test.

"What do you eat for breakfast when you're at Grandma's house?"

I got a smirk that hinted at an upcoming lie. "I really like frosted flakes."

"That's what you like, but what does Mom buy for you?"

The smirk disappeared. "Cheerios or corn flakes."

We cruised the cereal aisle buying Cheerios, corn flakes, and a couple varieties of "grown-up" cereals with fiber, fruit, and nuts. I found peanut butter, not that I was sure my peanut butter was moldy, but there was a chance Jenny would check the expiration and throw it away without further inspection. Jeremy picked out grape jelly. I bought bacon, eggs, sliced deli ham, and cheese. Jeremy chose a loaf of bread that was spongy and would probably never mold, even after decades buried in a landfill. I found a loaf of "sturdy" whole wheat bread, then we circled back to the produce aisle for apples and bananas.

I surveyed the cart that contained more food than I'd ever bought in one trip to the store. "Is there anything else we need?"

Jeremy looked at me with eyes that were near pleading. "Can we have cake? You said this was a special celebration."

We circled back to the bakery aisle and Jeremy picked out a six-pack of cupcakes.

* * *

Jeremy carried the light bags the first trip, then he filled Jenny in on our plan for pizza and cupcakes. She was shaking her head when I carried in the second load.

She unloaded the groceries and was still shaking her head as she inspected the cupcakes. "You're a pushover."

"Mom, this is a celebration. Peter...Dad said we could have cupcakes."

Jenny nodded, then pulled out the cereal. "At least you didn't fall for the story about frosted flakes."

I carried in a third load as Jenny took things to the giant pantry. I followed her in with some canned vegetables. She set the cereal boxes on the shelf and surveyed the long rows of empty shelves that had once held a year's worth of canning jars when some previous owners had grown a garden full of vegetables they would can for the winter.

Jenny put her arm around me. "It looks so empty."

"Compared to the tiny cupboard in my rental house, this looks like the Grand Canyon."

Jenny turned off the overhead pantry light and went back to the large kitchen. "This house is immense. The three of us will be like BBs inside a boxcar."

Jeremy unwrapped the pizza crusts, and we worked together to assemble two pizzas. Jenny was pre-heating the oven when I noticed smoke curling out of the cooktop. I pulled open the oven door and found three cast iron skillets left behind by Dolores, who'd given us the house and all its contents as a wedding gift. We scrambled to find hot pads, then realized that the smoke was coming from something that had spilled on the oven floor, so I scraped off a layer of burnt-on crud and scooped it into a coffee can left on the stovetop, apparently collecting bacon fat.

Jenny stood back as the smoke died. "When do you suppose Dolores last used this oven?"

I shrugged. "I don't think she'd been cooking much for a while."

Jeremy was watching us from a stool at the counter. "Are you going to put the pizzas in now?"

Jenny pushed her hair behind her ear and glanced at me. She bit back her response. "Sure, they're going in now. Go and set the table."

Jeremy left and I put the pizzas in the oven. "You showed great restraint."

Jenny smiled. "You're a nice buffer."

The smoke detector screeched as smoke continued to rise from the stove. I pulled a stool under it and took out the battery.

"Beer?" I asked.

"I'd fall asleep if I drank a beer. Milk, please."

I opened beer me, and then poured a glass of milk for Jenny and Jeremy. By the time we had the table set with dishes we'd carried over from my rental house, the kitchen timer dinged. We dug around to find a spatula and cutting boards. There wasn't a pizza cutter anywhere, so I used a giant chef's knife to cut the pizza into wedges.

We sat at one end of the giant dining room table and I raised my beer can. "Let's toast our new house and new family."

I'd just touched the can to my lips when there was a crash from beyond the kitchen. I raced through the kitchen, which seemed undisturbed, then into the pantry. The sealed cereal boxes were on the floor.

Jenny was right behind me, and Jeremy edged past her. "What happened?"

I picked up the cereal boxes and set them back on the shelf. "I don't know."

Jeremy left for the pizza. Jenny grabbed my hand and pulled me aside.

"Why would the cereal boxes fall off a flat shelf?"

"I don't know."

Jenny glared at me. "Then guess."

I thought for a minute. "I've got nothing short of poltergeists."

"Oh, great. We were given a haunted house."

"It's not that, but you asked me to guess."

"Make another guess."

I shook my head. "I've got nothing."

Jeremy walked back into the pantry, a slice of pizza in his hand. "Why are you arguing?"

"We're not arguing," Jenny said. "We're…"

"We're brainstorming. Your mom asked me why the cereal boxes fell off the shelves and I didn't have a good explanation."

Jeremy looked at the boxes and shrugged. "It was probably an earthquake. Lots of things fall off shelves in an earthquake." He walked away.

"There you go," I said. "It was an earthquake."

Jenny followed me back into the dining room and whispered, "There was no earthquake."

* * *

61

We were accustomed to the dishwasher in my rental. Our century-old "new' house was built before automatic dishwashers were invented. Jeremy handwashed dishes while I dried. Jenny continued to unpack dishes, pots and pans, silverware, and utensils carried over from my rental house next door.

"Mom, why are we washing all Peter's dishes? They were clean when we packed them."

"It's a good practice, and Peter is now your dad."

"Oh yeah," Jeremy said. "If we're going to use Dad's dishes, are we going to load the old ones back into the boxes to make space in the cupboards?"

Jenny kept piling dishes next to the sink. "I thought we'd load them on the pantry shelves, but that seems like a poor idea until we replace some screws."

Jenny called a moratorium on dishwashing and sent Jeremy into the dining room to do his homework. I pulled her close and kissed her. She wrapped me in a hug and I groaned.

She recoiled. "Sorry. I forgot about your broken ribs."

"They'll get better."

She kissed me gently, then checked on Jeremy who was concentrating on a math worksheet. She came back and took the dishtowel from me. "Jeremy will be in bed at nine. Maybe we'll be able to consummate our marriage after he falls asleep."

"I think that's a great idea. I'd like to see you in that nightie again."

Jenny grinned. "You want to see me out of the nightie."

Jeremy wrapped up his homework about eight thirty. It took a while to find the box with pajamas. After he brushed his teeth we talked about sleeping in a strange bedroom and then he settled under the covers.

Jenny kissed his forehead while I watched from the door. She walked away and started to close the door.

"Mom, can you leave the door open?"

"Sure."

"And a light on in the hall?"

"I'll leave the bathroom light on."

Jenny and I walked down the hallway to the master bedroom. We dug through our suitcases, loaded drawers, and hung up pants, shirts, scrubs, skirts, and dresses. Jenny went down the hall to the bathroom to clean up and change. I changed into boxers and a t-shirt in the giant walk-in closet.

I heard the bedroom door creak and the lock click. The lights went dark and I stumbled around the unfamiliar furniture until I finally found the old four-post bed. I slipped into the fresh sheets and snuggled up to Jenny. I was surprised when I put my hand on her hip and felt satin.

"Satin pajamas?"

"Silk."

"Mmm. They're very sexy, but unnecessary."

"They were a wedding shower gift. I thought they'd build more anticipation than the sheer nightie."

I had the top half unbuttoned when the doorknob rattled, followed by a knock. "Mom."

Jenny gathered her top together. "Good thing I locked the door." She buttoned her top as she crossed to the bedroom door. My state of anticipation made it inappropriate for me to get out of bed.

Jenny took a deep breath, unlocked the door, then opened it. "What's the matter?"

"Why'd you lock the door, Mom?"

I smiled and waited for the answer. "Well, you seem to have forgotten to knock when you come to a closed door, so I thought I'd help you remember. What's the matter?"

"I think there's someone walking around upstairs."

I jumped out of bed, stubbed my toe on the dresser, hopped on one foot into the closet, and was into a pair of pants and slippers in ten seconds. The adrenaline rush and pain of a possibly broken toe had resolved my potentially embarrassing amorous state. "Let's go to your room and check that out."

I led Jeremy and Jenny down the hall to Jeremy's bedroom. I sat on the bed and listened while my entourage stood by the door. I waited a minute, then heard the old boiler light in the basement. There was a faint sound of water running through the pipes followed by the creaking sounds of the old radiator as it expanded when the hot water ran through it.

"Is that what you heard?"

Jeremy shook his head. "It sounded like someone walking upstairs."

I looked at Jenny who shrugged. I went to the kitchen and found a flashlight. I climbed the stairs to the attic, checking the dusty steps for non-existent footprints. The attic was cold and dark. I found a pull chain for an overhead light, but the 40-watt bulb did little to light the dark expanse. I walked the length of the attic which was mostly empty. I turned the flashlight toward a row of boxes all labelled Christmas Decorations in Dolores' shaking penmanship. The dust around them had been disturbed, like someone might've slid them an inch, but there weren't any footprints or other evidence of human activity. I turned off the light and walked back down the steps.

Jeremy, who was determined to be independent and loathe to be touched or hugged, was clinging to Jenny's side. "Anything?" Jenny asked.

"It's mostly empty and dusty. There are a few boxes of Christmas decorations we should check out."

Jeremy looked spooked. "Can I sleep in your bedroom tonight?"

I looked at Jenny, who smiled. "Welcome to fatherhood."

"Sure," I said. "Gather up your pillow and blanket and you can sleep on our rug."

'Mom lets me sleep in bed with her sometimes."

So much for consummating our marriage tonight.

Chapter 7

Jeremy was the only one who got a good night's sleep. He climbed between us in the bed and twitched, twisted, kicked, and moaned all night. I moved to his bed after getting kicked in my broken ribs. I was tired, disoriented, and confused by the furniture and room when my mental alarm woke me. The window blinds showed no hint of light making me question my brain's message to get up. Then I remembered it was the winter solstice which meant driving to and from work in the dark on the shortest days of the year.

Moments later I heard the alarm go off, followed by running water. The bathroom door was closed, and I heard Jenny humming in the shower. I went to the master bedroom to get clothes and found Jeremy upside down in the bed and tangled in sheets. He looked like a mummy with only his nose and feet showing.

Jenny walked into the bedroom wrapped in a bathrobe as I pulled underwear and socks out of the drawer. Her light complexion and the dark bedroom make the dark bags under her eyes look like shiners. She flipped on the overhead light and I could see the red lines in the whites of her eyes.

I dug out a golf shirt, part of my usual business casual uniform. "Did you get any sleep?"

She pushed past me, into the walk-in closet. "I must've napped some, but Jeremy squirmed like a dog having a nightmare all night long. The accumulation of changes must've really got him wound up."

"I wonder if he heard the pipes creaking last night?"

"We listened to them, but he said that wasn't what he heard."

I took a pair of khaki pants off a hanger and walked toward the bathroom. "Whatever it was, I hope he sleeps in his own bed tonight."

The water pressure in the old pipes was poor, so the shower dribbled more than pounded. I toweled off questioning whether Dolores deeding the old house to us was a gift or a curse. I was shaving when the bathroom door opened and Jeremy, half asleep, walked in. He was standing next to me before he realized the only bathroom on the second floor was already occupied.

I glared at him. "We talked about knocking on closed doors last night."

Still only half awake, he looked at my face covered with shave cream. "Grandpa uses an electric razor."

"I prefer using shaving cream and a real razor."

Jeremy was shifting his weight from one foot to the other. "Are you going to be done pretty soon?"

I quickly finished shaving, wiped the lather off my face and snatched my shirt off the hook by the mirror. "I'm done." I closed the bathroom door as I left.

Jenny wore blue scrubs with yellow duckies. She was leaning against the counter yawning as the coffee maker gurgled. "I haven't been this tired since I used to get up to nurse Jeremy. How about you?"

I pulled two of Dolores' mugs out of the cupboard and set them next to the coffee maker. "Navy basic training was probably the most tired I've ever been. Part of the regimen is breaking the new recruits down through lack of sleep and fatigue, then building them back up into a cohesive team. I think I only got three or four hours of sleep a night for weeks."

The coffee maker stopped dripping and Jenny poured for us. "That sounds like torture."

I accepted a mug and took a sip to test the temperature before taking a gulp. "Yeah, those are some of the same techniques used to interrogate prisoners."

Jenny started to open the soft bread. I pointed to the bread box. "There's grown-up bread in the other bag."

Jenny paused, then opened the soft bread. "I need to make lunch for Jeremy anyway." Jenny found the lunch meat, but looked around, pulled bottles aside. "Did you buy butter or mayo?"

"Sorry, they never crossed my mind."

Jenny closed the refrigerator. "Could you run next door to the rental house and grab some out of the refrigerator?"

I tried to look pathetic, but quickly realized it wasn't going to work. "Sure."

I slipped on a pair of shoes and dashed across the frosty grass. I pulled a shopping bag out from under the sink and grabbed an armful of condiments, mayo, and other refrigerator stuff, then dashed back.

Jenny dug through the bag and loaded things into the refrigerator. She set the mayo on the counter then continued. "This is an...interesting mix of items. I might've waited for a later trip to bring over the expired ketchup and bloody mary mix."

I shrugged. "My brain isn't fully engaged."

Jenny closed the refrigerator door and leaned against it. "Mine too. I hope Jeremy will sleep in his own bed tonight."

"If he's still freaked out, maybe we should let him fall asleep in our bed. We'll move to his bed and all of us will sleep."

Jenny leaned into me. "I love that you're analytical. That solution would never have occurred to me."

A sound like elephants running down the stairs preceded Jeremy's arrival. He tore into the kitchen and froze, seeing us in each other's arms. "Are you two having sex?"

Jenny pushed away. "What?"

"My friend Maxwell said when married people hug they're having sex."

Jenny knelt down so she was eye-to-eye with Jeremy. "Honey, sometimes people who care for each other just hug. It's a hug, not sex."

Jeremy looked at her skeptically. "Grandma and Grandpa don't hug, so I thought that meant they weren't having sex."

I expected Jeremy's questions to go on, leading to "the sex discussion" but he moved on. "I'd rather have Cheerios than corn flakes." He stood on his toes and got a bowl from the cupboard. Then he went to the pantry and returned with the Cheerios.

Jenny got one of Dolores' sugar bowls out of the cupboard and checked the contents. She brought it to Jeremy who'd already found a spoon and the milk. He took a seat at the small kitchen table and read the cereal box as he ate.

I put two slices of "grown-up" bread into the toaster and topped off my coffee. "Would you like a piece of toast?"

Jenny shook her head. "I think my body would like something with more fiber." She retrieved a box of "grown-up" cereal from the pantry. She joined Jeremy at the table and ate without enthusiasm.

After breakfast we helped Jeremy pack his lunch and homework into a backpack. He stood by the door, expectantly. "Who's taking me to school?"

I looked at Jenny. "Jeremy's not taking a bus?"

"We haven't notified the school of his address change. I guess I'll drive him and stop in at the office. I'll add you as an emergency contact, too."

Chapter 8

I hung my coat behind the door and was checking emails when I sensed a presence in my doorway.

"There are two tuba players in a car. Who's driving?"

I turned and saw Brian Johnson, the tuba player from the Two Harbors city band. His face was cherubic and he was smiling broadly. When I didn't respond he said, "The policeman." He sat in my guest chair without invitation. "So, what's the consensus about the murder?"

"I haven't heard anything."

Brian leaned forward. "You're kidding. It's the hot topic all over town."

"I was busy yesterday and no one was throwing out theories to me." I lied, hoping to end the conversation.

"I had coffee at Judy's this morning and the guys were all sure Ole was killed by a jealous husband."

I took a deep breath, knowing the conversation wouldn't be over until Brian had aired all the rumors he'd heard and was satisfied that I'd listened and responded with what I knew.

"A jealous husband?"

73

"I was just a kid, so I didn't hear much about the murder. But, some of the old-timers said Lundquist fixed a lot of leaks and laid a lot of pipe." Brian wiggled his eyebrows like he'd said something suggestive. I missed it.

"Leaks and pipe are kind of the bread and butter of plumbing."

"He *laid a lot of pipe,* as in satisfied a lot of sexually frustrated women."

I rolled my eyes. "How would the old-timers know that?"

"It was common knowledge in the day."

"If it was common knowledge, why would any husband leave Lundquist alone with his wife?"

"He was the only plumber in town, and there's some thought that the husbands were maybe relieved that someone was keeping their wives happy when they were too tired to perform their duties."

I looked at Brian, who I guessed was about seventy. "I can't believe that any husband would be relieved to have someone take that burden."

Brian put up his hands. "Hey, times were different. Lots of men were working twelve-hour days, six and seven days a week. Plus, Ole was around during both WW2 and the Korean War and there were lonely war widows whose husbands were serving overseas. I'm sure more than one soldier came home to a baby born while they'd been overseas for a year or more."

I closed my eyes and tried to envision any scenario that would involve Jenny inviting the plumber to her bed while I was serving overseas and came up empty. "I'm sorry, Brian, but I'm tired and have a ton of work to do." I stood up.

Brian walked out of the door but stopped short. "Well, you jump on this. The Whistling Pines residents were adults at the time of the murder. I think one, or more, of them has an idea about who murdered the Swedish plumber."

"I'm sure they do," I said, "but I think most of what they remember is rumor and hearsay."

"Yup, but I'll bet one of them has the real scoop."

I walked to the dining room and drew a cup of coffee from the urn. The residents were coming in, seating themselves at their usual tables and there was a murmur of conversation. Experience said the usual topics were grandchildren, the food, health, and irregularity.

Wendy was at a back table with the crossword spread in front of her, wiggling her finger at me. "You look like you didn't sleep. The duties of a newlywed keeping you up all night?"

I had no interest in getting into a relationship discussion with Wendy, who was single, played in a band, had a reputation for showing men one or more tattoos hidden under her work clothes, and occasionally finding comfort in the arms of her band's drummer, bass player, or a cute fan.

"Jeremy was unsettled in his new room and climbed in bed between us."

Wendy was dubious of my explanation, but let it pass. "I need an eight-letter word for 'generous clowns.'"

"Shriners."

She gave me a skeptical look but wrote in the letters. "How does that even make sense?"

I got up with my coffee. "Shriners sponsor fund-raising circuses and drive around in clown cars."

Wendy waved me away, apparently having enough letters to fill in the other words. I sat at an empty chair at a table with Howard Johnson. As always, Howard was dapper, the creases in his pants as crisp as they'd been when he'd been an Army officer. He was the self-appointed mayor of Whistling Pines and spoke up for the people who were too shy or embarrassed to bring up their own issues. Because he didn't engage in rumors, I liked talking with him because he had the pulse of the residence and the information he shared was carefully filtered and with "delicate" conversations held in confidence when requested.

He spread strawberry jam on the last remnant of a slice of toast and smiled at me. "How goes the murder investigation?"

"That's what I hoped to find out from you."

Howard smiled. "All I've heard are rumors and vendettas."

"I expected rumors, but vendettas are an interesting twist."

"When you've lived your life in a small town, there are people who've rubbed you the wrong way. This is an opportunity for people to toss some garbage over the fence onto their unfriendly neighbors with the barking dog, the noisy kids, or the junk car in the backyard."

I looked around the dining room at the gray heads. "You'd think that when people get to a certain age they'd get over those things."

Bud Appledorn was sitting across from Howard shaking his head. "Oh, no. The petty slights from grade school and beyond don't run very deep. When you get to our age, you remember those things better than what happened yesterday or last year."

"Howard was in Korea at the time of the murder, what was going on with you, Bud?"

"I was a brakeman on the railroad, hauling ore from the iron range to Two Harbors and Duluth. I don't remember the specific day of the murder, but I remember the aftermath. The whole town was pointing fingers. Everyone thought they knew who the murderer was."

"And who was it?"

Bud laughed. "It depended on who you talked to. Everyone in town had a different murderer in mind and was happy to share that information with anyone who'd listen. I bet the cops were going absolutely crazy with every nut in town calling them to report their neighbor, brother-in-law, the local drunk, and the people who weren't very big on the Swedes in town."

"There was anti-Swedish sentiment?"

"Oh, yah. The Swedes were neutral in the big war, selling food to the Brits and iron ore to the Krauts. Any ship with a Swedish flag was untouchable, even if it was pulling out of South Hampton or Bremerhaven. They made money hand over fist, then pretended they were holier than thou. There was a lot of sentiment against the Swedes, and Ole Lundquist was getting a lot of it. People thought he should've volunteered for the Army or Navy, like so many of the miners' kids, but he claimed he was too old and he kept his Swedish passport handy in case anyone called the draft board to suggest his name."

I pondered that information. "That kind of attitude must've killed his business."

"Would've if there'd been another plumber in town, but all the others got drafted or were too old to do heavy work. Ole did okay for himself even if people were talking behind his back."

Howard smiled through Bud's monologue, making me curious. "You were gone, but you have suspicions."

Howard put his hands up. "Suspicions are only rumors. My suspicion is that Lundquist was as savvy a businessman as he was plumber and he knew how to make a buck. All the

78

rumors that are flying around are just that, rumors. Lundquist may have been accused of a lot of things, but he did good work and was a trusted craftsman. I'd take all the rumors about his philandering with a grain of salt. If he was bedding as many women as people claim, half the town would have blue eyes and blonde hair."

Bud was halfway through a sip of coffee when Howard made that pronouncement. Bud coughed and sputtered while covering his mouth. Once he caught his breath and people stopped watching, he leaned close. "You go back and look at the class pictures from the elementary school from the forties and see how many families have a blonde kid among their dark-haired, brown-eyed siblings."

"Wasn't Ole Lundquist married?" I asked.

Howard nodded. "That I can speak about as fact. Ole was married when he arrived in town, but he was a bit of a drinker and his wife wasn't. She loaded the kids on the train and went to live with her sister down in St. Paul. I don't know if Ole ever divorced her, but I know she deserted him."

Bud shook his head. "I saw her get on the train. She had two black eyes and a crooked nose from the beating Ole gave her the night before. She probably took the money from the cookie jar and high-tailed it out of town while Ole was working."

"When was that?" I asked.

"I think they must've moved here about 1940, but she was gone before the war. That's when the rumors were flying that Ole was bedding the women whose husbands were off fighting the Nips and Krauts."

I cringed at Bud's politically incorrect descriptions of the Japanese and Germans. It was probably no more hurtful than the epithets the residents threw back and forth, kidding each other about their ethnicity. Two Harbors was a cross section of the miners who'd moved to, or been brought to, the iron range to work in the mines. The mine owners liked to hire first generation immigrants who couldn't speak to each other, reducing the risk of unions organizing the men who couldn't even communicate with their co-workers. Whistling Pines, like Two Harbors, was home to people of Finnish, Slovenian, Slovakian, Welsh, English, and Italian heritage along with the Swedes and Norwegians who moved to Minnesota to farm.

"I heard Ole's house burned down."

"Damned druggies." Bud spat the words. "There were about four houses that burned down from those idiots cooking meth in the '80s. They should've been taken behind the barn and shot."

Howard made a steeple with his fingers. "I wonder if there's something more than Lundquist's plumbing business behind his murder."

"What are you thinking, Howard?"

"He worked eight or nine hours a day, leaving evenings and weekends free. I know he drank heavily and that tends to lower people's inhibitions. Maybe he was into something else or some other things."

"Like what?"

Howard cocked his head. "I don't know of anything, but if you limit your focus to his business, you're excluding two thirds of his life. We talked about vendettas over childhood slights, who knows what Ole might've said to someone in a bar or during a card game. Maybe someone thought he was cheating at cards."

Bud was shaking his head. "Nah, it wasn't him having a drink too many or an ace up his sleeve, it was his sleeping around that did him in. You mark my words."

I thanked the guys and got up. I'd hardly risen from my chair when I heard a woman calling my name. I knew Hulda Packer's voice and knew attempts to avoid her would only escalate the volume of her attempts to get my attention. I walked across the dining room, dreading Hulda's input. She was a confused former teacher, known among the staff as the source of all misinformation. If there wasn't a good rumor, Hulda would create one. If she had solid information, Hulda twisted it.

I pulled a chair over from a neighboring table and sat at the corner of Hulda's group. "What's up, ladies?"

Hulda cut off Helene Carter, who was about to say something. "Peter, are you involved in the Lundquist murder investigation?"

"Not really."

"See!" Hulda said. "I told you he was working with the police. Are you making any headway?"

"I'm not working on it. I have nothing to do with it. I have a new wife, a new son, and a new house. I don't have time or the interest in an ancient murder investigation."

Hulda leaned across the table. "Ole Lundgren was schlepping Daisy Preston."

I took a deep breath. "Schlepping means dragging. I'm sure he wasn't dragging Daisy Preston." I knew she meant schtupping, the Yiddish word for intercourse, but I wasn't going to offer the correction.

"Of course not! He was sexting her."

I closed my eyes and composed my response, trying hard not to let my tired brain scream out in protest over Hulda's misuse of terms she didn't understand.

"I'm sure Ole Lundquist wasn't sexting Daisy Preston."

Hulda frowned. I looked at the other three women at the table and they were all staring at Hulda, afraid to contradict her, and awaiting her next verbal assault.

Helene got her courage up during the break in the conversation. "I think Lundquist was quite a ladies' man. He was tall, blonde, blue-eyed, and liked to flirt. He had that big empty house after his wife left and there were some shenanigans going on in there."

Hulda leaned forward and pointed a gnarled finger at me. "See, I'm not the only one who thinks he was sexting the women in this town."

Ignoring Hulda, I turned to Helene. "What kind of shenanigans are you talking about?"

"There were people coming and going all the time, especially on paydays. There was some card playing, some drinking, and who knows what all else."

Hulda glared at me. "It was a regular den of inquisition!"

"I think the phrase is 'den of iniquity.'"

Hulda waved off my correction. "You know exactly what I meant. There was sexting, drinking, and carousing. I'm sure some jealous husband got drunk and stabbed him."

"He died of a gunshot wound," I said.

"Same difference. He was dead, D-E-A-D, dead." Hulda crossed her arms, a signal I had a chance to escape while she was angry with me and there was a lull in the conversation.

I was filling my coffee cup from the urn when I felt a hand on my bicep. "You should try to get some sleep."

Miriam Milam, dressed in her white kitchen outfit, was standing next to me looking concerned. She was caring and always had a friendly smile.

"Thanks. We're trying to get settled in Dolores' house and there have been some issues that've made the transition difficult."

Miriam glanced around to make sure no one was listening. "I heard about the ghost in the attic."

"You spoke with Jenny?"

Miriam broke into a smile. "She spilled on the attic ghost, the collapsing shelf, and the rattling pipes. She looks even more tired than you."

"I'm adjusting to having two extra people in the house full time."

"You'll get used to being married faster than you'll adapt to fatherhood. Most people have at least nine months before they have to deal with another person in the mix. Jenny arrived with a ready-made family."

A different voice called to me from the doorway. "Peter."

I walked over to the director, Nancy, who rarely sought me out. She nodded toward her office and I followed, closing the door behind me.

"Have a seat," Nancy said, as she sat in her chair behind the desk. "I had a call from Len Rentz."

I put up my hand. "Don't worry. I already told Len I didn't have time to get involved in his murder case."

Nancy leaned back and grinned. "Len offered me quite a proposition. He'd like you to help, but he wants to be very cagey about it. He suggested we set up some field trips to places where you could do some research and, perhaps, help our residents engage in the mystery investigation."

I closed my eyes and sank in the chair. "Like what?"

"We brainstormed and we think you should take a group of residents to the library. Turn them loose in the newspaper archives and each person who finds an article about the murder or the victim would win a prize."

"Nancy, I don't have enough prizes for bingo."

"Len said he'd buy you bags of hard candy, both regular and sugar-free, and you could hand the pieces out as prizes."

"Well, that'd be a hit with the residents. I'm more concerned about having dozens of people digging through old newspapers."

"Len says he can't afford to divert the police force into a full-scale investigation of a 1951 murder. But if someone could hand him the evidence for analysis, that'd be a workable solution. What do you think?"

"Could I consider it for a day? I'm dead tired and having a hard time reasoning through the value of bringing a crowd to the library."

"Tomorrow's perfect! There's nothing on the calendar tomorrow. Post a signup sheet and you can take a vanload of people."

Somehow thinking about something for a day had become let's start tomorrow. I nodded and got up from the chair. "Are you going to announce the trip at supper?"

"I'll have Wendy do it. I'll also ask her to think about where else we might take a group to do some sleuthing."

I paused at the door, questioning the wisdom of getting Wendy involved too.

I was about to protest when Nancy got up from her chair and patted my shoulder. "This will be fun!"

Like a root canal, I thought to myself as I walked toward my office.

* * *

I leaned on Jenny's office doorframe, feeling the effects of the day. It seemed like anyone with dementia or confusion had searched me out to offer theories about the murder or to ask repetitive questions about what I'd planned for the weekly activities. My face hurt from smiling while I wanted to scream.

Jenny looked up from a file on her desk, appearing as haggard as I'd ever seen her. "What's up, husband?"

"It's time to quit. I'm burned out."

"Why don't you pick up something for supper while I wrap up my charting."

A walker collided with my hamstring, causing me to nearly sprawl into Jenny's cramped office.

"I'm disappointed," said Hulda Packer, who pushed herself into the tiny space, running over my toes. "I haven't seen you in the matching sweaters I gave you for a wedding present. Your thank you note said that they were very pretty, but I haven't seen you wearing them."

Jenny smiled, knowing we hadn't even purchased stationery for thank you notes. "I have to wear scrubs at work."

"Hmph. Maybe you should take a picture when you're wearing them."

"They're packed while we're moving, but once we're settled, we'll take a picture and post it in the newsletter with photos of some of our other gifts."

I saw that Hulda wasn't satisfied with that answer, but she let it slide, backing her walker out of the cramped space and running over my toes again.

"We had homemade pizza last night, how about a roasted chicken from the grocery store deli?" I suggested.

Jenny looked at me with fatigue. "I'd already forgotten about last night. Sure, a roasted chicken would be great. Pick up a bag of salad, too."

Jenny jumped when her cellphone buzzed next to her hand. "This is Jenny." She listened for a second, then said, "I'm so sorry. Peter will be there in a few minutes to pick him up."

I took a step toward the door. "Jeremy missed the bus?"

"Worse. He got on the wrong bus. He's eating a peanut butter sandwich with my mom."

* * *

Barbara met me at the door with a smile, holding Jeremy's backpack. "I knew we'd be seeing you. I didn't think it would be today."

Jeremy buzzed past, snatching the backpack out of Barbara's hand as he went by.

"It's been a transition for all of us," I said, pecking her on the cheek.

"Try to get some sleep, Peter. You look tired."

"Yeah, we are adjusting to the noises in the new house."

She nodded. "Jeremy told me about someone walking around in the attic."

"There wasn't anyone there. I went up with a flashlight and the dust was undisturbed."

"He says he heard something."

"I'm sure he did, but it was probably the creaking radiator."

Barbara waved goodbye as we backed out of the driveway.

Jeremy pushed his backpack off the seat, onto the floorboards. "What's for supper?"

"You just ate a peanut butter sandwich with Grandma."

"That was an after-school snack. I'm hungry again," he said as he buckled himself in my back seat.

88

We cruised through the grocery store, got a roasted chicken, a bag of salad, some dinner rolls and a six-pack of beer. Jeremy rushed into the house while I carried in our two bags of groceries. I closed the kitchen door but froze when I saw newspaper from our boxes of dishes strewn on the kitchen floor. I was certain we hadn't unpacked anything that morning, so the loose newspapers were a mystery. I reasoned that I'd taken Jeremy to school before Jenny left, so I assumed she'd unpacked dishes after I'd left.

After getting Jeremy started with his homework, I unloaded the groceries and picked up the crumpled newspapers we'd used to pack the dishes. I pulled all the dishes out of the boxes and washed them, then set the table. After surveying the cupboard space, I took down Dolores' dishes and wrapped them in the crumpled newspaper and put the boxes on the floor of the pantry. I put our clean dishes in the now empty cupboard.

Jenny walked in like she was in a stupor. "Hey," she said as she hung her coat behind the door.

I hugged her and steered her toward the dining room. "Go change and I'll get supper on the table."

She nodded wearily and glanced at Jeremy, who was engrossed in a school worksheet. I heard her scraping around upstairs and running water as I put out silverware and sliced the chicken.

Jeremy abandoned his homework when he smelled the chicken. He was sitting at the table when Jenny came downstairs wearing a pink sweatshirt and sweatpants. I'd hardly set the chicken down when Jeremy's hand darted out and grabbed a drumstick.

"Would you like a beer?" I asked.

"I'll fall asleep before I'm through eating if I have a beer," Jenny replied. "Just bring me a glass of water."

I brought water for Jenny, milk for Jeremy, and a beer for me. Jeremy had taken the second drumstick before I was seated. Jenny looked mildly annoyed but was apparently too tired to admonish him. I let it slide.

Halfway through supper Jenny looked around. "Where'd the boxes of dishes go?"

"I unpacked them, washed them, and put them in the cupboard."

She reached out and touched my hand. "I wouldn't have had the energy to deal with them tonight."

Jeremy washed the supper dishes and I dried. Jenny scraped plates and took the garbage to the curb for pickup. We sat in front of the television, not really watching, but marking time until we could send Jeremy to bed.

Jenny tucked him in and kissed his forehead. "Sleep tight."

We were crawling under the covers, both too tired to consider consummating our marriage, when there was a crash downstairs.

Jeremy was at the top of the stairs looking spooked. I brushed past him, taking the steps two at a time. I stopped at the bottom step, breathing heavily and listening, the heavy breaths causing stabbing pains in my ribs. The lights were off and the house was silent except for the creaking pipes.

I flipped on lights and wandered around, not finding any broken windows. I was walking into the kitchen as Jenny opened the cupboard and our unbreakable Corelle dishes spilled out onto the counter and floor. She was too stunned to even back up as they fell to her feet.

I picked them up as she stood frozen.

Jeremy stood at the doorway between the dining room and kitchen, watching. "What happened?"

"I think we overloaded the shelf," I said, standing up with the last of the dishes from the floor.

Jenny glanced into the cupboard and shook her head. "I don't think the Corelle weighs any more than the china Dolores had on the shelves."

"I imagine we loosened the brackets when I removed her old dishes and put the new ones in their place. We also have more Corelle than settings of the china Dolores left for us."

Jeremy almost whispered, afraid to say the words out loud. "Do we have a ghost?"

"Why would there be a ghost here?" I asked, shooing him toward the stairs. "Dolores lived here forever, and she's very much alive and happy in her new apartment."

"I want to sleep in your bed again," he said, stopping short of the door to his new bedroom.

Jenny pushed him toward the master bedroom. "That'll be fine for tonight, but you're going to have to sleep in your own room eventually."

"Maybe after the ghost stops breaking things."

* * *

Jeremy was asleep within minutes. I snuck off to his bedroom as soon as the kicking started. Jenny followed five minutes later.

Jenny snuggled into my back. "He'll raise holy hell if he wakes up and we're not there."

"Maybe we can get a couple hours of sleep before that happens." If Jenny said anything more, I wasn't awake to hear it.

I was dreaming about Iraq. I'd gone back in time, before the attack that had wounded my body and mind, and turned my life upside down. The colors were vivid, and the hot wind blew in my face as I looked out over the desert. My eyes popped open and I was staring into someone's eyes. The hot desert wind was someone's breath. I clenched my fist to punch the face in front of me when Jeremy whispered, "Why are you and Mom sleeping in my bed?"

I was disoriented and foggy from the Iraqi dream. I looked around and felt Jenny's body stirring behind me.

"What time is it, Jeremy?"

"I don't know. Your alarm clock woke me up."

I swung my legs out of bed and walked down the hall to turn off the alarm that had been buzzing for almost ten minutes.

Jeremy bumped into me when I stopped at the nightstand. "Do I have to get up or is that the grown-ups alarm?"

"You're already up, buddy. You might as well get dressed and eat breakfast."

"But I'm still tired."

Chapter 9

I walked into the Whistling Pines dining room and sat at a large table where several men were having a serious discussion.

"His name is pronounced like Whiskey," said Lee Westfall. "He told me that yesterday. But he's not Polish, so it's not spelled with an S-K-I at the end. He spells it with S-C-H-K-E."

"That sounds Polish," said Bud Larson.

"It's not," replied Lee.

"What is it?" asked Hank Lundberg.

"I heard him say it was Lithium," said Paul Peterson.

"You mean Lithuanian," corrected Bud.

"No," said Paul. "It wasn't that long of a country."

I put my hand up to stop the conversation. "Who are you talking about?"

Hank looked at me like I was dimwitted. "Ole Lundquist's brother-in-law, John Weschke."

"It's probably Latvian," said Bud. "My butcher was Latvian. He used to cut the best pork chops I've ever had. He said he learned from his father in Beirut."

"Beirut is in Lebanon," said Lee.

"Maybe it was Damascus," said Bud. "I know it was one of those old Russian occupied countries next to Poland."

"Damacus is in Syria," said Paul. "That's nowhere near Poland."

"I'm sure he said Damascus. Is that in what they used to call Bohemia?"

"What's Bohemia got to do with it?" asked Hank.

I stopped the conversation again. "What about Ole's brother-in-law?"

Paul frowned at me. "He was Bohemian."

Bud snapped his fingers. "That's where my butcher came from."

"Liechtenstein!" cried Hank.

"What's in Liechtenstein?" Lee asked.

I stopped the conversation again. "There's something about Ole's brother-in-law that started the conversation. Was it something related to the murder or time capsule?"

The men looked at each other. Bud nodded. "We just remembered Ole had a brother-in-law because I went to school with his son, Alex. I'm not sure the conversation was going anywhere other than that."

Lee leaned forward. "Sure it was. You said Alex had a cute sister who dated your brother."

Bud snapped his fingers. "That's what it was. They broke up and he married Leah Menard."

Hank shook his head. "Her maiden name wasn't Menard, it was something Finnish, like Ahonen or Saarinen."

"She wasn't Finnish, she was Slovenian! I should know, it was my brother who married her."

I looked at my watch and stood up, stopping the conversation. "Are any of you signed up for the library trip?"

Bud snorted. "I haven't been in a library since I graduated from the eighth grade."

Hank smiled. "Do they have any picture books?"

"I need people to dig through the newspapers. I don't need you to read a book."

Lee got up. "I can read a newspaper for you."

"Thanks. Any other takers?"

The others shook their heads and went back to their conversation.

Lee followed me out of the dining room. "There wasn't any discussion about the murder. They just like to argue."

"You're from Iowa, why were you in the discussion?"

Lee smiled. "I sometimes like to throw a little gas on the fire just to keep them revved up."

I shook my head. "Grab your coat. I'll pull the van around."

I scraped the frost off the van's windshield while the engine warmed up. When I climbed in, the interior was toasty. I pulled under the portico and carried the signup sheet inside where my volunteers were lined up. Lee and Howard were the only men out of the dozen people who'd signed up for the library. I checked off the names as people stepped onto the van.

With everyone accounted for, I closed the doors and faced my volunteers. "I expect it will be easier to explain my plan before we get to the library. The librarians have pulled out the newspapers from 1949 to 1952. I need you to read through them and let me know if you find any articles that mention Ole Lundquist, his plumbing business, or his murder."

Elaine Paulson raised her hand. "And we get a prize for every article we find, right?"

"That's right. The sheriff is buying a bag of hard candy and everyone finding an article will get a piece of candy."

Howard smiled. "I think everyone should get a piece just for showing up." Several heads nodded agreement.

"I'm sure Len will be generous with his candy."

I drove to the library and pulled to the curb behind Len's unmarked patrol car. Len got out and helped people step down from the van. Ardis Arnold, the librarian, met us inside the door and helped me gather coats, then we directed people to the tables where she'd set up the yellowed newspapers.

Ardis waved her hands to get everyone's attention as the residents sat down. "These are fragile old papers. Please handle them gently because they flake easily."

I steered her aside as the reading began. "Are you afraid the papers will be destroyed?"

She shook her head. "This is the first time anyone's looked at these old newspapers since I arrived twenty-three years ago. I had to dig deep into the piles in the basement to find them and I think they're all backed up on microfiche."

"Do you have a microfiche reader?"

"No, but I'm sure there's one somewhere in the library system."

A hand shot up. "I've got one!"

Len walked over to the person who'd raised their hand and offered her a choice of the candy assortment he'd brought. He used his cellphone to take a picture of the article.

It took less than three hours for my crew to get through all the newspapers. They'd found five articles, most about the murder, and made eleven trips to the bathrooms.

Len thanked everyone and offered them all their choice of candy as they got on the van. He folded the top of the bag and handed it to me. "My donation to your bingo prize stash."

"Did you find anything interesting?"

"I've got more background on the murder than I had from the old police files, but nothing that was an 'aha' revelation. I'll print out the articles and read through them when I get back to my office, but I don't expect a breakthrough."

* * *

I gave each of my riders a couple more pieces of candy as they unloaded from the van. Len thought he was giving me a cheap bag of candy, but each person smiled and accepted the gift as if I was handing out dollar bills. Howard Johnson was the last to exit the bus. He took two butterscotch hard candies. He put one in his pocket and unwrapped the other, popping it into his mouth and depositing the wrapper in the wastebasket next to the front door. I was ready to park the van and go to the warmth of my office, but he looked at me expectantly.

"What's up, Howard?"

"What's our next adventure?"

"I haven't thought that far ahead. Do you have a suggestion?"

"It might be interesting to go to the historical society and look for information about the murder and band shell construction. Was it really being remodeled when Ole died, or did someone just stuff the box in a hole that was covered later?"

"That'd be interesting. I'll try to set something up and post a sign-up sheet for a field trip." When Howard didn't walk away, I was curious. "Is there something else?"

"I don't think you understand the depth of the reaction this time capsule has elicited."

"What am I missing?"

"It's the topic of discussion at every table during meals and in the commons."

"I knew that was going to happen, but I don't think it's a bad thing."

"It wouldn't be, except that it's dredged up some old animosities. A few people are using it as an excuse to point fingers and cast aspersions."

"I hope you're interjecting some reason."

"I throw oil on the disturbed waters when I can, but…let's just say that some of the rumors are very hurtful and may cause some rifts that won't heal quickly."

"Is there something I need to do?"

Howard stared at the sign next to the door for a moment. "I think Nancy will have to adjust a few dining table assignments to separate the accusers from the victims. I'll talk to her about that. I think you should join in when you see a group of people in deep discussion. The residents respect you and value your calming input."

"I can do that, but I'm not sure my voice brings a lot to the discussions. Many of the women have very tightly knit cliques and I'm unwelcome."

Howard patted my arm. "That's exactly why you need to step in. People respect you and your voice, even if they don't want to hear it."

He walked inside, and I pondered his words while I parked the van. I went to Nancy's office when I got inside. She was on her computer, so I knocked on the doorframe."

"Hi, Peter," she said as she shut down her email screen. "What can I do for you?"

I closed the door and sat in one of her guest chairs. "I had an interesting talk with Howard Johnson after our field trip to the library. He said the time capsule has stirred up the residents. He's going to talk with you about rearranging the dining table assignments, but he also wants me to step into the discussions people are having."

"He mentioned changing dining assignments. What are you supposed to do?"

"He'd like me to step into the discussions some of the cliques are having to stop the hurtful rumors that are being spread."

Nancy leaned back and closed her eyes. "How bad are things?"

"Some residents are using the murder as an opportunity to open some old wounds. People with old vendettas are pointing fingers and causing pain."

Nancy got up from her chair. "Let's find Wendy and Jenny and meet back here in fifteen minutes."

I hung my coat in my office and found Wendy talking with a resident who was having her hair done in our tiny beauty parlor. "Nancy wants to meet with us in her office."

Wendy apologized to the resident for the interruption and followed me into the hallway.

"What's up?"

"The residents are in turmoil over the time capsule and some of them are being victimized by the rumors that are flying around."

"I've walked up on a couple discussions that ended abruptly when I showed up. I figured something unpleasant was underfoot."

I stopped in the dining room and got a carafe of coffee and four cups. Wendy, Jenny, and Nancy were gathered around the small table in Nancy's office. I closed the door and handed out cups.

Nancy smiled when I handed her a cup. "Bless you," she said, taking the carafe and pouring coffee for the four of us.

"I understand the rumor mill has run amok," Nancy said, leaning back with her cup. "I'd like your suggestions on how to get it under control before irreparable damage is done to the relationships between our people."

Wendy grimaced. "It's difficult for us, as staff members, to get into the discussions. I told Peter that I walk up to groups and their conversations stop until I leave."

Jenny nodded. "I made the dispensing rounds with medications this morning. People who are usually pleasant and engaging looked at me like I was an ogre. Conversations just stopped and residents glared at me until I left. I tried to engage them, but it's like a wall went up." Jenny paused, then added, "Poor Genevieve Lange was sitting at a breakfast table by herself in tears. I asked her why and she just shook her head."

Nancy looked at me. "Peter, tell them what Howard Johnson said."

I repeated my conversation with Howard and his suggestion that I step into conversations.

We all stared at each other, coffee cups in hand, waiting for someone to propose a plan of action. Nancy broke the silence. "I'm calling a residents' meeting this afternoon and I'm going to address this head on. I want the three of you there, and I'm going to make it clear that the hurtful rumors will end. Once it's over, I expect the residents will break into their usual cliques to mull over my comments. I want you three to step into those groups and reinforce my message."

Wendy took a deep breath and set her cup on the table. "Your message won't be well received, and our interference will be intrusive."

"I don't care. People like Genevieve are being hurt and it has to stop before the damage is irreparable. If we don't nip this in the bud, people are going to call their families and they'll be moving out. If this doesn't end, word will get into town and people won't want to move here."

I shook my head and Nancy glared at me. "I'm not disagreeing with you. It's just a sad situation. The reality is that our jobs depend on getting this under control. We have to get into this before it gets worse."

Jenny had been silent. I saw the pain in her face. "I don't have the time to get into this. I'll support whatever you three are trying to do, but I've got a staff to supervise, doctors to call, and meds to dispense."

Nancy nodded. "Then it's up to the three of us; Wendy, Peter, and me, to be out among the residents and setting things straight. Wendy, put up signs announcing a meeting after lunch. Peter, set up the theater for the meeting. I'll gather my thoughts and prepare a presentation. At one o'clock, I want all of you to be herding people to the theater." Nancy stood, ending the meeting.

Jenny took my arm as I stepped out of Nancy's office. "Talk to Len. If he needs you to take a bigger role in solving this murder, do it."

"But..."

"We're fine. Your relationship with Jeremy is great. I'll deal with getting the house unpacked."

"You're sure about this?"

Jenny nodded. "I've got our outside lives under control. You help Len."

"The murder happened almost seventy years ago. I doubt it'll ever be 'solved.'"

Jenny shrugged. "Get involved and make sure the residents know that you're working with Len. I think they'll stop pointing fingers if they think the real murderer might be caught."

"I doubt that. People like to gossip."

Nancy had been standing next to her office door and overheard our discussion. She took a step towards us and whispered. "Jenny's right. Talk to Len and get this off the table and out of the rumor mill. Do whatever you can."

"I'm no detective!"

Nancy smiled. "You're the best detective I've got."

"I'm the only detective you've got."

* * *

I closed my office door and called Len's cellphone. He answered immediately and I relayed my conversation with Jenny and Nancy. He listened and waited for more.

"That's it," I said. "I don't know what I can do, but I'm supposed to do something."

"Follow your nose."

"That's it? Those are your only words of advice?"

"That's all any detective does," Len replied. "I'll email the newspaper articles to you. Read through them and see if there's anything that strikes you. I'll give you a call if anything turns up here."

I was hoping Len would tell me to back off, but now I was committed. "Okay. I'll read the articles, but I'm not sure what to do after that."

"Peter, trust your instincts. You would've made a good cop. You may discover something nobody else has considered."

* * *

The residents' meeting went as expected. There were a few questions. A few clutches of people whispered back and forth between Nancy's comments, but for the most part, people seemed to understand and respect what was said.

The meeting broke up and several groups immediately gathered in the atrium. I stepped up to a group of women gathered around Hulda Packer. Hulda glared at me.

"We're having a discussion, Peter."

"I understand, and I'd like to be part of your discussion."

"It has nothing to do with you," Hulda hissed.

"It has to do with the residents and that has everything to do with me." I let that sink in for a second. "The rumors about who might've been sleeping with Ole Lundquist have to stop. Now."

"I don't think…"

I cut Hulda off and the other women looked shocked. "Listen to me. You don't know who was or wasn't sleeping with Ole Lundquist. Period." Then I looked directly at Hulda. "Unless it was you who was sleeping with Ole, shut up. Okay?"

Hulda sputtered. "How dare you! I wasn't sleeping with anyone!"

"Then leave it at that." Hulda tried to turn away, but I put my hand on her walker, forcing her to look at me. "None of you know what was going on with Ole Lundquist. Do you?"

The other four women shook their heads. Hulda glared at me. "Do you, Hulda?"

Hulda continued to glare at me but shook her head.

"Then leave it alone. The rumors you're spreading are baseless and hurtful. They have to end. Do you understand?"

It was obvious that Hulda, who was a former teacher, was unaccustomed to hearing anyone order her around.

"I'll talk to Nancy about this," Hulda hissed.

"Please do that. She's the one who told me to talk to you about ending the rumors. I'm sure she'd like to hear that I've accomplished that mission."

A crowd gathered around us, listening to the escalating voices. A few people looked surprised. Most of them were smiling. I took the opportunity to jump on the issue with both feet.

"Hulda, unless you were the one sleeping with Ole Lundquist, you have nothing to say. Period. Please talk with Nancy and tell her that and tell her you're through using the time capsule to hurt other people."

Nancy broke away from another group, probably having the same discussion. I waved at her and she joined us.

"Hulda wants to talk to you about her affair, or lack of affair, with Ole Lundquist and how she's not going to spread anymore rumors about other people."

Nancy smiled, getting my drift. She put her hand on Hulda's shoulder. "Come to my office. I'd love to talk with you about the nasty, hurtful rumors people have been spreading."

Hulda was fuming, red, beyond angry. "Peter is trying to dictate what we..."

Nancy put her hand on Hulda's walker and steered it toward her office. "Peter is trying to tell you that it's unacceptable behavior to spread malicious, hurtful rumors. I asked him to communicate that to everyone, so he's doing exactly what I directed him to do."

Hulda shuffled along as Nancy steered her walker away from the group. "But he has no right to talk to me like that!"

"Hulda, you were a teacher. You understand how important it is to keep control of an unruly classroom and how hurtful children can be of others who look, talk, or dress differently."

Their voices faded as they entered Nancy's office. "I am not an unruly child!"

"I didn't say you were. I was simply using the classroom analogy to point out how you, of all people, can understand the importance of containing hurtful rumors."

Nancy's door closed and I looked at the surrounding group. "Did you get the message about the Ole Lundquist rumors being through?"

All the heads near me were bobbing.

I went to my office, closed the door, and held my head in my hands. When I closed my eyes I saw a drill instructor with his face inches from mine, spittle flying off his lips, as he yelled at me because the sheets on my bed weren't tight enough to bounce a quarter. The pain of that experience was etched in my brain, and I felt terrible that I'd used much the same technique on Hulda.

There was a gentle knock and my door opened as I lifted my head. Jenny walked in, closed the door, and pulled me into her arms. Without saying a word, she communicated that things would be okay and that I was loved. I knew then that her love was the most important thing in the world, and she'd silently reminded me I had to keep my priorities in order.

* * *

The rest of the day was a whirlwind of people patting me on the back or glaring at me. Hulda Packer retreated to her room as soon as she left Nancy's office. Nancy and Wendy moved from table to table, chatting with people as they gathered for supper. I took up a station near the aviary and spoke with dozens of residents. The early conversations were about Hulda getting her comeuppance. Later conversations were about Ole Lindquist. By the time I left for home, conversations were back to grandchildren, doctors, bodily functions, and finally what the kitchen was serving for supper. Nancy had defused the ticking timebomb, although we were all anxious about backlash from Hulda and her allies.

I drove directly home, not receiving a call that Jeremy had missed or taken the wrong bus. Jeremy was sitting at the kitchen table with an open package of bread, peanut butter, jam, a butter knife, a carton of milk, an empty glass, and crumbs everywhere.

He looked up from his homework and smiled. "What's for supper?"

"You just had a sandwich." I closed the bread bag and swept the crumbs into my hand.

"Don't you remember what I told you at Grandma's house, that's just an after-school snack. It's got nothing to do with supper."

"How do you feel about frozen lasagna." I turned toward the refrigerator and saw that the sugar bowl and butter dish were tipped over. Sugar was spilled on the counter and it looked like someone had run a giant finger across the butter, smearing it around.

I grabbed a paper towel, started the cleanup and glared at Jeremy. "What's up with the sugar and butter?"

"You didn't do that."

"No. I put them away after breakfast."

Jeremy shrugged. "They were like that when I got home."

Looking at the countertop, I realized a row of canisters had been moved away from the wall about two inches. A cookie jar, left behind by Dolores, was turned almost ninety degrees and away from the wall.

"Did you move the canisters?"

"Uh, uh."

I pushed the canisters back and straightened the cookie jar, a chill running down my spine as the comments about ghosts came to mind.

I took a pan of lasagna from the refrigerator freezer and started the oven. While the oven was pre-heating I looked into the pantry. The cereal boxes were on the floor again and I got a very eerie feeling. I picked them up and put them on a higher shelf. After putting the lasagna in the oven and starting Jeremy on his homework I went upstairs to change.

Jenny walked into the bedroom when I was pulling on jeans. She pecked me on the cheek and pulled a sweatshirt and jeans out of a drawer.

"Did you move the canisters this morning?"

She pulled off her scrubs and cocked her head. "Why would I move the canisters?"

"They were away from the wall. The butter and sugar dishes were tipped over and someone smeared butter on the counter."

"Why would Jeremy do that?"

"He said he didn't"

Jenny pulled the sweatshirt over her head and froze. "If he didn't do it?" Jenny pulled on her jeans and put on slippers. "This is getting kind of creepy."

"Have you seen a house key while you're been going through drawers?"

"I have the one Dolores gave me at the wedding reception." Jenny thought for a moment. "I suppose it's still in the purse I had at the wedding. Do you think we need to start locking the doors?"

"That key hasn't been in the lock for decades, so I doubt if the tumblers would turn. Even if they did, I doubt the hardware store could make copies. If we wanted to lock the doors, we'd be better off installing new deadbolts."

I heard feet on the stairs and Jeremy appeared at the bedroom door. "The kitchen timer is buzzing. The lasagna must be done."

Jenny nodded. "Set the table. We'll be right down."

When Jeremy was gone she turned to me. "Do you really think someone was in here while we were at work?"

"I'm trying to figure out *why* someone would come in while we were working. It's not like we're rich. Would someone break in to steal the Corelle dishes?"

Jenny's eyes went wide. "The Hummels!"

We walked to the one room that was undisturbed since our move, Dolores' "display" room. We opened the door and flipped on the light. Rows of Hummels stared at us from cabinets, along with Tobie mugs and an empty gun case. The guns had been removed after Dolores used them to shoot at rabbits, deer, and other animals she considered "vermin." She'd shot at them, unsuccessfully, from her porch, and after each incident, Len and I removed all the guns we could find. Somehow, she always found one more.

I surveyed the room. "Nobody's disturbed anything in here."

Jeremy's voice called from downstairs. "Dad, I think the lasagna is burning!"

Supper was quiet. Jeremy's monologue about schoolmates dominated the conversation. Jenny said her mother had called her at work, not wanting to disturb her at home, to see how married life was going. We all skirted around the issue of the ghostly events. Jeremy and I washed dishes while Jenny went to my rental house and carried over a box of pots and pans.

A knock on the back door preceded the entry of Jenny's parents. Barbara came in with a basket of fruit and Howard carried in two suitcases. Jeremy seemed subdued and hung back as we hugged.

Howard knelt down. "Hi, buddy. How's your new bedroom?"

Jeremy shrugged.

"I've got a suitcase of your clothes. Let's go upstairs and you can show me your room."

Jeremy walked out of the kitchen. Howard gave me a questioning look and I shrugged.

Jenny unwrapped the fruit basket. "Thanks, Mom. Peter's been doing the grocery shopping and his tastes run toward Italian pasta dishes, chili, and pizza. I'm dying of tomato and onion poisoning, and scurvy."

Barbara laughed, which was far out of character, and signaled her comfort with us. "I'd never let Howard do the grocery shopping. He'd come home with a car full of steaks, roasts, ham, and potato chips."

Jenny peeled an orange and pulled the sections apart. She handed pieces to Barbara and me. "We're a little spooked. There's some strange things going on."

"Like what?"

Jenny looked at me, then spoke. "The cereal boxes have been falling off pantry shelves and a cupboard shelf collapsed in the middle of the night. Peter came home and found the sugar bowl and butter dish turned over with butter smeared on the counter."

I nodded. "Someone pulled a bunch of newspaper packing out of an open box of dishes and moved all the canisters away from the wall while we were at work."

Barbara's happy look turned to concern. "Someone's been coming into your house?"

Jenny looked at me, then added, "Jeremy thought he heard someone walking in the attic

114

the first night he tried to sleep in his room. He's been in our bed every night since then."

"I checked the attic, but there was no one and nothing up there. Just dust and a few boxes of Dolores' Christmas decorations."

Jenny decided to change the conversation. "What's in the other suitcase?"

Barbara smiled. "I was doing my own Christmas decorating and found some things for you. They're an early Christmas present."

Barbara carried the suitcase to the kitchen table and opened it. She handed a box to Jenny who pulled it open and stared at the contents.

Jenny looked like she was afraid to touch whatever was inside. "It's Grandma's ceramic Christmas tree."

"It was the first thing you took out every year. I thought it could be your first Christmas decoration in your new home."

Jenny handed the box to me and hugged her mother. It was the first time I'd seen Barbara actually wrap her arms around anyone and hug them close. Barbara immediately pulled a tissue out of her pocket to dab tears from her eyes before they ruined her makeup.

The rest of the boxes contained Lenox Christmas decorations I'd seen on the shelves of Barbara and Howard's house. They were tasteful, but breakable. Barbara and Jenny were finding places to set them when Jeremy thundered down the stairs with Howard close behind. Clutched in Jeremy's hand was something red, green, and white.

"Mom, look! Grandpa brought my Christmas stocking!" Jeremy ran to the fireplace and surveyed the mantle for a place to hang the stocking.

Howard had a sly smile, taking a threaded hook from his pocket. "I thought you might need this."

I looked over the front surface of the old wooden mantle looking for an existing hole. "Dolores never had children, so there probably weren't any stocking hung here."

Howard ran his fingers under the bottom edge and smiled. "Let's use the one right here, in the middle."

He handed the hook to me and I screwed it into the hole and Jeremy hung his stocking.

"Look, Mom. It's all ready for Santa."

Howard leaned close to me. "I felt six holes under the edge. The owners before Dolores must've had a big family." He paused, never looking away from Jenny and Barbara. "You know, we wouldn't feel bad if you and Jenny had a reason to put hooks in all the holes."

I glanced at Howard who had a sly grin.

"We haven't talked about more children," I whispered.

Howard nodded. "I find that hard to believe. You and Jenny have been dating for a couple years. I expect the topic has come up. If not, it's time. Your biological clocks are ticking."

116

I was speechless. "You and Barbara have discussed this?"

"It might've come up."

After Jenny's parents left, Jeremy turned on the television. Jenny looked at me with resignation. "We have to start writing thank you notes for the wedding presents."

I groaned. She brought a box out of the pantry and peeled off the tape. On top of the pile was the book Barbara had used to record the names of guests and the present each had given. Under that were a roll of postage stamps and boxes of embossed thank you notes matching the wedding invitations.

"It appears Mom thought we might not be prepared to write thank yous." She opened a box of stationery and the book. "You reopen the presents and I'll write a few appreciative lines."

I opened a box and pulled out a knitted rectangle, two-thirds blue and one-third orange. "What do you think it is?"

Jenny flipped through the book and stopped at the last entry. "Evelyn Marris gave us knitted placemats. Are there more in the box?"

I pulled out another that was all orange, followed by one that was green and orange. The next one was all green. "I think she knitted until she ran out of one color, then continued with her next ball of yarn."

Jenny was writing as I put them back into the box and set it aside. "What did you write?"

"Dear Evelyn, Thank you for the colorful placemats. They go nicely with our dishes."

"That's really what you wrote?"

Jenny nodded. "What's next?"

I opened the box with what we'd decided were the crocheted can cozies and held them up. "What are you going to write about these?"

Jenny closed her eyes. "Well, since we're not sure they're can cozies, I guess I'll just thank them for sharing their crocheting talent with us. Who are they from?"

"Janet Heberg."

Jenny jotted the note while I put the cozies away and took out another, larger box. "Oh, oh. I found the matching sweaters from Hulda Packer. What are you going to write about these?" I held them up, showing Jenny the hideous shade of cranberry. The knitted rows were uneven, like Hulda had dropped a few loops, making the surface lumpy and irregular.

"I think we're off the hook. Hulda said she'd already received our thank you note."

I shook my head. "I don't think we dare do that. She'll see everyone else getting thank you notes and go searching for hers. Come up with something clever."

"You promised to show her a picture of us wearing them, Peter."

"I'm betting she'll forget that promise, and if she doesn't, she'll forget that she hasn't seen the picture."

"Jeremy, come here for a minute."

Jeremy walked into the dining room with one eye still on the television. Jenny handed him

118

her phone while I pulled the larger sweater over my head. "Take a picture of us with my phone."

Jenny pulled her sweater over her head and we started laughing. My sleeves were about two inches too short and hers were equally too long. My sweater fit around my torso but didn't reach my belt. Hers was long enough to wear as a dress. She bunched the sleeves up and pulled the cuffs to her wrists. I hunched my shoulders to make the sleeves look longer.

"Jeremy! Take a picture."

Jeremy took the phone and looked at us for the first time. "You want a picture wearing those things?"

"Just take the picture, honey."

We smiled and the camera flashed.

Jeremy's eyes were already back on the television. "Am I done?"

Jenny took the phone back. "You'll have to go to bed at the end of this show."

"Okay, Mom."

I pulled the sweater over my head. "Are we going to donate these to the clothing drive?"

"We can't. Hulda shops the thrift shops and she might see them there."

"Maybe my mother can give them to one of the Duluth charities."

"Peter, it'd be even worse if Hulda saw some indigent person wearing one of them on a trip to Duluth."

"So, we burn them in the garden."

Jenny threw the pen at me and giggled. "We're done for tonight."

"Why? Did you run out of polite lies?"

"Be careful, Navy boy, your ribs are already sore. I can make them worse."

Jeremy's show ended and he started watching another. Jenny took the remote and turned the television off.

"It's bedtime. Put your pajamas on and brush your teeth."

I put the presents back into the pantry and got to Jeremy's room in time to watch Jenny kiss him goodnight.

"You're sleeping in your own room tonight. Right?"

"I'll try, but if the ghosts start making noises again…"

Jenny ran her hand over his hair. "There aren't any ghosts."

"That's what you say, Mom."

I changed into fresh boxers and t-shirt while Jenny used the bathroom. She came out wrapped in a bathrobe with the hem of a flannel nightgown reaching her ankles.

"What happened to the nightie you wore at Lutsen?"

"There's no way I'm wearing that when there's any chance Jeremy will see me."

"I'd like to see you out of it."

"I saw you take a Percocet. You're neither ready nor able to perform your husbandly duties tonight." She walked to me and brushed her hand over my hair just as she'd done to Jeremy. "How bad is the pain?"

"On a scale of one to ten, I'd put it at a three."

Jenny looked into my eyes. "Where does being thrown from a Humvee and being shot at fall on that scale, dear?"

"About fifteen."

Jenny closed her eyes. "I can't imagine what you've been through."

"Don't try."

Footsteps came running down the hallway and Jeremy stuck his head in the bedroom. "There's someone downstairs!"

I rushed down the stairs and stopped in the living room. At first there weren't any sounds, but a second later I heard scraping noises in the kitchen. I stood in the dark kitchen with Jenny and Jeremy peeking around me.

"The ghost is in the pantry," Jeremy whispered.

I agreed that something was in the pantry, but not believing in ghosts, I picked up a kitchen knife. I stepped into the pantry and turned on the light. One of Hulda's sweaters was on the floor and the other was partially out of the box.

Jeremy looked around my hip and whispered, "The ghost doesn't like new stuff in his house. All our new stuff gets moved around and knocked down."

I looked at Jenny who raised her eyebrows like he had a point.

Scratching noises came from the box and the second sweater started moving. Jenny gasped when the second sweater fell out of the box. I stepped closer to the box and pulled the sweaters aside. The box started to vibrate and a can cozie started to rise from the box as if it was levitating.

I grabbed it and stepped back, waiting to see what would happen. I nearly fell over backwards when a black nose and two beady eyes appeared. It took a second for me to process that I was seeing a chipmunk's striped head.

I didn't realize I'd been holding my breath, but I let out a gasp.

Jenny started to laugh. "I think we've found the ghost. Now, how are you going to get rid of him?"

I backed out of the pantry and closed the door. "I'm not doing a thing tonight."

"You're leaving him in there with our wedding presents?"

"Jeremy, go back to bed and I'll tuck you in."

Jeremy ran upstairs and Jenny poked my chest. "The wedding presents?"

"I think he's looking for nesting material. With any luck, he likes cranberry sweaters."

"Really? That's all you're going to do?"

"I'll go to the hardware store tomorrow and buy a rat trap."

"You'll do no such thing! You're not going to kill a chipmunk in the pantry!"

"Okay, I'll buy a live trap, but then we have to figure out where to release him."

"It's December. He's supposed to be hibernating. He'll die if you release him outside."

I waved off her concerns. I'd broken ribs during an incident with my neighbor Dolores and a moose the night before the wedding. I felt the pain when I got tired or strained. "Let's deal with this tomorrow, Okay?"

Jenny followed me up the stairs. "No. I want to hear your plan."

"I'll have a plan tomorrow. My Percocet is kicking in and now I need to sleep."

I walked into the bedroom and saw a lump huddled under our quilt. "All clear. There's no ghost. It was a chipmunk."

Jeremy pulled back the covers and looked at me skeptically. "Really?"

"Yes, really. I left him in the pantry and closed the door. Tomorrow we'll decide how to trap him and what to do after we catch him. Don't open the pantry door when you come home from school."

Jenny sat on the edge of the bed and ran her hand over Jeremy's hair. "You're not ready to sleep, are you?"

Jeremy shook his head.

Jenny took a deep breath and looked at me. "And you can't stay awake. Sleep in here and I'll lay down with Jeremy."

Jeremy pulled the covers around himself. "I'd rather sleep in here, in your room."

Jenny looked at me with sad eyes. "Do you mind?"

"It doesn't matter where, but I'm going to be asleep very soon."

Jenny walked me to the other bedroom and put me through the same tuck-in procedure she'd used on Jeremy.

"Are you going to ask if I've brushed my teeth?"

She stroked my face. "I'm so sorry. Is this what you thought you were signing on for when you asked me to marry you?"

I touched her face. "This is a pretty small bump in the road. At least we know we aren't dealing with a ghost."

"I love you." She kissed me. "One of us should get some sleep."

Chapter 10

I hid in my office, re-reading the email attachments from Len and trying to find anything in the newspaper articles that would hint at the murderer's identity. The stilted newspaper prose, popular in the day, led nowhere. I called Len.

"Okay, I've read everything and I've got nothing. Do you have any other information?"

"I've got a police report that looks like it was written by a schoolchild, and the coroner's report, which isn't much better."

"What did the doctor say about the body and wound?"

"Well, the coroner was the funeral director, and his report is pretty brief. I'll send that too, but you'll get more out of the three pictures he took of the body before he embalmed it."

"Email them to me and I'll take a look at them."

I went to the dining room for coffee while awaiting Len's email. Most of the breakfast crew was gone with the exception of people at two tables who were drinking coffee and talking.

"Peter! Come over here if you have a second."

I recognized Dolores' voice, having been her neighbor for a couple years. She'd been a polite, friendly neighbor, who was struggling to stay in her house long after she was unable to continue with upkeep and repairs. I'd spent many evenings patching things together for her. In return she sent me home with casseroles and cookies, most of them inedible, made from expired or questionable ingredients. In one instance, she'd cleaned out her spice rack, sending me home with a box of tiny cans, some from a grocery store that had gone out of business when I was a child. Others were so old they didn't have expiration dates. I'd accepted them with a smile, then quickly dumped them into my trash, as I'd done with the casseroles and cookies she'd given me.

I brought my coffee to her table and pulled up a chair. "Good morning, ladies."

"Peter, I assume you know my friends."

I nodded to the other three women, who I knew as some of the most polite and thoughtful residents. Dolores had only moved to Whistling Pines a week earlier, having given Jenny and I her huge old house and all its contents, as a wedding gift. She said it was in partial payment for all I'd done for her. In her short time as a resident, Dolores had chosen her friends carefully.

"Are you settled into the old house?"

"We're still unpacking boxes and moving things over from my rental. We're getting there, but it's a process."

"I realized last night that you'll be spending your first Christmas there as a family. I hope it will be wonderful. I have many fond memories of Christmas at the house." She paused. "Jenny's son, I forget his name, was excited about having a bedroom. I hope he's happy with it."

I hesitated a moment too long.

"Isn't that going well?" she asked.

"The new house has strange noises and they've got him a little spooked."

"Ah. The old boiler and radiators make noises he's probably unaccustomed to. I'm sure he'll get used to them over time."

Maureen Breslin leaned forward, smiling. "The house isn't haunted, is it?"

I smiled and shook my head, then looked at Dolores, who'd lost her smile.

"What's the matter?" I asked.

"The previous owners told me their children had been spooked by the house, but I think it was just the poor lighting and dark corners." She paused, then added, "They were convinced there were gremlins in the radiators trying to get out when the pipes pounded. The older children had fed that fear and I think it got out of control."

I took a sip of coffee, then said, "You never had any ghostly encounters."

Dolores stared at me, like she was trying to frame her response. "Well, there was the previous owner who was killed in the kitchen with an ax. Is that what you've seen?"

I opened my mouth, but her comment had me tongue tied.

"Gotcha." She smiled, then added, "I've never heard anything but creaking pipes and I've seen nothing scarier than a cobweb."

I shook my head as she walked away. Dolores was sometimes confused, but she was sharp enough to yank my chain when I least expected it.

Len's email was on my computer and I opened the attachments and read the police and coroner's reports. As predicted, they were brief, poorly written, and offered nothing new. I looked at the three pictures of Ole Lundquist's body. I'd never seen his face and his autopsy photo was hardly complimentary, leaving me wondering why that picture had even been taken unless it was intended for identification. The second black and white picture was of Ole's clothed body. The image did little to tell me about his death. What I assumed was blood, appeared black on his light-colored shirt. The third picture was of Ole's naked body. Because it was taken to capture everything from his head to his feet, the only thing of interest was a tiny black hole in his chest. My battlefield experience as a Navy corpsman said the bullet had passed either through the top of his heart or had ripped through the aorta and he'd died quickly.

There were no crime scene photos, none taken with his chest opened, nor was there a picture of his back, where I assume the bullet exited his body.

A final attachment was a crude hand-drawn diagram of his body, front and back, with tiny holes indicated by dots at the tip of arrows.

I closed the attachments, frustrated by their cursory observations and poor police and forensic procedures. Watching television CSI dramas, I knew how much information hadn't been recorded or captured in the photos or reports.

I called Len. "Where are the crime scene photos?"

"There aren't any in the file. You have copies of everything I have."

"By today's standards, this was hardly an investigation."

"Listen, Peter, I'm as frustrated with the information as you are. But there just isn't anything more. I pulled a couple other police reports from that era and they're no better."

I was frustrated when I got off the phone, but then realized Len was working on Ole's murder too. He was as a law-enforcement officer and was just as frustrated as I was. I stood up, trying to figure out what to do.

I shook my head. "What in hell am I going to do now?"

There was a knock on my doorframe.

"A tuba player asks his friend if he'd seen his last recital."

I turned to Brian, his cherubic face smiling. "His friend says, 'I hope so.'"

Brian flopped into my chair and closed the office door.

I remained standing, hoping he'd catch the hint I wanted his visit to be short. "I'm a little busy."

Brian looked around. "It looked like you were talking to yourself."

I gave up and sat down. "What's up?"

"You're investigating Ole Lundquist's murder, right?"

"Who told you that?"

Brian smiled. "It was one of the topics at this week's band practice. If you'd show up, you'd hear all the local news."

"Let me guess; it was the clarinet player. Right?"

Brian put up his hand. "What happens at band practice stays at band practice."

"That's Las Vegas, not the Two Harbors band practice."

"You'd learn many things, and make many friends, if you came to band practice. We could use another tenor sax player." Brian paused. "Are you sold yet?"

I shook my head. "I'm helping the police, but there's not much to go on."

"I was only a couple years old back then, but my parents were living down the street from Ole."

"Are they still alive?"

"My dad died a couple years ago, but my mom lives a couple blocks from the lighthouse. I asked her what she remembered about the Lundquists. She went to school with one of Ole's daughters and remembers when they disappeared."

"I heard his wife packed up the kids and jumped on a train while Ole was working."

"Mom said that happened after Ole beat his wife one too many times. I guess Ole had quite a temper when he was drinking."

"Did your mother stay in contact with Ole's daughter?"

"I don't think Mom knew how to contact the girl, so they lost touch."

"There's all kinds of rumors flying around. I assume most of them are suppositions and lies. If your mother has any concrete knowledge of Ole, his family, or his life after the family left, I'd like to know it."

Brian reached over to my desk and took a note pad. I handed him a pen. "Here's Mom's phone number. She's retired and around the house most days and all evenings."

"Thanks, I'll give her a call."

Brian got up and opened the door, then paused. "It's been kind of crazy for you and your wife since the wedding. Maybe you can come to a practice after things settle down."

"I appreciate your interest in my participation, but I don't see that happening."

"You can't say I didn't try."

I put out my hand. "You tried, but I just don't have the time right now."

"Merry Christmas, doc."

"I've hardly thought about Christmas yet." I grabbed the note pad. "We need to get a tree and decorations. Thanks for reminding me. Merry Christmas to you."

Brian's visit broke my train of thought. I looked at his mother's phone number for a second, then logged onto my computer. The screen opened to the coroner's drawing of Ole's body and I stared at it, disappointed at the quality of the drawing and the coroner's report. I moved from screen to screen, looking at the photos and the reports. I wanted another opinion of what I was seeing. I needed another medical opinion, and the only person who came to mind was Jenny.

I emailed the files to Jenny and walked to her office. She wasn't there, so I stuck a note to her computer screen, explaining the email and asking for her opinion of the coroner's notes, photos, and the police reports.

I walked to the dining room and drew a cup of coffee. Wendy was the only person in the dining room. She was engrossed in a crossword and I weighed walking away against the chance to bug her, repaying some of the jokes she'd played on me.

I sat down at the table and set my cup down a little harder than necessary. She jumped and her pencil flew out of her hand. "Jeez, Peter. You scared the crap out of me."

I picked up her pencil and handed it back to her. "Sorry."

"Don't even pretend you're sorry." She paused, then smiled. "You know I'll get even."

"Oh, no. I was getting even with you."

She waved off my argument. "As long as you're here. I need a three-letter answer. The clue is 'Multiple of LXVII.' It's a Roman numeral. What's an L?"

I did the math in my head. *Sixty-seven times two is one hundred thirty-four, CXXIV. Three times sixty-seven is two-hundred one, CCI.*

"Try CCI."

Wendy penciled in the answer, then looked up. "A ten-letter word for autopsy."

"It's actually two words, post mortem."

Wendy was quickly penciling the crossing words and waved me off. I took my coffee cup and topped it off.

Miriam Milam came out of the kitchen carrying a bowl of apples. "Hi Peter, you and Nancy did a great job defusing the rumors that were flying around. Everyone's back to talking about their grandchildren, gout, and bunions."

"That's great to hear. I just wish I had an actual thread that would lead me to the murderer."

"You don't have anything?"

"I got a bunch of stuff from the police chief, but it's pretty much worthless. I'd like to have a medical examiner, or at least a medical doctor, look at the coroner's pictures and notes."

"You must know a doctor or two. Isn't there someone from your corpsman training or school you could call?"

Wendy walked up behind us, catching the last of our conversation. "Why don't you call that doctor who was French-kissing you at Hugo's?"

"Yes! Thank you." I rushed to my office and closed the door. My old high school chemistry lab partner had shown up at a gig I was playing with Wendy's band. She'd flirted with me, knowing I was engaged to Jenny, so not available. After high school, she'd blossomed from an ugly duckling, with big glasses, braces, and acne, into a pretty redheaded M.D. who worked in the E.R. of a hospital on the Iron Range.

I was ready to pull up the hospital's phone number, then couldn't remember which city she'd said she was in. I searched for her, Roberta Carlton M.D. and found her listed as a resident in the Eveleth hospital.

I was referred from the hospital receptionist to the emergency room. A woman answered and I asked for Doctor Carlton.

"Who should I say is calling?"

"Peter Rogers…no, wait. Say her high school lab partner is on the line."

I was on hold for nearly five minutes and started to think I'd been cut off.

"Peter Rogers? Is it really you?"

"Hi Bobbie. I need some help."

She laughed. "Sorry, I don't fool around with newlyweds."

"Seriously, I need a medical opinion, and I hope you can help."

"I won't give you a prescription for oxycontin or penicillin to treat an STI."

"I'm working with the Two Harbors police on an old murder. I need a medical opinion about an old coroner's report."

Her voice became serious. "I've got your number on caller I.D. Can I call you back in two minutes from my office?"

"Sure."

The phone rang one minute later. "Hi Peter. Sorry about kidding you, but it's quiet right now and the nurses were in stitches as I was ribbing you. I have a sense you can take it."

"I'm glad I could provide the Eveleth E.R. with comic relief."

"So, what's up?"

"Give me your email address and I'll send you a couple reports and some coroner's photos."

"You do know I'm an E.R. doctor and not a forensic pathologist."

"Have you ever seen a gunshot wound?"

"Not as many as you have, but some."

"Give me your email address, then call me back after you look at the pictures."

I hung up and emailed Len's files, then sat at my desk staring at a picture of Ole's dead body displayed on my computer screen.

The phone rang. "Peter."

"Okay, I'm looking at some black and white photos and a crude drawing. What is this?"

"A guy was murdered in 1951 and this is the entire file on his death."

"Is this the time capsule thing?"

"Yes. We think this is the guy who was killed with the gun in the time capsule. His murder wasn't solved."

"Yeah, considering the police and coroner reports, I can see why it wasn't solved unless there was an eye-witness."

"What can you tell me about this guy's death?"

"Hang on. I'm going to blow up the photos to see how much bigger I can make them without losing resolution. I'm putting you on speaker.

"Okay, I see a single gunshot wound to the chest. No sign of ligatures, no other blunt force trauma, no bruising, contusions, nothing. I see one entry wound that probably pierced the pericardium and may have ripped through the left atrium and maybe the aorta. If they'd cut him open, they would've known, not that it would've made much difference. The guy was dead as soon as the bullet hit him although it probably took a couple minutes for him to bleed out. There are powder burns on his shirt and stippling on his skin, so the gun was very close to him, less than six inches away, when it fired."

"So, it was someone he knew, who got very close before firing the gun."

"It's really hard to say, Peter. It could've been a pizza delivery guy who shot the victim when he opened the front door."

"Bobbie, I don't think restaurants delivered in 1951."

"I go by Roberta now. Bobbie was a flat-chested insecure high school girl."

"I'm not Petey anymore, either."

"Was he shot at the front door?"

"The police report doesn't say, but the newspaper said he was murdered in his basement. I don't even know if they recovered the bullet."

"Good luck. There's not much here. Sorry I couldn't be more help."

"Roberta, you added more than the mortician/coroner or the investigating cop. Thank you."

"You're welcome." She paused. "You got married as planned?"

"There were a few complications, including a trip to the ER on the evening of the groom's dinner. But we're married and we've moved into a haunted house."

"Peter, I'm really pleased for you. Jenny seems like a really nice person and I understand she came with a ready-made family. I see a lot of marriages fall apart when people don't work at it. I think you've got your head screwed on, and so does Jenny. I hope you're happy and your marriage lasts forever."

"Thank you, Roberta. That's very kind of you."

She laughed. "And if it doesn't work out, give me a call because I haven't met anyone who'd be as good a catch as you."

"Merry Christmas."

"Merry Christmas to you and your family, Peter. I imagine the first one with a new spouse and kid will be one you'll remember forever."

Howard Johnson was standing in my door when I hung up on Roberta. "I assume you heard some of that conversation."

Howard smiled. "I heard nothing."

"Just like Sergeant Schultz on Hogan's Heroes."

Howard shook his head. "I hope I'm a little more on top of things than Schultz." He paused. "Are we going to the historical society today?"

"Oh, crap, I forgot about that. I haven't posted a sign-up sheet."

"Warm up the van. I'll round up a couple volunteers."

I called the historical society from my office and connected with Molly Schroeder, the president. I explained my plan to have some senior citizens search for archival information about the murder and work on the band shell.

"Peter, I'm pleased you're pursuing the information in the time capsule, but we're in winter mode, and I'm here alone and not really prepared to deal with an influx of people."

"I'm only bringing a few of my mentally sharper residents and the scope of our research is limited."

"Why don't you try the library," she suggested.

"We were there, and we went through old newspaper for pertinent articles, but I'm sure your archives are better." I had no idea what the historical society archives contained, nor did I know who I'd be bringing for the search other than Howard Johnson. I was embarrassed by how quickly I could make up plausible lies.

Molly sighed. "Can you come after Christmas? I'll try to get a couple volunteers here to help."

"Molly, I messed up. I have people lining up for the van as we speak. Is there any way you can let us into the archives today?"

"This is not convenient."

"We're trying to figure out the mystery revealed by your time capsule."

"Fine. I'll be here and I'll unlock the archives, but I have to stay close to the front door. I trust you'll supervise the people and return everything to where you find it."

"Of course!"

I ran out the back door and started the van. It was starting to warm as I pulled under the portico. Howard Johnson had only three volunteers. We were loading when I spied Wendy, so I drafted her, then drove to the Lake

County Historical Society building on South Avenue.

Molly, a middle-aged woman who'd taken over the chairman's position several years ago, met us at the door. She was wrapped in a heavy sweater and looked unhappy as she held the door for us.

"I have the heat down for the winter," she said as she took us to the archives. "Here are the archives. Please return everything where you find it." She walked away quickly, leaving us in a large room with books, photo albums, ship models, and dusty memorabilia.

I looked at my volunteers. "Let's see if there's anything that relates to band shell construction, reconstruction, or Ole Lundquist's murder."

I went to the bookshelves and read book spines, virtually all histories of the Minnesota Iron Range, the railroads, and shipping. Many were one-of-a-kind books, and a few were loose-leaf binders of typed or handwritten pages. Nothing I saw looked pertinent to our search.

"Peter." I looked across the room where Howard had a photo album spread on a countertop.

"What did you find?"

Howard turned the album so I could see the pictures of construction people working on the band shell. "This says it was the 1952 repair of the basement stairs and stucco."

140

"Bingo! That helps fill in part of the story. We know there was construction going on when the time capsule was put in the building. Is there a list of the construction workers?"

Howard flipped through a few pages and shook his head. "No, this moves ahead to other civic projects in '53. There's no list of the workers, but I recognize my friend, Oscar Ledin."

"Any chance he was Ole's killer?"

"I'd say it's unlikely. He was a happily married young man with a couple kids."

"Do you know any of the others?"

Howard flipped through the two pages of '53 bandshell pictures. "Some of the other faces look familiar, but I don't remember their names."

"Where's Oscar Ledin? Maybe he'll remember some names."

"Oscar's in the Catholic cemetery, so he won't be any help."

I took out my cellphone and shot photos of the album. "Maybe someone back at Whistling Pines will remember some of these faces."

Howard was flipping through the photos when I turned away. His voice stopped me. "There was construction in the '60s, too. It looks like there were some repairs on the backside of the bandshell."

"My gut says the box was put in the wall in '52. The newspaper was from the week after the murder."

141

Howard smiled. "The newspaper was put in some time after the murder. Who's to say it was placed there in the '50s versus the '60s, or even last year?"

"The hinges on the box were rusty," I replied.

"How long would it take for steel hinges to rust enough to squeak when you opened the box? Maybe they were squeaky when the box was placed in the wall."

"You're breaking down all my nice clean theories."

Howard closed the photo album. "Isn't that what a good defense attorney would do?"

"Yes, but there's never going to be a trial."

"I've guessed there aren't many nice clean murder investigations that can be solved in an hour unless you're filming a television drama."

"Touché."

We gave up after forty minutes without finding any additional information about Ole's murder, the '52 bandshell reconstruction, or the workers.

I sent Len an email with the photos and gave him Oscar Ledin's name, then printed out the pictures and put them on my office door with a note asking if anyone could identify the men in the picture.

Chapter 11

After being admonished about my menus leaning heavily on tomato and onions, I picked up groceries, shopping heavily in the produce aisle. I drove home with two bags of salads and vegetables. Because we were at the winter solstice, it was already dark and I noticed that nearly every house had outside Christmas decorations or their drapes were open to display the glowing Christmas tree in their living room. I felt guilty for not having the Christmas spirit.

Jeremy was watching television. I turned off the set and got him started on his homework. As I pulled out a large bowl to assemble a tossed salad, I heard scratching noises from the pantry.

I kicked myself for not buying a live trap to deal with the chipmunk. I made sure the pantry door was still closed, listened to rustling noises that sounded like paper being shredded, and left well enough alone, going back to supper preparations.

Jenny, whose job routinely required her to spend an hour or more updating medical charts after her scheduled work hours, cruised in looking tired and haggard. She appraised the salad bowl as she went past on her way to change.

"Ooh, green stuff for supper," she said, pecking me on the cheek. "I'll be back in a couple minutes."

I heard the shower running as I set the table and reflected on a conversation from our months of dating. She'd arrived at my house fresh from work and I had dinner sitting on the table. Despite my protests she insisted on changing before eating. I'd argued that supper would be cold. She'd responded that she'd been in contact with a variety of bodily fluids and was going to change and shower before eating. I found her argument compelling and filed that away, always having supper close to ready, but never sitting on the table when she came home.

I heard her footsteps on the stairs and I pulled a pork tenderloin and sweet potatoes out of the oven.

She stepped into the kitchen in a clean long-sleeved t-shirt and jeans, looking refreshed and pretty. "Mm, that smells heavenly. What can I do?"

"There's a bottle of wine in the refrigerator. You could open it and pour for you and me."

She took down a wine glass and a two tumblers, then froze when she heard noises from the pantry. "Did you buy a trap?"

"I got side-tracked buying groceries and making supper."

She leaned against the counter. "So, what's your plan for dealing with Chipper?"

"Chipper?"

"Well, since we're going to live trap him and we can't set him loose outside, I suppose he's going to be a pet."

"A pet chipmunk? Really?"

"Do you have a better solution for Chipper?"

I let out a sigh. "Open the wine and we'll talk about it after supper."

She poured wine for me and milk for herself and Jeremy. Based on my poor history of dealing with past-expiration dairy products, she sniffed the carton before pouring the milk.

"I bought that milk two days ago. It's fine."

She carried the glasses of milk past me and grabbed the salad bowl. "I know, dear, but it's hard to break old habits."

I sliced the pork and was putting the sweet potatoes into a serving bowl when she returned for the wine glass. "Are you talking about my habit of not checking the expiration date on the milk, or your habit of sniffing everything before it's served?"

Jenny paused as she passed me. "Yes."

I set the serving bowl and platter of meat on the table and dished greens into my salad bowl. Jeremy dug into the pork and had it cut up before Jenny prompted him by passing the salad. He put a piece of meat in his mouth, then put one small lettuce leaf in his salad bowl.

I took the salad and heaped a pile of lettuce, tomatoes, and cucumber into his bowl, garnering a glare. Then I set a baked whole sweet potato on his plate.

Jenny watched with amusement. "I hope you're not planning to take a Percocet after the wine."

I sipped my wine, having thoughts of evening romance, not Percocet, in my future. "I think the pain is better today."

Jenny, knowing that a bottle of wine usually led to a romantic evening, glanced at Jeremy, who was trying to scrape the sweet potato out of the skin without burning his fingers. I caught her meaning and nodded. Then I shrugged and mouthed, "Who knows?"

I got a skeptical look in return.

"No wine for you?" I asked.

"I'm dead tired. I'd fall asleep and fall face-down in my supper."

I had a forkful of pork halfway to my mouth when I saw motion under the dining room window. My first thought was that Chipper had escaped, but it was a gray mouse scooting across the floor. He paused to pick up a bread crumb, probably left over from Jeremy's after school snack, then ran to the corner to eat it. I looked at Jeremy, who was focused on his food, then at Jenny who'd seen the mouse and sighed.

I closed my eyes, then whispered, "I'll get mousetraps tomorrow."

146

"A live trap and mousetraps," she whispered back.

I nodded and made a mental note.

We ate supper, getting an update on school activities, then cleared the table. Jeremy and I were washing dishes when Jenny pulled the drying towel from my hand.

"I'll dry dishes. Go figure out how to deal with Chipper."

I heard music outside. It took a second until I recognized "Good King Wenceslaus" being carried through the evening air by carolers and a couple instruments. I took the towel from Jenny and threw it on the counter, then grabbed Jeremy's hand.

Jenny opened the front door to a dozen carolers dressed in heavy coats and stocking caps, with a small group of musicians, including Brian, the tuba player.

They moved on to "Deck the Halls" as Jenny pulled Jeremy and me close. "This is our first Christmas as a family," she whispered.

Brian handed off his tuba when the song ended, and he bent down behind the carolers. There was a flurry of activity and when the carolers parted, Brian marched up our steps carrying a Christmas tree.

"The band figured you've been kind of distracted with the wedding and move, so we got together and decided you probably hadn't had time to cut a Christmas tree."

He pushed past me, tracking snow and a trail of pine needles across the living room. The clarinet player followed with a scarred Christmas tree stand, and behind her came two carolers with boxes of lights with tangled wires and a box of mismatched ornaments. We watched in stunned silence as the tree was screwed into the stand, the lights untangled, and the ornaments set out on the fireplace hearth.

The group stepped back, displaying what was possibly the ugliest tree since Charlie Brown's Christmas. The balsam was nearly bare on one side and the trunk had a kink that made it lean to the left. I surveyed it, wondering how it managed to stay in the stand without tipping over.

The carolers and band members gathered around us, all their faces red from the outside cold.

Brian glowed. "We figured you probably didn't have any lights or decorations, so we each picked a couple of the more hideous ones from our own collections and brought them. No one will feel bad if you replace them next year and donate the old ones to the Methodist Church rummage sale."

Jenny, with tears in her eyes, hugged Brian, then moved on to the others. I shook hands, thanking people as I moved along.

Brian bent down and shook hands with Jeremy. "Do you know how to fix a broken tuba?"

Jeremy shook his head.

"With a tuba glue." Brian snickered.

It took Jeremy a moment to get the joke, then he smiled and looked at me. "I'm going to tell that tomorrow at school."

Brian shook my hand. "I guess we'll go and let you guys decorate your tree."

"Thank you. You've made this a Christmas we'll never forget."

Jenny hugged him again and kissed his cheek. "Thank you. I think you've helped us find our Christmas spirit."

Brian stepped back. "Unless there's something else I can do..."

"Christmas spirits!" I said, snapping my fingers. "We could use some help catching a ghost."

The whole group looked at me like I was crazy.

"We've had strange noises since we moved in and Jeremy thought we had a ghost. Last night we caught the ghost and he's locked in our pantry."

Brian smiled, assuming I was joking. "I'd be happy to exorcise your house with tuba music, but an accordion or bagpipe might be more effective at driving a spirit away."

I shook my head. "Our ghost is a chipmunk. I closed the pantry on him last night, but he's loose in there and I need to catch him. Do any of you have a live trap?"

The carolers shook their heads, but Brian smiled. "It's actually pretty easy. Get a blanket."

Jenny looked skeptical but ran upstairs.

"What's your plan?" I asked.

"You hold the blanket up in front of you, so the chipmunk can't see your face. Then, you sneak up to him, drop the blanket over him, clutch him gently in the blanket, then carry him outside and let him go."

"You're joking?"

"No. I've actually caught rabbits and a baby racoon that way. I've heard it works with skunks, too, but that's an experience I'll leave to someone else."

Jenny appeared with the blanket. "What now?"

"Hand the blanket to Peter and you open the pantry. He's going to hold the blanket up and drop it over the chipmunk."

The entire band and caroler entourage followed me into the kitchen, all interested in seeing the chipmunk capture. I held up the blanket and Jenny opened the door. The theory sounded implausible, but then became unworkable when I realized having the blanket up so the chipmunk couldn't see me, meant I couldn't see the chipmunk either.

I lowered the blanket, trying to locate the chipmunk, but he was nowhere in sight. Assuming he was in the box of wedding gifts, I raised the blanket and walked toward the box, planning to cover the whole box and carry it outside.

With my face carefully hidden, I advanced slowly down the long pantry. I heard paper crumpling and scratching, then Chipper flashed past me, running down a pantry shelf. Cereal boxes flew off the shelf and a woman shrieked in the kitchen. I turned and took a step toward the kitchen, stepped on cereal boxes that slid under my feet, then fell, trying to catch myself with my hands tangled in the blanket.

My ribs hit the doorframe and I saw stars as I tumbled to the floor. My mind numbed with pain, heard women shrieking and men yelling as they dodged around the kitchen. I saw a flash of Chipper racing down the counter and behind the sink. The crowd followed him into the living room as I lay on the floor, clutching my ribs.

Jenny bent down. "Can you take a deep breath?"

"I don't think so," I croaked as people yelled at each other in the living room.

Someone shouted, "Ralph, keep him off the stairs!"

I looked at Jenny. "Oh, please, don't let him upstairs."

"He's in the Christmas tree!"

Jenny was staring at me, but I knew she was focused on the shouts coming from the living room.

There was a crash, more shouts and screams. I lost track of the running chase as I tried to push myself up from the floor.

"Pick up the tree. Don't let him back in the tree!"

"He's in the couch! Lift up the cushions before he digs in!"

Jenny grimaced. "Not the couch."

"I've got the kitchen blocked!"

"Ralph, look out! He's headed for the stairs!"

Jenny helped me to my feet and we shuffled to the door between the kitchen and the dining room. People had their coats off and it looked like we had a dozen toreadors racing around the living room, trying to corral the chipmunk.

"Open the front door!"

I felt a cold gust as the front door opened.

"He's coming back toward the fireplace! Judy, grab him!"

"I'm not grabbing him. You grab him!"

I saw one of the men leap forward, his jacket extended. "I missed him!"

We got to the edge of the living room and watched the band and carolers, who now looked like a rugby scrum in the middle of the room. A man was on the floor with the others stepping on, over, and around him while he spit expletives and tried to get up.

I saw a flash of tan on top of the mantel, followed by decorations and lights crashing to the floor. Then Chipper disappeared. A hand reached out and grabbed Jeremy's wiggling Christmas stocking and pulled it down. I saw a man trying to run toward the front door through the crowd. The door slammed and the riot seemed to end.

Brian walked through the front door a moment later, smiling broadly, and carrying the empty Christmas stocking. "He's out!"

The carolers and band members straightened up and gathered their coats. None of them were spring chickens, and there were a lot of groans and oaths as they gathered themselves together.

Jeremy took the stocking from Brian and hung it back on the mantel.

"The good news is he's out," Brian said, picking up the lamp and returning it to the table next to the couch. "The bad news is that Ralph's truck was open, and Chipper ran into the cab of the truck."

"Why'd you let him do that?" Ralph asked, leaving his post guarding the stairs.

"I was focused on keeping him out of the house. I let him loose in the middle of the yard and he made a run for the open pickup door."

Ralph shook his head. "I guess I'll put some peanut butter on my gopher trap and set it on the floorboards tonight."

Jeremy looked stricken. "You're not going to kill Chipper?"

Ralph shook his head. "It's a live trap. I'll catch him and set him loose out back. I've got a big brush pile and he'll find a cozy spot in there for the winter."

Jeremy accepted that, but Jenny looked skeptical.

Our guests started moving to the front door and I got my first look at the living room. The tree was on its side, with pine needles spread over half the living room. There were broken ornaments on the hearth, and the Persian rug was bunched up. The couch cushions were on the floor and a chair was tipped over. All in all, it looked like the living room had been ransacked by vandals.

Brian stood at the door as the last people left. He looked at the living room and shook his head. "I feel bad leaving you with this mess, but we did get rid of the chipmunk."

Jenny left me leaning on the dining room door frame and gave Brian a hug. "We'll never forget this Christmas. Thank you."

She closed the door, then looked around the room. "Where's grandma's ceramic tree?" She threw couch cushions aside while I clutched my ribs and searched around the dining room.

Jeremy shouted, "Found it!"

Jenny was kneeling at the end of the couch, picking up pieces from the floor. My heart sank, then I saw the ceramic tree on the couch. Jenny stood, holding out a handful of the tiny plastic inserts that glowed like Christmas lights on the ceramic tree when the lightbulb in the base was lit.

"It's intact?" I croaked.

Jenny nodded, then realized I was bent over, taking shallow breaths, and holding my ribs.

She set the tiny bulbs on the coffee table. "I assume we're going to the emergency room."

"I can take a Percocet and go to bed."

"You can't take a Percocet on top of wine. Jeremy, put on your pajamas and slippers, grab your quilt, and meet us in the car."

I was slipping on my shoes when I heard talking downstairs. The male voice was indistinct but seemed very real.

Jenny looked at me. "Are the carolers back?"

The voice stopped and a country western song started.

"Well, that's not chipper and it's not the carolers and band."

Jenny and I walked down the stairs and followed the music into the kitchen. An old radio, left behind by Dolores, was sitting at the end of the counter, playing Patsy Cline's version of "Crazy."

I turned the volume knob until it clicked and the music stopped.

Jenny shivered. "Chipper didn't do that."

I shook my head and Jeremy bounded down the stairs and saw us standing by the radio. "Why'd you turn the radio on? I thought we were going somewhere."

I closed my eyes, not wanting to address the situation. "I wanted to see if it worked."

Jenny led me to the car and helped me into the passenger seat. Jeremy came flying out of the house, slammed the door, and ran through the snow in his puppy slippers, the ears flapping like Dumbo trying to take off.

He jumped in the backseat and slammed the door. "Where are we going?"

"We're taking your dad to the hospital."

Jeremy buckled his seatbelt. "Why? Did Chipper bite him?"

"Chipper didn't bite anyone. Dad hurt himself."

"When? He wasn't even in the living room?"

"Earlier."

"When, earlier? When we were washing dishes?"

Jenny drove down the street, trying to focus on her driving. "In the pantry."

"How did he hurt himself in the pantry?"

"I slipped on the cereal boxes," I said, a little too sharply.

"What cereal boxes?"

"Give it a rest," Jenny said, trying to break the cycle of question. "We'll talk about it when your dad is in with the doctor."

"But I just wanted to know…"

"Shh. Later."

* * *

We got home from the emergency room shortly after midnight. Jeremy was asleep in the backseat. Normally, I would've carried him to bed, but even lifting my arms caused pain. Jenny woke him up and led him to his bedroom. He was in a deep stupor and didn't resist sleeping in his own bed.

156

I unbuckled my belt, unfastened my jeans, and let them drop to my feet. Sitting on the edge of the bed I pushed off my shoes and pulled my feet out of the jeans, then rolled into bed. Jenny had to pull the sheet and quilt out from under me, then spread them over me.

She kissed my cheek. "I think I'll sleep on the couch so I don't accidentally poke you or throw and arm over your chest."

I didn't argue. I drifted into oblivion, carried on the numbing effects of the morphine I'd got in the ER.

Chapter 12

I rolled over, getting a sharp pain from my own elbow tucked under my ribs. The bleary red digits on the alarm clock showed 4:50. The room was dark and the other side of the bed was empty. I lay on my back and tried to fall asleep but gave up after twenty minutes.

With effort, I took off my shirt and boxers and stepped into the old claw-foot bathtub. I got a stabbing pain when I reached for the shower curtain. The hot water poured over me and I closed my eyes. A second later the water was icy and I nearly fell, scooting away from the cold spray. I steadied myself, ready to step out of the tub, but the water turned warm, then back to hot. After cursing the century old pipes, I quickly shampooed, scrubbed my torso, rinsed, and turned off the water without getting another jolt of cold water.

Jenny walked into the bathroom while I was drying off.

"Why are you up?" I asked.

"I heard you moving around and thought I'd better check on you. How's your pain this morning?"

"Not as bad as last night."

Jenny shook her head. It's hard to lie to a nurse about pain. "Pain is always worse the day after the injury. Always."

I wiped my torso and bent to wipe my legs, but gasped.

Jenny took the towel from me and wiped my legs and feet. "You don't have to be a hero. Take a pain pill and go back to bed. Whistling Pines will survive without you for a day."

"I'd rather have the diversion of work than sit here in a drug-induced stupor watching game shows on television."

Jenny ushered me out of the bathroom and got clothes out of her drawers. "Get dressed as best you can while I shower. I'll help with your socks and shoes when I get dried off."

"Be careful in the shower. It went from hot, to cold, back to hot on me."

"Gremlins," she said with a smile. "Or, I might've flushed the downstairs toilet while you were showering."

"Ah, mystery solved."

I was dressed, except for socks and shoes, when she stepped out of the bathroom in her scrubs. She got a pair of my socks out of my dresser and rolled them onto my feet, then put my shoes on and tied the laces.

"There's coffee downstairs," she said as she picked up my dirty clothes and put them into the hamper.

I often had cereal for breakfast, but the pantry light illuminated the cereal boxes on the floor, all crushed in my rush to catch Chipper. Some had broken open and spilled onto the floor. I decided on toast as a better option, not wanting to bend and reach down.

I was eating toast and drinking coffee when Jenny came downstairs. Although her clothes were neat and fresh and she'd put on a touch of makeup, her eyes said the emergency room trip had cost her most of a night's sleep. I heard her picking up the cereal boxes and sweeping up the mess on the pantry floor.

She set the corn flakes box on the table, then sat down with her coffee, a bowl, sugar and the carton of milk. "The corn flakes were the only cereal that didn't break open. I threw the other boxes into the wastebasket."

I watched her pour cereal into her bowl, then add sugar and milk. "You must be *very* tired."

"Did the dark bags under my eyes give it away?"

"No. You didn't sniff the milk before you poured it on your cereal."

She stopped with the spoon halfway to her mouth, thought a second, then put the spoonful in her mouth. "You only bought it like three days ago."

I picked up my plateful of crumbs and walked to the kitchen. "You *always* sniffed the milk at my house before you poured it."

I brought back the coffee carafe and topped off both our cups.

"Did you take a pain pill with your toast?"

"I took a couple aspirin. I'll bring the bottle to work and take more with lunch."

"Put the Percocet in your pocket, too."

"I can't function or drive if I take the narcotics."

Jenny carried her bowl to the sink. "Take it if you need it. I'll drive you home. I'm going to roust Jeremy out of bed. Can you pack a lunch for him?"

I sat down at the dining room table, exhausted from the pain and exertion of eating and clearing the dishes. "I think it should be a school hot lunch day."

Jenny shook her head, then went upstairs. I was halfway through my second cup of coffee and reading the news on my cellphone when the kitchen radio came on halfway through a Shania Twain song. I jumped as it blared out "Any Man of Mine."

I got up, walked to the kitchen, half expecting Jenny to have slipped past while I was engrossed in the news about New Zealand's young Prime Minister and her plans to overhaul their social services.

The kitchen was empty. I grabbed the volume knob, but it was already turned off. I hesitated a second, then pulled the plug out of the wall socket.

Jenny's footsteps pounded down the stairs and she flew into the kitchen. "Why did you have the radio on so loud?"

I paused, looking at the radio. "It turned itself on again."

"How?"

I shrugged. "The knob was turned off. I had to unplug it."

Jenny stared at the radio. "What happens if you plug it in?"

I looked at her, then at the radio. I picked up the plug and put it into the socket. Sparks shot out of the radio and the lights went out. I pulled the plug.

Jenny stepped back. "That was exciting."

Feet thundered down the stairs and Jeremy raced into the kitchen. "Hey! Who turned out the lights?"

I fumbled through the "junk drawer" until I felt the flashlight. "I guess we're buying more fuses at the hardware store."

Jeremy followed me to the basement. I let him identify the burned fuse and he screwed the new one in while I held the flashlight. The lights came on and he beamed.

I heard the radio go into the wastebasket as we walked up from the basement.

Jenny was wiping up blackened bits of plastic and wire insulation when I put the

162

flashlight away. "I take it you've put an end to the radio gremlin."

"It looked like Chipper had chewed the insulation off the wires where they went into the radio. I think we can call him the gremlin in this case."

I nodded toward the waste basket. "Jeremy, please take the garbage out."

"Aw, that's my after-supper job. I'll do it tonight."

"I'm afraid there might still be some hot wires in the radio and I'd rather have it in an outside metal garbage can than in the kitchen wastebasket if it started a fire."

He thought about my argument for a second, then pulled the plastic bag out of the wastebasket.

While he was outside Jenny smiled. "You handled that better than I would've. He and I would've had an argument about who was the mom and who was the kid, and it would've dragged on until he'd been in danger of losing television privileges. Your logical explanation was very slick. Thank you."

Jeremy walked in, unhappy, but with the task done. Jenny smiled at him. "Did you get any homework done last night?"

"I did it before supper."

"Can I see it?"

Jeremy let out a sigh, then pulled open his backpack and removed a stack of papers. Jenny was reading through them when she stopped abruptly. "You didn't tell us there is a Christmas play."

Jeremy shrugged. "I thought I had."

"What part do you have?"

"I'm an elf."

Jenny looked at the announcement again and her eyes went wide. "The play is tonight!"

Jeremy nodded. "I guess."

"How would we have known about it if I hadn't found this announcement?"

"I s'pose I would've told you at supper."

Jenny walked to the calendar we'd just put up. "Luckily, there's nothing else going on."

"What time does it start?" I asked.

Jenny picked up the notice. "Seven o'clock."

I pulled out my cellphone and hit Mother's number in the directory. She sounded like I'd woken her. "Mom, you've got grandma duty tonight."

"What? Peter?"

"Yes, it's your son, Peter. Your grandson is in a Christmas play tonight. It's at seven o'clock in the elementary school auditorium. We'll save a chair for you if you're running late."

"What are you talking about?"

"Yes, he's an elf in the play. I'm sure it'll be delightful."

"Hang on. I have to put on my glasses and look at the calendar."

"That's great, Mom. I'm sure Jeremy will appreciate you rearranging your calendar so you can come to his play."

"You're railroading me."

"That's right. Seven o'clock in the grade school auditorium."

I disconnected before Mother could argue with me, then I turned off my cellphone.

Jeremy's eyes lit up. "Grandma Rogers is coming?"

I was about to say yes, when I realized she might not respond to my new pushy demeanor. "She's trying to rearrange her calendar and she hopes to make it."

"Cool! Mom, will you invite regular grandma and grandpa?"

Jenny cocked her head. "Regular grandma and grandpa?"

"I'm calling Dad's mother Grandma Rogers. I think my other grandma and grandpa are the 'regular' ones."

Jenny smiled. "I'll call regular grandma when I get to work. They'll probably come to the play too."

We drove Jeremy to school, where he was in before-school activities. We'd agreed that he wasn't responsible enough to get out the door and on the bus by himself, but we'd acquiesced to his argument that his friends all rode the bus home from school and spent the afternoons home alone until their parents got home from work. I handed him two dollars to buy a hot lunch, then he ran up the sidewalk to the school.

"He always seems excited to be at school in the mornings," I said.

"He plays chess with a friend before school. He looks forward to it." Jenny paused. "Do you think Audrey will actually come to the play?"

"I don't know. I turned off my phone so she couldn't argue with me about it. I figure the odds are about three to one against her showing up, but we should save her a chair, just in case."

Wendy wasn't in the dining room when I got coffee, but Howard Johnson was sitting at a table with Lee Westfall. Howard waved me over and pulled out a chair.

"We heard you were in the emergency room last night. Any major damage?"

I sat down and shook my head. "You're joking. Who told you I was in the emergency room?"

Howard smiled. "There's not much point in divulging my secret source. If I do, he or she, won't be a source anymore."

Lee looked concerned. "You grimaced when you sat down. Are you sure you should be here?"

"I banged my ribs again. I'm okay."

Lee smiled. "Oh, when you were chasing the chipmunk?"

"All right, you two. Were you window peeping?"

Howard looked at Lee. "I guess we're busted. I told you we shouldn't be looking in his windows."

Lee slapped his knee and laughed.

I saw Miriam peek out of the kitchen when she heard Lee laughing. She came to the table carrying three saucers with poppyseed Danish pastries. "These just came out of the oven, so the frosting is going to run all over when you eat them." She winked at me and retreated.

Lee took a bite of his Danish. "You got something going on the side with her? She only brings us hot baked goods when you're here, Peter."

I shook my head. "She's just a very special, caring friend."

"How's the murder investigation going?"

"There's not much to go on."

Lee took the last bite of pastry and licked frosting off his fingers. "The cops should have some records to look at."

"They do, but they're incomplete and the coroner was a funeral director. All he did was make sure Ole Lundquist was dead and snap a couple photos of the body. There's nothing but dead ends and rumors."

"Did the police find any clues when they searched Ole's house?"

"If they did, they didn't write it down."

"Sounds like pretty shoddy police work to me."

I rolled my shoulders and got a stabbing pain in return for the motion. Howard and Lee

167

looked at me with concern, but I waved them off. "I think the state of forensic investigations was pretty thin back then, and unless someone witnessed the murder or there were fingerprints on a murder weapon, most crimes went unsolved."

"Were there fingerprints on the murder weapon?" Howard asked.

I froze. "I'll have to ask the police chief. I'm not even sure the old gun in the time capsule was the murder weapon. I don't know if they can get fingerprints off a rusty old pistol, but I should ask the question."

Lee smiled. "Sounds like you're on a wild goose chase."

"More like a scavenger hunt but I don't know what I'm supposed to find."

Howard's eyes lit up. "I think you've just solved your problem with the rumormongering. Put together a scavenger hunt. Everyone will be too busy to spread rumors."

I smiled, but I was grimacing inside. "Throw out a few ideas of items we could search for."

Howard immediately saw my problem. "We're in a pretty closed environment. You don't want people chasing around outside, nor do you want them damaging things or fighting over things that are rare."

Lee nodded. "There are some things that would take some time, but everyone can find, like an obituary notice and an ad for denture cream."

I took out a pen and a small notepad. "Okay. Give me some more."

Howard pointed at my pen. "A pen, a cancelled stamp on an envelope, a black & white photo."

Lee's eyes lit up. "Everyone's got a picture of a grandchild, niece or nephew. A popcorn kernel, a leaf, a paperback book, a feather, a staple."

After five minutes we'd developed a list of thirty things that would be relatively common but would challenge people to roam around the building in their search.

I thanked the men, refilled my coffee, and walked back to my office. I took out my cellphone to call Len and ask about fingerprints, but realized I'd turned it off when I'd ended my call with Mother. As it powered up there were chimes, telling me I had three messages from Mother. I dialed my voicemail and listened.

"Peter. Why would you sandbag me like this? I can't just drive to Two Harbors on a few hours' notice. Call me."

"Are you screening my calls. Call me back. I've got commitments tonight, and I don't want to change them to attend a grade school Christmas play. Call me as soon as you get this."

"Peter. I understand that you want me to be Jeremy's grandmother, but you've got to give me some notice. You can't call in the morning and expect me to show up this evening. Call me."

The phone chimed while I was listening to the third message. By the time the message was over, there was a new voicemail.

"Okay. I'm getting the message. I'm either a grandmother, or I'm out of your life." There was a pause. "I'm cancelling my plans for tonight. I'm not sure where the school is, but I'm coming. Please call me with directions when you get this message." There was another pause and I thought she'd been looking for the key to end the call when her voice came over the phone again. "I'm sorry I wasn't much of a mother, and it's a little late to say this, but I do love you, even if I haven't said it with my actions. Please call me." Her voice cracked at the end.

I punched in Mother's number and she picked up on the first ring. "Peter?"

"Hi, Mom. You left a couple messages."

"Peter…"

"What, Mom?"

"Where's Jeremy's school?"

I gave her directions and an estimate of how long it would take to get from Duluth to the school.

"Okay. Save a chair in case I'm running late."

"Mom, Jeremy asked if Grandma Rogers would come. He told us his 'regular' grandma

170

and grandpa would be there, but he wanted you there too. I told him I wasn't sure."

There was a long pause. "This is what you meant when you told me it was time to quit mailing in my parenting."

"I'm sorry about the short notice, but we literally found out about the Christmas play at seven this morning. But that's the way parenting, and grandparenting goes. I've learned to be flexible and do whatever it takes to be there so Jeremy knows he can count on me. That's what it means to be his father."

"I'm starting to understand. Please bear with me, it's a learning process."

"And it's not without discomfort. See you tonight, Mom."

"Peter..."

"Yes."

"I'll be there."

"Why don't you plan to come over to our house after the play. You can see our Christmas decorations. Howard and Barbara brought Jeremy's stocking over and we hung it over the fireplace."

"I'd like that. I'm embarrassed to say this, but I don't know where you house is."

"You can follow us home from the play."

* * *

171

I posted notices about the scavenger hunt, advising that the list of items would be handed out at lunch. I was filling my cup in the dining room when Wendy called my name. She was at her usual morning spot in the back corner. The tablecloth was folded back, and she had a pencil poised over the crossword puzzle.

I handed her a stack of papers listing the scavenger hunt items. "Please hand these out at lunch."

"Where are you going to be?"

"I've got to run into town and buy mouse traps."

She scanned the list. "Most of these things should be pretty easy to find."

"That's the point. I want it to take some time, but I hope virtually everyone will complete the list and win a prize."

"What are the prizes?"

"Len Rentz gave me a couple bags of hard candy. All the winners get their choice of one piece."

Wendy nodded and set the stack aside. "I need an eight-letter word for, 'poem with vertical name.'"

"That would be acrostic."

"Spell it."

"A-C-R-O-S-T-I-C."

As she filled in the letters my mind raced to the poems in the time capsule.

"I've never heard that word before. How do you know that stuff?"

172

I set my cup on Wendy's table and dodged around the people coming in for breakfast. I pulled up the *Duluth Times* website and typed in "poem." The results were stories about the newly appointed Wisconsin poet laureate and the poet who was the runner-up in the Northeastern Minnesota Book Award competition. I retyped my search, this time asking, "Two Harbors murder." The results went back to the Whistling Pines resident who'd been kidnapped and killed over rumored gold coins. I typed in a third search for "Two Harbors time capsule" and got the article about the time capsule recovered during the demolition of the band shell. Buried in the middle of the article I found the list of the contents: A pistol. A newspaper. Two poems. The article didn't print the poems, just said they were hand-written and faded.

I dialed Len Rentz's cellphone and waited impatiently for him to answer. It rolled over to his voicemail and I left a message asking him to email the poems found in the time capsule.

I stared at the phone, willing Len to answer my message, but my ESP was malfunctioning. He didn't get my brainwaves. I ran my hand over my hair, searching for another avenue to get the text of the poem.

I Googled the phone number for the local newspaper and dialed from my cellphone, not tying up my office phone if Len returned my call. A young woman with a perky voice answered.

"*Two Harbors News,* this is Jenn. How can I help you?"

"Hi, did you publish the text of the poems found in the time capsule?"

"I'm not sure. Let me get Sally, the editor." The line went quiet while I waited on hold.

"This is Sally."

"Hi, I'm Peter Rogers. I was wondering if you published the text of the poems found inside the time capsule."

"Peter, from Whistling Pines. I remember you from the murder investigation last year. Hang on." I heard keys clicking, then paper rustling. "I did a short article last week but didn't put the poems in it. I was holding it for this week's edition, waiting to see how much room we had when I did the final layout."

"Can you email a copy of the poems to me?"

"I'm doing the final layout of this week's edition right now. Can you wait until Thursday?"

"It might be critical to finding the murderer. Can you at least read them to me?"

Sally sighed. "I'm busy. Can you wait until tomorrow?"

"Hand them to Jenn. She can read them to me or email me."

"This is Jenn. Sally just handed me two poems and I'm not sure why."

"Please scan them and email them to me right away." I gave Jenn my email address and she promised to get them to me immediately.

I sat impatiently, waiting for the incoming mail to pop up on my computer screen.

"How do you call a tuba player?"

I looked at the door. Brian, the tuba player was the last person I wanted to see. Well, maybe Hulda Packer would've been worse, but Brian, with a bad tuba joke, was next to last. I shook my head.

"Euphonium him." Brian sat in my guest chair, uninvited. "You get it, right? It's a play on words with euphonium, a baritone horn."

"Yeah, I got it. But I'm a little busy right now."

"You're staring at your computer screen doing nothing. That's hardly busy."

"I'm sorry. Busy is the wrong word. I'm preoccupied."

Brian's cherubic face and infectious smile were disarming. "Let me change your preoccupation to an occupation. I need an accordion player Friday for a wedding reception. I thought you might be willing to sit in."

"Sorry, I never learned the accordion."

Brian reached around the doorframe and slid a battered accordion case into my office. "I thought you might say that, so I came prepared. You're a musical genius and I thought you could figure out an accordion if I gave you a couple days to play with it."

I shook my head. "I'm up to my eyeballs. I've got a new wife, a new son, a new house, and the police chief has me trying to solve a seventy-year-old mystery. I don't have the time or interest in learning the accordion."

Brian got up and slid the accordion case into the corner. "I'll leave this in case you change your mind." He was gone before I could protest.

My computer dinged, signaling the arrival of an email. The screen identified the sender as Jenn at the newspaper. I opened the email and read the poems.

Sunshine beams through windowpanes
A bedroom mirror, your beauty frames
Raven hair drapes slender hips
A pretty smile, inviting lips
Houses close, yet far apart
Stolen glimpses pull at my heart
I've felt we should be lovers
My heart fears you belong to others
Please look my way and blow a kiss
Steal a moment, no one will miss
Only then can our passions flare
Nothing could your love compare

Just glimpses stolen
O'er garden walls
And lips pressed sweet
Names whispered, please call
Never ending warm embrace

Even though our meet forbidden
Passionate touch
Our love remains hidden
Spend the night here 'neath my quilt
Then my lust for you will full be felt

I retyped them, highlighting the first letter of each line.

Sunshine beams *through windowpanes*

A bedroom mirror, *your beauty frames*

Raven hair drapes *slender hips*

A ready pretty *smile, inviting lips*

Houses close, yet *far apart*

Stolen glimpses pull *at my heart*

I've felt we should *be lovers*

My heart fears you *belong to others*

Please look my way *and blow a kiss*

Steal a moment, no *one will miss*

Only then can our *passions flare*

Nothing could your *love compare*

Just glimpses stolen
O'er garden walls
And lips pressed
sweet

Names whispered,
please call

Never ending warm
embrace

Even though our
meet forbidden

Passionate touch
Our love remains
hidden

Spend the night
here 'neath my quilt

Then my love for
you will full be felt

I powerwalked to the dining room and stood at the door. "Does anyone remember women named Sarah Simpson and Joanne Post who lived in Two Harbors in the nineteen fifties?" I yelled.

Four hands went up, including Dolores'. I ran to her table.

"Where did they live?"

"Simpsons and Posts lived in the old part of town, but I think Simpsons moved before the fifties."

"Tell me about Mrs. Simpson."

178

Dolores looked puzzled. "I thought you wanted to know about Sarah Simpson, not Mrs. Simpson."

"Sarah wasn't Mrs. Simpson?" I asked, sitting down.

"Sarah was their daughter."

"How old was she when they moved?"

"I don't know. I suppose we'd both just graduated from the eighth grade, so I suppose she was thirteen or fourteen."

"Where did they live relative to Ole Lundquist?"

"I'm not sure. They lived nearby."

August (Augie) Paulson came over to the table. "They were neighbors. Their houses were right next to each other."

"Did any of you stay in touch with Simpsons after they moved?"

Everyone shook their heads.

"Sarah's father was a railroad engineer," Augie explained, "so they might've moved anywhere there were tracks."

"How about Joanne Post?"

Dolores answered briefly. "They lived by Lundquist."

"There's something you're not saying."

"It's not my place to comment on Joanne."

"Why not?"

Augie smiled. "She got knocked up and gave up her baby for adoption."

I looked at Dolores for confirmation and she glared at me. "I've got nothing to say."

"But Augie…"

Dolores stood up, signaling the end of our conversation.

I flashed back to a conversation I'd had with Brian Johnson after my very brief tenure as band director. I ran back to my office, dodging people and walkers.

"Damn it, Brian. You're always here when I don't want you, and now that I need you, I don't even have your phone number."

I grabbed the note I'd made when Brian Johnson spoke about his mother's memories and punched Eleanor Johnson's number into my cellphone while I paced in the hallway outside my office.

"Hello."

"Mrs. Johnson, my name is Peter Rogers. I'm Brian's friend from the band. I'd like to get his phone number."

"Peter. You're the one who filled in as the band director last year."

"Yes, that was me. I need Brian's number."

"You did such a nice job, and the piccolo duet you played with that schoolgirl was wonderful."

"Thank you, but I need to talk to Brian and it's rather urgent."

"That's right! He told me you were working on Ole Lundquist's murder investigation. He said you might call. How is that going? Can I help?"

I was about ready to reach over the phone and choke the woman, but I knew patience was key to dealing with senior citizens. "It's going well, but I'm at a critical point and need to speak with Brian immediately. Can you give me his number?"

"Well, certainly. Do you have a piece of paper?"

I lunged into my office and grabbed a marker and stripped a sheet of paper out of the printer. "Go ahead."

She told me the number and I scrawled it on the sheet. "Thank you."

I was about to disconnect when I heard my name. "Peter."

"Yes, Mrs. Johnson."

"If it's urgent, wouldn't you rather have me hand the phone to him rather than calling him. He's right here having a cup of coffee with me."

I rolled my eyes but forced my voice to be calm. "Yes, that would be great."

"Hi, doc. What can I do for you?"

"You told me that people never retired from the band, they just became inactive."

"Right. Are you ready to reactivate?"

"Not right now, but you might be able to help solve Ole Lundquist's murder. Is there a roster of members from the fifties?"

"There's a roster going back to when the band was formed."

"Who has it?"

"The band secretary keeps the roster."

"Who's the secretary?"

"Well, there isn't a secretary right now."

"Let me rephrase the question. Who has the roster right now?"

"I do."

"I assume it's not with you."

Brian laughed. "It's a big old ledger. It's at my house."

"Can you drop everything and run to your house?"

"I'm in the middle of a story, but I suppose I could finish my coffee and head home. What do you need?"

"Where's your house? I'll meet you there."

"It's kind of complicated. We live in a rural area near Hugo's Bar, where you've played with Wendy's band. The addresses are only fire numbers. It'd be easier if I picked it up tonight and brought it to your office tomorrow morning. I'm meeting a couple trombone players at Judy's for coffee. Will you be around mid-morning?"

I pressed my hand to my head. "Is there any way I could look at it tonight?"

"What's the rush? I thought we were talking about Ole Lundquist's murder in 1951. What's the difference between tonight and tomorrow when we're talking about a seventy-year-old murder?"

I took a deep breath. He was right. There was no rush except in my mind. But I really was so close to a possible answer. "Tell you what. Look in the roster tonight and call me if you find anyone named Simpson who was a band member in 1951."

"So, I can finish my coffee and story?"

"Yes, Brian. You can finish your coffee and story. Call me later."

I disconnected from Brian and realized Jenny was standing at my door. "Are you okay? Dolores said you ran from the dining room like there was an emergency."

I turned my guest chair so she could see my computer screen, then entered my password to open it. "Read the poem."

It only took her a second, then she looked at me. "So?"

"Read the name spelled by the first letters of each word."

"Okay. It says Sarah Simpson. So what?"

"This is the poem from the time capsule, and the Simpsons lived next door to Ole Lundquist. Sarah was their daughter. Dolores said Sarah was about fourteen when Ole was killed. Joanne Post lived nearby, too."

Jenny's eyes went back to the computer and she reread the poems. "You don't think…"

"I think Ole wrote the poem about peeking through his drapes into Sarah's bedroom window. I suspect her father found the poem and killed Ole."

"How would it get into the time capsule?"

"I called Brian Johnson. He's going to check the band roster for 1951 to see if any of the Simpsons were in the band at the time of the

183

murder. They might've had access to the band shell and slipped the box into the wall."

"That seems like a stretch."

"It's the only theory anyone's got."

My desk phone rang, and I checked the caller ID. It said, "TWOHBRS PD."

"I hope this is Len calling. I'll fill you in when I get home."

"Hi, Len."

"I got your message and I'm reading the poems. They're a little creepy and suggestive, but it doesn't seem to point to anything or anyone. I don't see anything criminal in it at any rate."

"I can help with that. They're acrostic poems. If you read the first letter of each line, they spell Sarah Simpson and Joanne Post. They were teens who lived near Ole Lundquist about the time of the murder."

I waited while Len reread the poems and processed the information. "Well, hell. If Ole wrote these, it sounds like he'd been window peeping. But that's quite a jump."

"The tuba player from the band has the membership roster. He's going to look at the membership in 1951 to see if anyone named Simpson was in the band. That may explain how the time capsule got placed in the band shell wall."

Len was silent. "So, *if* Ole Lundquist wrote the poems, and *if* a member of the Simpson family put the box with the gun and poem in the wall, and *if* we thought Sarah or Joanne, their fathers, or mothers killed Ole because they read the poem, what will we do with that information. It's been seventy years since the time capsule was put in the wall. The killer was probably an adult, and he's probably dead or sitting in a nursing home wheelchair drooling on himself." Len let out a deep sigh.

"Len, it was a murder, and we might have the pieces to the puzzle that closes the case."

"Peter, so what? The murder case files are worthless, as is the coroner's report. The pieces you've pulled together are intriguing, but they aren't enough to take to the county attorney, even if the murderer is alive. And even if I arrested someone, no jury would convict an old man in a wheelchair on the evidence we've got."

I thought back to my discussion with Lee and Howard. "Are there fingerprints on the gun from the time capsule?"

"It's a rusty mess and we don't even know if it's the murder weapon. I'm not going to spend anyone's time or money to check it for fingerprints." Len paused. "Peter, even if someone could lift prints off the pistol, they have to be matched to prints in the system. If this was a crime of passion, the chances are that the murderer's prints aren't in the federal AFIS database."

"One of my residents said Simpsons lived next to Ole Lundquist. The first poem sounds like Ole wrote it looking in her bedroom window."

"Okay. What do you want me to do with that information?"

"I heard Lundquist's house burned down. Is the Simpsons' house still there?"

"If you've got an address, I can check. But again, what if it is?"

"Maybe there's some evidence there. I mean, maybe Sarah hid something in a hidey hole, or maybe there's a shoebox of poems in the attic."

"Peter, the murder was seventy years ago. Seventy years! The house has probably been sold five times since then and every family that moved out cleaned out everything they owned when they left."

"Len, work with me. What do we have to lose but a little time while we stick our hands into the basement rafters and maybe check behind the drawers in the built-in china cabinet?"

"You want me to walk up to people in a house and tell them the neighbor was killed in 1951 and I want to search their house for evidence."

"It sounds kind of stupid when you put it that way."

"It sounds stupid because it *is* stupid."

"Len, humor me. Let's knock on their door and ask permission. Tell them it's a long shot, but they might be able to help us solve an old mystery."

Len sighed.

"It's Christmas. Consider it my present."

"You just won't let this die, will you?"

"Not at this point."

"I heard about the chipmunk chase. Did your Christmas decorations survive the turmoil?"

"Most of them are intact. Some didn't."

Len paused. "What the hell. The city council might do me a favor if they fired me. Let me check around to see which house was Simpsons'. I'll call the current owners and see if I can sweet talk them into helping with our wild goose chase."

"Thanks."

"I'll see if I can arrange something for tonight."

"No! Jeremy is an elf in the Christmas play tonight. I have to be there."

"Hallelujah! You do have your priorities right. I'll see what's possible and get back to you."

I drove to the hardware store and studied the mouse trap options. I'd expected to see the ones I remembered as a kid with the spring-loaded metal hoop that snapped on your fingers when you tried to set them. That was one option, in single, double, and four packs. There were also plastic traps that didn't require putting your fingers in peril, metal boxes, disposable plastic traps that put the victim out of sight, sticky traps, and more.

A pleasant man wearing a red vest approached me. "Can I help you?"

"I need a couple mouse traps, and I'm overwhelmed with my choices."

He smiled politely. "I can point out the features, but the choice is up to you. Do you have one mouse, or are you getting a steady stream of them?"

"I hope there's only one, but I don't really know. Let's assume I have one and that I'll come back if more show up."

"So, you're in a new house and someone left the door open."

"No, I'm in a big old house. Does that make a difference?"

"If you've got one mouse the sticky trap works well, but if you've got many, you might want to consider poison, but only if you don't have any pets."

"If I poison them, where do they go when they die?"

He smiled. "Mouse heaven."

I shook my head. I had to get the Two Harbors comedian. "Do they die inside a wall, or do they go outside to die?"

"My experience has been that they seem to look for water, so I find them in the toilet."

"I think that wouldn't go over well with my wife. What's the next option?"

He held up a four-pack of traditional mouse traps. "These are cheap and reusable."

"I hate snapping my fingers in them."

He put those back and handed me a two-pack of traps claiming to be the easiest and best ever. They were expensive, but reusable. "Do they work as well as the metal hoop style?"

He smiled and shrugged. "I don't know. I'm too cheap to buy these. It says they're good, but I've never tried them."

"And the mouse gets trapped inside and you throw it away?"

"No. It snaps on them like the originals. You still have a dead mouse in the jaws in the morning and someone has to take it out and rebait the trap."

"How about the sticky pads?"

"The mouse gets stuck to the goo."

"Can you see it?"

"Sir, I get the impression you want something that's cheap, kills the mouse quickly, and leaves it invisible. Am I capturing your specifications?"

"Yeah. Which of these does that?"

"You need a cat, although some cats like to deliver the mice to you after they catch them."

"I need to think about this overnight."

"Not a problem. We sell a lot this time of year, especially to people who own old houses, and we restock the shelves twice a week."

I drove to Culver's and bought a lunch combo. I sat in a back corner with my mind wandering from mice, to poetry, to hidden

189

caches of clues, and the rumors about Ole Lundquist. There was no way Ole was as much of a Romeo as people claimed or someone would've killed him or run him out of town decades before his murder. On the other hand, there must've been a thread of truth to the rumors and the poems in the time capsule certainly made it sound like he was window peeping or more.

I was mulling the Lundquist murder when I swung my legs out of the booth to stand up. In my deep concentration I missed seeing the child toddling ahead of his mother. I was halfway to my feet when I stepped out and touched him with my shoe. Reacting to the child, I pulled my foot back but my momentum kept going and I reached over the child's head to grab the chair across the aisle. Pain shot into my ribs as I tried to support myself on one foot and one arm while not crushing the kid who was oblivious to me.

The boy's mother saw my plight and grabbed my other arm which made me roll, eventually falling to the floor, missing the kid. With one hand on the chair and the child's mother grasping the other I had no way to break my fall, so I twisted to land on my back. The wind was knocked from my lungs and my head banged against the floor causing me to see stars. People rushed to help me get up, but the rib pain left me panting, not wanting to take a deep breath or grab any of the hands offered to help me up from the floor.

I'm not sure exactly how I got up, probably using the chair and going from knees to my feet, but I was standing with a group of concerned strangers looking on. A man offered to call an ambulance, but I refused. The Culver's manager, in his blue apron, rushed out and offered to drive me to the hospital. I waved off their offers and put up a brave façade.

I threw away my burger wrappers and went to my car. I called Jenny and told her I was going home to take a pain pill and wouldn't be back to work. She said she'd get a ride home with one of the nurses. I drove home, took a Percocet, and fell asleep on the couch. The next thing I heard was the slamming back door when Jeremy arrived home from school.

Chapter 13

I made chili and mixed up a batch of baking powder biscuits while Jeremy worked on his homework. I was pre-heating the oven and cutting out baking powder biscuits when Jenny walked in. She pecked me on the cheek and turned to go upstairs, then paused.

She pointed to the accordion case in the corner. "What's that?"

"Brian, the tuba player, dropped off an accordion. He asked me to sit in with his band Friday."

"I've never heard you play the accordion."

"I don't. He left it so I could learn."

"Before Friday? I hope you declined."

"I did."

Jenny went upstairs and showered while I set the table. Jeremy finished his homework and packed it into his backpack.

"Show me how an accordion works," he said, pulling the accordion case into the dining room.

I had a few minutes before the biscuits were done, so I opened the case and pulled out the accordion. I put it on my lap and unlatched it, then squeezed hard and got a sharp pain in my ribs. I squeezed easier and played a few notes on the keyboard.

"That's cool. What are the buttons?"

I pushed the chord buttons, then played a few notes on the keyboard while pressing the chords. It took a while before I caught onto the chord sequence, but it was pretty straightforward.

Jenny came down the stairs just as the timer signaled the end of the biscuit bake time. "You can play the accordion."

I latched the accordion and set it into the case. "Not really. I was just showing Jeremy how it worked."

"It sounded good."

I pulled the biscuits from the oven and set them on the plate. "Playing a couple chords and a few notes does NOT make me an accordion player."

Jenny carried the pot of chili to the table and scooped up bowls for each of us. Jeremy chattered about school and a new kid who'd just moved to Two Harbors from North Dakota. We heard about his father's electrician job on the oil fields and how they moved here so the father could work on the railroad. Jenny talked about the new computer system Nancy had suggested for tracking patient records.

I was clearing the table when Jenny looked at the clock. "Set the dishes down. We have to get to school for the play!"

I glanced at the clock. "The play won't start for almost an hour."

"Jeremy has to get in costume. and we need to hold seats for five people."

We were among the first cars in the parking lot, parking alongside one of the angels, who came dressed in her costume. Her mother struggled to protect her angel wings while wrapping her in an over-sized parka.

Jenny closed the car door and zipped Jeremy's coat as he tried to run for the school. "Do you know the angel?"

Jeremy glanced at the girl and her parents, then made a face. "That's Lindsey."

Jenny struggled with the zipper. "You don't like her?"

"Mom, she's a girl."

Jeremy raced ahead of the angel and her family, slipping through the door without holding it for the angel's family. Jenny shook her head.

I smiled and took her hand. "In ten years, he'll be asking Lindsey to the prom."

Jenny squeezed my hand. "Let's not rush things. I hope the 'I don't like girls' stage lasts a few more years."

We wound through the hallways, following handmade signs pointing the way to the gymnasium. A stage had been positioned under a basketball hoop, and parents were unloading folding chairs from racks and setting them in rows. Jenny hung our coats on chairs in the

194

second row and we helped set up chairs, chatting with other parents who were members of the PTA or whose children were also in the play.

By the time all the chairs were up, the gymnasium was starting to fill and voices echoed in the space. Jenny waved to Barbara and Howard, then she led them to our seats while I helped the fathers stow the chair racks in a back room.

"Peter, I'm Kerry. We met at the VFW."

Kerry's face and left hand bore burn scars. He wore a cap that I knew covered the scars on his scalp. "Hi, Kerry. Do you have a child in the play?"

Kerry rolled his eyes. "My son's a pine tree. How about you?"

"Jeremy's an elf."

The right side of Kerry's face smiled. The scars on the left side hid damaged muscles that didn't flex. "Your son must be more talented."

I put my hand on Kerry's shoulder and we walked back to the gymnasium together. "I find that hard to believe."

We stopped at the door and let a group of people pass. I was about to say goodbye when Kerry pulled me aside. "How are you holding up?"

"What do you mean?" I asked.

Kerry's eyes darted around, making sure no one was close. "I'm having a hell of a time with the holidays this year. My wife is trying to be upbeat and cheerful, but..." Kerry held up his scarred left hand. "I can't even screw in a lightbulb. I feel useless."

When I didn't respond immediately Kerry stepped back. "It's not your problem."

"Kerry." He turned back toward me. "I have nightmares and sometimes I'm back there. I feel guilty because I'm back and lots of guys…"

Kerry looked at the floor. "Sometimes I think it would've been better if…"

"No, it wouldn't have been better, Kerry. You're here with your family and you're here for your son's Christmas program, even if he's only a pine tree."

Kerry stared at the crowd, shaking his head. A tear leaked from his right eye. I knew his left eyelid had been rebuilt from skin grafts and I wasn't sure if it made tears or not.

"You're not thinking about hurting yourself?"

Kerry shook his head, but I could see the pain in his eye that said, "Yes."

I pulled a dog-eared card out of my wallet and handed it to him. "Call them."

He fingered the card. "It looks like you've been carrying this a long time."

"I called them dozens of time after I got back. Between Vern, at the VFW, and the guys on the suicide hotline, I got my shit together and…well, I'm still here."

He looked at the card but seemed unconvinced. I put out my hand. "Give me your cellphone."

I took his phone and put my number into the memory. I handed it back to him.

"You put in the hotline number?"

"I put in my number. Call me anytime. I mean anytime, day or night."

"The nights are worst. Some nights I'm afraid to fall asleep because I don't want…"

"My phone's on at noon or midnight, Kerry. It doesn't matter what time of day it is I'll talk to you."

Kerry put his phone back in his pocket. "I heard you were a Marine, right?"

I shook my head. "I was a Navy corpsman."

"Vern said you got a purple heart."

"It doesn't make any difference. I'll take your call."

"Peter, it *does* make a difference." He swung his hand, gesturing toward the gathering crowd. "These folks don't have a clue. They say, 'Thanks for your service,' but they don't know what we went through."

I drew a breath, then grimaced with the pain. Kerry put his hand on my shoulder. "Are you okay?"

I waved it off. "I'm fine."

"Lingering Iraq shit?" he asked.

I smiled. "Hardly. A chipmunk was loose in the house and I slipped on cereal boxes he knocked off the shelf when he raced by."

Kerry's half smile appeared. "You're shitting me."

I held up my right hand. "Honest. I was trying to catch him in a blanket and it turned into a riot. The city band was there caroling, and they all tried to help. The Christmas tree tipped over and about half the ornaments broke."

"Did they catch him?"

"They took him out the door when he ran into a Christmas stocking. When they released him he ran into the trombone player's open pickup truck."

Kerry shook his head. "That must've been something to see."

The sound of bangles caught my ear and I saw Mother searching the room for us. "There's my mother. You have my phone number. I'm serious, call me anytime."

Kerry nodded as a cute blonde came out of the crowd, looking concerned. Kerry grabbed my sleeve. "Hang on."

The blonde approached us. "It's almost seven. Marcia's watching our chairs."

"Deb, this is Peter. I met him at the VFW. He was a corpsman in Iraq."

Deb smiled and shook my hand. "Do you have a child in the play?"

"Mine is an elf."

Deb smiled. "Yours must be talented. Our boy is a pine tree."

Kerry grabbed Deb's hand. "I'd like to have Peter and his family over after the holidays."

198

Deb nodded. "Sure. Do we have your phone number?"

Kerry nodded. "Peter programmed it into my phone." He paused, looking into his wife's eyes. "He told me to call him anytime."

The gravity of Kerry's words wasn't lost on Deb and she grabbed my hand and squeezed it. "What's your wife's name?"

"Jenny. My son is Jeremy."

Deb's face lit up. "You just got married last Saturday. I heard the ceremony was a hoot, but the reception was even more fun."

"Yup. That would be our wedding."

Deb took Kerry's hand. "We'll call, but we need to get to our seats."

Mother looked lost. The crowd was mostly seated and she looked around, trying to find Jenny or me. I waved and eventually caught her attention as I fought my way toward the door.

"We've got seats in the second row," I said, taking her hand.

I helped her take off her coat at the end of the row, then we waded past the dozen people seated near the aisle. The lights dimmed as Mom hugged Jenny and squeezed Barbara's hand.

I'd been to the previous Christmas play, so my expectations were low. The acting was poor, the music was out of tune and the dancing out of synch. The crowd laughed when kids bungled their lines, and overall, it was everything a grade school Christmas play should be. Mother was initially shocked by the kids dropped lines and missed cues, but she eventually started laughing with the other parents at the gaffes.

The scene changed to Santa's workshop and Jeremy, dressed in candy-striped legging and a green hat, raced out with a half dozen other elves, Santa, and the reindeer. He was standing behind as a well-rehearsed sixth-grader, dressed as Santa, delivered a monologue, reciting all the reindeers' names.

Jeremy searched the sea of faces, looking anxious. He finally spied Jenny, then looked across the row, first spying Barbara and Howard, then seeing Audrey and me. He broke character and waved at us just as he was supposed to deliver his only speaking line. We heard a teacher cue him from the side of the stage, getting laughs from the crowd. Undeterred, he stared right at Mother, smiled, and delivered his line.

Mother beamed and turned to me. She reached past me and tugged on the sleeve of the man sitting next to me. "That's my grandson!"

* * *

Like the other parents, Jenny and I stood around waiting for the kids to get changed out of their costumes. The cafeteria opened and PTA served hot cider and cookies. Jenny and our parents got in line for the treats while I broke down chairs.

I found Jenny and our families standing in a clutch sipping cider while Jeremy gushed about the play, the students, the cider, the cookies, and pretty much anything else that came to mind. Barbara and Howard listened and smiled. Mother tried to get a word in but failing that, she stood by smiling. Against all odds, she seemed to be enjoying herself.

I grabbed a Styrofoam cup of cider and one of the last broken cookies as the PTA parents were breaking down the tables and cleaning up the spilled cider and crumbs. I joined the family and tried to interrupt Jeremy, without success.

I felt someone at my shoulder and turned. Kerry's wife, Deb, was standing next to me. She nodded toward the cafeteria and I followed her away from the crowd.

"Thanks for talking to Kerry. Christmas has been tough every year since he got back, but this year has been the worst. I think having your number will make a world of difference. Even if he never calls you, he knows you've got his back."

"My demons are nowhere near as challenging as his, and I sometimes struggle."

Jenny walked over and put out her hand. "Hi, I'm Peter's wife, Jenny."

Deb smiled. "Your wedding is legendary. I don't know how you pulled it off, but you created something that will be in everyone's memory forever."

"Hang on for a second," Jenny said. She tapped Barbara's shoulder and whispered to her. They walked back to Deb and me.

"Deb, this is my mother, Barbara. She's responsible for the wedding planning."

Deb put her hand on Barbara's arm. "Peter and Jenny's wedding has become the milestone that all other weddings will be measured against."

Barbara was speechless, having planned the perfect wedding, then watched it turn into the most memorable wedding for all the wrong reasons. "Um, great."

"I don't know how you pulled it off, but it must've been absolutely incredible! A half dozen of your guests have told me they laughed until they cried. The reading from Ogden Nash, "If I said you had a Beautiful Body" as the song, the dropped ring, the minister pretending to be confused. My gosh, I can't imagine the planning that must've gone into it. You should go into the wedding planning business. You'd be swamped!"

Barbara smiled. "Thank you, but it was a one-time endeavor."

Kerry joined us and Deb grabbed his good arm. "Kerry, this is Peter's mother-in-law, Barbara, the one who planned the wedding of the century."

Kerry smiled with the right side of his face. "I guess it was really something."

Deb and Kerry's son found us in the crowd. He nodded at his parents, then went over to Jeremy. They stepped away from the adults and started chatting.

Deb leaned around us, looking at the boys. "It looks like Jacob knows your son."

Jenny nodded. "I think they're in the same class. I remember Jacob from a field trip."

Deb looked at Kerry. "I suppose we should get Jacob home."

"Mom, Barbara, and Howard are coming over," I said. "Why don't you join us? You can see the site of the great chipmunk chase."

Kerry looked at the boys, avoiding the topic, but Deb smiled. "What was the great chipmunk chase?"

Jenny saw Kerry's reluctance and glanced at me, guessing there was something tied to Kerry's scarring that was at play. "I found an old-fashioned hot chocolate recipe in the cupboard and I bought all the makings. I bet Jeremy would like to show Jacob his new bedroom and tell him the ghost stories."

Kerry looked at me. "Ghost stories?"

"It's easier to explain at the house. Come over."

Deb entered our address into her iPhone and gathered Jacob. I found Mother talking to another set of grandparents who'd been seated near us.

"Are you ready to follow us to the house?"

Mom said goodbye to the other people and joined us. "It'd be easier if Peter rode with me."

Jenny nodded. "Good idea."

Mother led me to her Cadillac and clicked the remote. I directed her to the parking lot entrance and got her started toward the house without a word from her. She finally glanced at me, then back at the road. "I think I'm starting to understand what you were trying to tell me. Jeremy lit up when he saw us in the audience."

"He'll remember tonight forever."

"I had to cancel out of my bridge club to come here."

I looked at her. "Was it worth it?"

Mom didn't answer. I guided her to our house and she parked behind Jenny's car. She stood in the driveway for a moment, looking at the house.

"This is the house your neighbor gave you as a wedding present?"

"It is. Let's go inside."

I took Mother's coat and was about to lay it over a kitchen chair when there was a knock on the door. Jacob rushed in when I opened the door. Deb came in and looked around the kitchen.

"This is a huge old house. It's lovely."

I took her coat and hung it behind the kitchen door. Kerry put his coat on top of mother's coat and shook my hand. "Thanks for the invitation. We don't go out much."

I put my hand on his shoulder. "You, Deb, and Jacob are welcome at our house anytime."

He nodded but didn't smile. Barbara and Howard were right behind him.

Jenny shooed us out of the kitchen and put Deb to work opening cans of evaporated milk while she got out a can of cocoa and a bag of marshmallows.

Mother was examining the ornaments on the tree when the rest of us walked into the living room. Jacob and Jeremy raced up the stairs and within minutes I could hear the distinctive sound of an electronic game.

I introduced Kerry to Mother, who blanched when she saw his scars up close, but she didn't say anything inappropriate.

Howard stood back and looked at the tree. "That has to be the ugliest tree I've ever seen. Is that the one the band brought over?"

"Yes, they brought the tree, the lights, and the assortment of ornaments."

Barbara saw the ceramic tree glowing on an end table. "Oh good, I was afraid Grandma's tree might've been a casualty of the chipmunk escapade."

I shook my head. "Somehow, the ceramic tree got knocked onto a couch cushion and was saved."

Kerry looked around the living room. "This is where you were chasing the chipmunk?"

Jenny and Deb came out with trays of steaming mugs full of cocoa, marshmallows floating on top. "This is too hot to drink, so maybe Peter can give you a tour of the chipmunk trail of destruction, then we'll drink the cocoa."

Mother was shaking her head. "What chipmunk trail of destruction?"

I started with the band and carolers showing up, then led them into the pantry and explained the plan to capture Chipper in a blanket, followed by the mayhem in the living room. By the time I finished, Mother was laughing, Deb was in tears, and Kerry was smiling and shaking his head.

We drank cocoa without the boys, talked about our family Christmas traditions, and then Jenny told them about the ghostly incidents, explaining each in terms of the chipmunk.

The boys heard the laughter and came downstairs. Jenny got them mugs of cocoa and topped off our mugs.

Kerry noticed the accordion case in the corner. "You play the accordion?"

"No, I play guitar and saxophone."

Jenny shook her head. "He's being modest. Peter has a degree in music. He plays piano, clarinet, flute, piccolo, and saxophone."

Jeremy jumped up and unlatched the accordion case. "It's really hard. Dad could play the keyboard because it's just like a piano."

"Leave it in the case, Jeremy," I said. He ignored me and carried the accordion to the table.

Jenny leaned close and kissed my cheek. "Play a Christmas carol."

I saw no escape, so I strapped the accordion on and immediately knew squeezing the accordion hard caused stabbing rib pain. Using slow, easy squeezes I played "O Little Town of Bethlehem" softly, using only the keyboard. After a couple bars I experimented with the chords. Barbara started singing and everyone joined in for two verses.

I was latching the bellows when Mother said, "Play something else fun that we all know, like Jingle Bells."

I played that and two more songs before setting it down. My ribs were unhappy and telling me it was time to end the concert. "That's enough! It's Jeremy's bedtime."

Kerry watched me put the accordion away while the others got their coats. "You played all that without music, even though you'd never played the accordion before last week."

I shrugged. "It's pretty easy because I know the piano."

He made sure all the others were busy and pulled me over to the Christmas tree. "Thanks for having us over. I...we don't socialize a lot because..."

"I get it," I said.

He nodded. "Yes, you do get it, and...this has been fun. Thanks."

Deb walked in with his coat and held it out. "What are you two conspiring about?"

Kerry took his coat. "I was just saying thanks."

Deb helped him into the coat and started the zipper for him. She guided Kerry toward the dining room. "Honey, can you make sure Jacob helped Jeremy pick up his room?"

Kerry nodded. "Jacob, let's make sure you guys didn't leave a mess."

"Aw, Dad."

"C'mon, let's check it out."

Kerry went upstairs with the boys. When they were out of sight Deb hugged me. "Kerry's been in a dark place since Thanksgiving. I don't know what you did or said, but this is the first time I've been able to get him to socialize since he got out of the hospital. He actually laughed tonight, and I haven't heard him sing since..." She buried her face in my shoulder and said, "Thank you." Then she fled to the kitchen.

Mother hugged everyone as they left, like a good hostess, then she helped Jenny carry the mugs to the sink. Jenny refused to let her wash dishes, instead explaining the menagerie of tree ornaments while Jeremy got ready for bed. I washed the mugs and set them on the drying rack.

Mother and Jenny were walking down the steps when I was wiping off the table. "Is Jeremy in bed?"

Mother sat down at the table. "We tucked him in. Then I did something you're not going to like. I asked Jenny what she knew about your time in Iraq."

I looked from Mother to Jenny, then saw the wooden box that contained my Navy memorabilia under Jenny's arm. I glared at Jenny, but she unlatched it and lifted the top, displaying my Navy insignia, service bars, and medals. She spun it around so all three of us could see inside.

"I know a little about these, but it'd be better if you told Mom about them, Peter."

I reached out to close the box, but Jenny pulled it out of my reach. "Audrey wants to know what you did in the war." Jenny glared at me. "Tell her."

I sat down but wasn't ready to deal with the topic in front of Mother. "I was a Navy corpsman assigned to the Marines. I treated the men who were wounded."

Jenny waited for me to go on. When I didn't, she slid her fingers under the purple heart. "Peter was awarded this when he was wounded. The little oak leaf means he was wounded a second time."

Mother looked at me. "I didn't know..." Then she looked back at the box. "What's this star?"

Again, Jenny waited for me, but explained when I didn't speak. "It's a silver star, the third highest award for battlefield bravery. Peter pulled wounded Marines to safety after their vehicle was blown up. He did that while they were being shot at. Your son is a hero."

Mom reached out and fingered the star, then looked at me. "If I'd met you at the airport when you flew home from Iraq, I would've seen you wearing these."

"I had the ribbons on, not the actual badges." I tried to find words, but I was embarrassed. "Mom, it's people like Kerry who deserve the medals, not me. I was just doing what I'd been trained to do."

Jenny closed and latched the box. "Soldiers like Kerry were wounded, but they lived to come home because of people like you."

My cellphone buzzed and I took the call to break away from further discussion of my service.

"This is Peter."

"How many tuba players does it take…"

"Now's not a good time, Brian. Can we talk tomorrow?"

"I'm sorry I interrupted you."

"No, it's okay. We were just having a discussion. Actually, your timing may have been perfect. What's up?"

"I looked at the membership rolls, and there's no one named Simpson who was active after World War Two. It appears someone named Rudy Simpson was a trumpet player from '39 until '42, but I assume he got drafted and never played in the band after that. Is that what you needed to know?"

"Yeah, what I needed to know, but not what I wanted to hear."

"I can bring the book down and we can look through the years around then to see if

210

there's another name that connects with the murder and stuff."

"Sure. That'd be good. I don't know what we'd find, but I'm running out of theories."

"Can I buy you a cup of coffee at Judy's tomorrow about ten?"

"Sure, I'll see you then." I paused for a second. "Brian, would you mind if I bring a friend?"

"Sure. What instrument does he play?"

"His left hand was badly burned in Iraq, and I'm not sure he played anything before his military service."

"Sounds like a perfect candidate for a Euphonium. You support it with your left arm and push the valves with the fingers of your right hand."

"I'll see if he's available in the morning and you can pitch that idea to him. His name is Kerry."

"You know me, I'm always looking for another musician."

I dialed Kerry's number. "Are you available to meet me at Judy's tomorrow morning at ten?"

"I don't know of anything else going on, but I don't go out a lot."

"I'm beating my head against a wall trying to figure out who killed the town plumber in 1951."

"I thought you worked at the old folks home."

"I'm doing a favor for the police chief."

"Listen, Peter. I appreciate you offering your ear if I'm in a bad way, but I don't need you to make work for me."

"This is hardly work. Neither of us will be paid. All I'm doing is poking around an old murder investigation, trying to see if there's something that's been overlooked. I'm stuck and a fresh set of eyes might catch something I've missed."

When he didn't immediately answer I added, "We'll be meeting the tuba player and he's always got a sick tuba joke that makes me laugh, and he offered to buy coffee."

"A tuba joke?"

"Yeah, he asked Jeremy how to fix a broken tuba. With a tuba glue."

I heard a chuckle. "Jacob came home from school with that joke yesterday. Your friend the tuba player told it to Jeremy?"

"Yeah. He'll have a new one tomorrow."

"Do they get any better?"

I knew Kerry was interested and would meet me. "Naw, they never get any better, but he's always got a new one."

"Ten o'clock at Judy's?"

"That's the plan." I paused. "Do you play a band instrument?"

"I played a trombone in high school. Why do you ask?"

"Brian is always recruiting for the city band."

"I'm not a candidate. I played a horn owned by the school, I was never particularly good, and I haven't played a trombone since the spring concert my senior year."

"That won't deter Brian."

"Should I bring anything?"

"Do you know any trombone jokes?"

"That's a thing?"

"I'm sure they're out there."

"I'll work on it. See you at ten."

Chapter 14

I had breakfast, packed Jeremy's lunch, dropped him off at school, and drove to Whistling Pines. The entryway was surprisingly quiet except for a resident chatting with the receptionist, so I slipped past and hung my coat up in my office. I checked for messages and urgent emails, then went to the dining room for a cup of coffee.

The only person in the dining room was Wendy who was sitting at her usual table working on a crossword puzzle. I drew a cup of coffee from the urn and tried to slip out unnoticed.

"Peter, I need a six-letter word for Pacific weather phenomenon."

I sat down at Wendy's table. "El niño."

She wrote in the answer and started filling in the crossing words.

I watched until she'd finished. "Tell me about Genevieve."

"I don't know what you want to know. She's quiet, keeps to herself, doesn't make any waves, is polite, and doesn't cause any problems for me."

"Is she from Two Harbors?"

"I don't know. She seems to know quite a few of the residents, so I assume she is. I've never specifically asked her." She paused. "Why do you want to know?"

"She doesn't seem to indulge in all the rumors, so I thought she might be a reliable source of unbiased information."

Wendy shrugged. "She could be. I just don't know."

"Does your band have any gigs over Christmas?"

"Our next engagement is Hugo's on Christmas Eve. Would you like to sit in?"

"I think Santa might need help getting down our chimney and stuffing stockings."

Wendy got a sly smile. "You're an old married person now. You'll probably be asleep before the news comes on."

I stood up and put the chair back in place. "That's probably exactly what we'll do."

I took a step away and Wendy stopped me. "I heard your house is haunted."

"Who told you that?"

"Someone overheard you talking to Dolores and the word has spread."

"Our ghost was a chipmunk. He's gone now." Wendy's sly smile made me uneasy. "What's going on?"

"I heard a rumor there's going to be an exorcism."

"Firstly, there's nothing to exorcise. Secondly, there's no priest here to do an exorcism."

"Roxie Gilbert has a tarot deck. I heard she did a spread and confirmed there's an evil spirit in your house. Hilda Swanson is reading up on exorcisms and seances. I think they'll come up with something before Christmas."

I sighed. "I don't need anyone trying to drive off the spirits, and I'm pretty well booked up through Christmas."

Wendy put up her hands. "I'm not the one in charge of this. I'm only telling you what's in the rumor mill."

People were starting to fill the tables and Miriam was pouring coffee. I waved at her, but she pointed to the coffee urn.

I topped off my coffee. "What's up?"

"I've got a Ouija board. Do you want to borrow it?"

"Does this have something to do with the rumor about my house being haunted?"

Miriam smiled. "It might." She raised her eyebrows and walked away.

I finished reading my emails and realized it was time to leave for my meeting with Brian and Kerry. I slipped out the back door and drove to Judy's café.

* * *

Judy's breakfast rush had cleared so I had no problem finding a street parking spot. I was first to arrive, so took a table near the back and ordered a cup of coffee. Kerry walked in two minutes later. I waved and he joined me.

"Tell me more about Brian, the tuba player."

"He's retired, energetic, enthusiastic about the band and everything else he touches, and a little eccentric. All in all, he's a nice guy whose spring might be wound a little too tight."

"But you like him."

"Everyone likes Brian. His smile is infectious."

Brian walked in with a large book under his arm. He spied me and signaled to the waitress. "Decaf, please."

"Brian Johnson, this is Kerry." I paused. "I'm sorry, but I don't even know your last name, Kerry."

"Kerry Stone," he said, shaking Brian's hand.

"I don't know any Stones around here. Where did you grow up?"

"International Falls. My dad worked in the paper mill."

"A hockey player?" Brian asked.

"Hockey, football, and baseball. I wasn't good enough to get a scholarship to a division one school, so I went to Concordia on an ROTC scholarship and played hockey there."

The waitress brought a cup and a coffee carafe with a green rim.

"You're drinking decaf?" I asked as the waitress poured Brian's coffee.

"Believe me, you don't want to see me fully caffeinated."

Brian leaned close to Kerry. "Why did the chicken cross the road?"

"To get to the other side?"

Brian laughed. "No, to avoid the tuba recital."

Kerry shook his head but smiled.

"So, Kerry, what instrument do you play?"

Kerry shot a look at me liked I'd leaked information. "I played a trombone a long time ago, and I wasn't very good."

"Great!" Brian replied. "We've got a rehearsal Wednesday evening at the high school."

"No, no, no. I don't even own a trombone."

"Not a problem. I'll check with John Carr, the band director. I'm sure he knows someone who has a spare."

Kerry laughed. "I'm not interested in bringing back that lost skill."

"Ridiculous! We always need another trombone player and it's really not a big commitment of time. Besides, the band has great camaraderie. It's fun! Isn't it, Peter?"

I evaded the question and pointed at the book. "I'll let you two sort out the details of the band later. Show me the band roster from the late forties and early fifties."

Brian spun the book around so I was looking at the signatures. "Like I said, there's only one Simpson in the band during the forties or fifties."

I ran my finger down the pages, sometimes pausing to try and decipher the handwritten names.

Brian let me concentrate on the book but kept needling Kerry. "Either your wife is from Two Harbors or you've got a job here."

"My wife used to be Debbie Albertson. My in-laws live near the high school. Deb moved here with my son while I was recuperating in Army hospitals on my way back to the States. After I got discharged, it made sense to come here where we had a support network."

Brian nodded. "I assume your scars are from Iraq."

Kerry nodded and signaled for more coffee. "IED rolled my Humvee. I didn't get out until it was in flames."

"Infantry?" Brian asked.

"Army CID. I was investigating a reported rape."

Brian's eyes lit up. "That's why Peter enlisted you, so he'd have someone competent to help with his investigation."

"To be honest, I accepted his invitation to get out of the house. Peter offered coffee and some conversation."

I closed the book and pushed it back to Brian as the waitress arrived to top off our coffee. I waited for the waitress to leave, then I explained the time capsule, my discovery of the poem, and my suppositions about Ole having a crush on the neighbors.

"I talked to the police chief and told him we should approach the people who own the Simpsons' house and ask if we could search around in the nooks and crannies for some forgotten clue."

Kerry looked at me skeptically. "You're hoping to find a seventy-year-old clue lying around in a house that's been continuously occupied?"

"Hearing you say it out loud makes it sound pretty ridiculous."

Brian leaned forward. "My mother said Ole Lundquist was known as the passionate plumber."

"Your mother said that?"

"She claims he used it in his advertising."

Kerry and I looked at each other like neither believed that story.

"C'mon," Brian said. "My mother's a reliable source."

"Why don't you bring her down to Whistling Pines. She'll fit in with all the people creating rumors if there isn't one to pass."

"What do you do at Whistling Pines?" Kerry asked.

"I'm the recreation director. I plan activities, schedule shopping trips, pop popcorn for the movies."

Brian nearly snorted his coffee. "Kerry, Peter is the second most talented musician in Two Harbors. He filled in when the band director was injured and learned how to play the piccolo in a week when we needed a second person for the "Stars and Stripes Forever" piccolo duet. He plays at least five other instruments and fills in on guitar with one of the local bands."

Kerry looked impressed. "That explains you on the accordion last night."

Brian slapped his hand on the table. "Ha! I knew you wouldn't be able to resist playing that old accordion if I left it with you. Are you ready to fill in for our wedding gig?"

I shook my head and changed the topic. "Who's the most talented musician in Two Harbors?"

Brian beamed. "Me! I play six instruments!"

Kerry looked impressed, so I had to pop the bubble. "Brian, how many of those six instruments are tubas?"

Brian frowned. "One is a Sousaphone."

We were all laughing when Len Rentz walked in and spotted us in the back. He waved at the waitress and she immediately brought over a mug and the coffee carafe.

Len introduced himself to Kerry, then shook hands with Brian and me.

"You've got an upgrade from Peter's investigative skills," Brian announced. "Kerry was an Army investigator."

Len looked impressed. "Really? You were an MP?"

"I was in CID. I primarily investigated crimes on military bases."

Len smiled. "Why are you hanging out with these two? Association with them might sully your reputation."

Kerry smiled. "Peter invited me out for coffee and that morphed into a discussion of the old murder."

Len hung his coat on the back of his chair and sat down. "Be careful. They might stick you with the bill."

"To be perfectly honest, chief, I'd be happy to pay the bill. I haven't been out for a cup of coffee with 'the guys' in three years. Peter invited my wife and me over for hot chocolate last night and I think that was the first time I've laughed since…"

I jumped in during the pause. "I told him about Brian's plan to catch the chipmunk in a blanket and how the band almost demolished my living room."

Brian put up his hand. "In all fairness, we brought the tree that got tipped over when we were chasing the chipmunk. You wouldn't have been out anything if you hadn't been able to use it."

Len shook his head. "We didn't have any 911 calls about a chipmunk on the loose, or the band ripping anyone's house apart. Did you catch the chipmunk?"

222

Brian waggled his hand. "Catch might be too strong a word. The chipmunk ran into a Christmas stocking. I took it out of the house and when I released him he ran into the trombone player's pickup."

Brian picked up the band roster and threw a ten-dollar bill on the table. "I've got to run. You'll notice I left enough to cover at least two cups of coffee and a generous tip. The three of you can fight about who pays for the rest.

He shook our hands but held Kerry's hand an extra second. I expected him to make another plug for the band, but he surprised me. "Kerry, it was a pleasure to meet you. I sincerely appreciate your service. If you're interested in the band, that's great. But, if you ever want to grab a cup of coffee and just talk, I'd be proud to buy."

Brian took a step, then turned back. "How many tuba players does it take to change a lightbulb?"

We all shook our heads.

Brian grinned, "Three. One to hold the lightbulb and two to drink until the room spins." He waved and left.

"Does he always arrive with a tuba joke?" Kerry asked.

Len and I both nodded.

Kerry stood and looked at us hesitantly, "I should let you two deal with your business."

Len pulled out Kerry's chair. "Sit down. Nothing we're talking about is confidential, and it'd be nice to get a fresh perspective."

Kerry sat down. "Peter said that last night. I thought he was being polite."

Len smiled and signaled for more coffee. "Peter is polite, but this murder has sat unsolved for seventy years. There's nothing secret about it, and if you can offer a thought, I'd be happy to hear it."

Len reached into his inside coat pocket and pulled out an envelope. He handed it to Kerry. "This is the entire file on the murder."

Kerry opened the business-sized envelope and pulled out two sheets of paper and three black and white photos. He flipped the pictures over and read the police and coroner reports while the waitress topped off our coffee.

He flipped over the reports, looking for additional notes on the back. "This is it?"

"That's everything," Len said.

"You've got nothing to go on."

Len reached over to a nearby table and picked up the Two Harbors weekly paper. He spread it on the table. "Here's the newspaper story. There was more in the time capsule than there is in the police and coroner reports."

Kerry read the newspaper story, looked at the coroner's photos, then slipped the reports and photos back into the envelope. "Where are the crime scene photos?"

Len put the envelope back in his coat. "There aren't any in the file."

"I don't suppose you found an eyewitness or had someone come in to confess."

Len shook his head. "You've seen it all."

Kerry blew out a deep breath. "I've worked some cases without much evidence, but I've always had more than this to work from."

Len swirled his coffee in the cup. "Me too. But Peter at least gleaned something from the poems we didn't have before. We think Ole was watching his neighbor's teen daughter's bedroom."

"I suppose window peeping is a crime, but it's probably not a murder motive."

Len smiled. "It depends on who found out, how mad they were about it, and if they were sober. On the other hand, there could be a hundred other motives."

"Ole was a plumber," I explained to Kerry. "I wouldn't think someone would kill him over a botched leak repair."

"Brian said he was called the passionate plumber. A jealous husband seems like a more likely motive." Kerry thought for a moment. "The newspaper mentioned a pistol. What kind of pistol was in the time capsule?"

"It was a German 9mm Luger."

"So, you're thinking it was a WWII vet?"

Len shook his head. "The vets were shipping souvenirs home from Germany and Japan. They gave them to their brothers, their buddies, and sold them to collectors. They were all over the place by the fifties. I wouldn't eliminate anyone based on the origin of the pistol."

"Well, that was my one contribution." Kerry started to stand.

Len put his hand on Kerry's arm. "Do you need to get back to work or something?"

"Not really. I just…"

"Join us. I want to do some brainstorming. The closer I get to retirement the more I feel like I've only got half a brain to contribute."

Kerry smiled. "I'm not sure I can contribute anything, but I can listen."

Len signaled the waitress for more coffee. "Karla, do you have a cinnamon roll left?"

Karla smiled. "I've got two frosted cinnamon rolls, one pecan caramel roll, and three caramel rolls without nuts."

Len looked at us. "I'm having a frosted roll. I'm buying if you'd like something."

The scarred fingers on Kerry's left hand twitched, as if he was testing them. I sensed his reluctance to attempt to eat a roll using his stiff, scarred fingers. "Any pie?" I asked.

"The blueberry just came out of the oven. It'll be a while for the rest."

I hoped that eating pie one-handed would be easier than dealing with a cinnamon roll. "I'll have slice of blueberry pie with a scoop of vanilla ice cream. How about you, Kerry?"

"A piece of pie would taste good. I'll skip the ice cream."

Karla left and Len pulled out a dog-eared notebook and flipped to a blank page in the back. "We've got an old pistol, a newspaper

226

article highlighting the story about Ole Lundquist's death, poems that appear to be written by someone who was window peeping in bedroom windows, incomplete coroner and police reports, and three pictures of a corpse. Where do I go next?"

Karla delivered the roll and slices of pie, and I used the time to think.

"I suggested going to the Simpson house and asking the new owners for permission to search. I thought there might be something in a nook or cranny."

Kerry used the edge of his fork to cut a piece from his slice of pie, steadying the plate with his scarred hand. "Are any of the old neighbors still in their houses?"

Len made a note. "If they are, they're in their nineties."

Kerry ate his pie and thought. "Well, if we knew the names of the other neighbors, we might be able to find their children. Maybe they'd have memories about Ole, Simpsons and the murder."

Len smiled. "Kerry, you just earned your pie. I suppose the easiest way to do that is go to the courthouse with the addresses and check the property records." Len smiled at me. "Do you have time to do that?"

I nearly choked on my pie. "Len, I already told you that I have a job, a new wife, a new house, and Christmas is only days away. "

Kerry waved his fork. "Do you need a subpoena to see those records?"

Len licked frosting from his fingers. "They're public records. If we have the addresses, the assessor's office can pull them. The records that old are probably paper files. The hardest part might be getting the correct addresses. The assessor might be sticky about someone showing up and asking for all the property records on Maple Street."

Kerry nodded. "Do you have Lundquist's or Simpson's address?"

Len flipped back a couple pages in his notebook and flipped it toward Kerry. "Here's Ole's address."

"The Whistling Pines rumor mill said Ole's house burned down, so it's probably an empty lot."

Kerry finished his pie and was obviously thinking. He looked at Len earnestly. "Were you serious when you said you could use another set of eyes?"

"Hell, yes."

"I've got nothing but time on my hands. Write down that address and I'll drive through the neighborhood and note the addresses of the neighboring houses. I can take that to the assessor's office this afternoon and look up the owners from the late forties and early fifties."

Len tore out a fresh sheet of paper and wrote down Lundquist's address and handed it to Kerry. "I'll call the assessor's office and let them know you're coming and that you're working with me on a murder. That should grease the wheels."

Kerry took the note, folded it, and put it in his shirt pocket. "When are we meeting again?"

Len smiled. "I don't know how long it'll take you to get through the old abstracts. How about next week, after Christmas."

Kerry stood up. "How about tomorrow."

Len shook Kerry's hand. "I like you, son."

Kerry smiled. "I'm happy to have a mission...and to get out of the house. *Thank you.*"

Kerry left and Len threw a twenty on the table. He grabbed my shoulder. "Where did you meet him?"

"He has a son the same age as Jeremy. We met at the school Christmas program."

"He's professional, polite, bright, and available. I like that."

We walked out together, and I stopped at Len's car. "You keep trying to talk me into working for you. You may have met someone more qualified and who might be interested in a job."

Len smiled. "I'm always looking for talent. Let's see how this Lundquist thing goes."

* * *

I drove back to Whistling Pines, parked, and sat in the car thinking about Ole Lundquist,

Sarah Simpson, and the old band shell. I had no doubt that Ole had written the poem and was peeking at Sarah in her bedroom. I'd heard many people accuse him of sexual escapades, and sadly, the rumors sometimes have a thread of truth to them. The term 'passionate plumber' kept coming to mind. In context of his wife leaving him, I had to wonder if she'd caught him cheating, or if someone had put her wise to his activities. At a loss for any path to follow, I walked across the parking lot thinking about our ghost and wondering if Chipper was really responsible for everything that had happened.

How do you deal with a ghost?

I'd barely cracked the front door when someone shrieked, "Close the door!"

I stepped back, pulling the door shut. Someone threw themselves against the door. All I could see was her back, and that her arms were waving erratically. There was commotion inside and several people were moving around, yelling, and waving their arms. I realized the person with her back to the door was waving a giant colander around.

Nothing made any sense of the situation. There wasn't a fire. No one seemed in a hurry to get out, so there was no threat they were escaping. It was as if they were all stricken with sudden dementia. Then I wondered if someone had slipped LSD into the drinking water. All this passing through my head in about three seconds.

230

I realized the person against the door was Soon Yung, one of the kitchen workers with English as a second language, and her excitement led to bursts of Chinese among her English directions to me. I pulled the door open a half inch.

"What's going on?"

A woman yelled, "It's in my hair. Help me, it's in my hair!"

A shoulder pushed against the door as the giant metal colander clanked against the glass.

I tried to open the door again, only to have it slammed in my face. Inside the chaos continued.

I took out my cellphone and was looking for Len's number when I received a call from Jenny.

"What's going on?"

The noise in the background made it hard to hear what she was saying. "Go to the hardware store and get a couple landing nets."

"What?"

"Get landing nets and maybe butterfly nets."

"Why?"

"Just go quickly. Call me back when you're at the front door." Jenny disconnected without further explanation.

I drove to the hardware store, where an employee suggested I try the bait store. December wasn't the season for boat fishing or butterfly collection. The bait store brought two long-handled landing nets from the back room. I negotiated a short-term loan, pending discovery of what was going on.

As I drove back to Whistling Pines, I had the sinking feeling that a bat had gotten loose and they were trying to catch it. I dialed Jenny. "I've got two nets. Open the front door."

I waited five minutes for Jenny who opened the door for only a second and I slipped in.

"What's going on?"

"Someone opened the aviary to get a feather during the scavenger hunt and all the birds escaped."

"But it's always locked except when they're being fed or during cleaning."

"Bingle unlocked it to feed them. Someone saw him unlock it and they snuck in while he was getting the bird food out of the cabinet. The birds went crazy when a stranger walked in and started poking around to get feathers."

The pandemonium had slowed as most of the residents hid in their rooms. A lovebird zipped past and veered up, joining its mate, sitting on the right antler of the moose. The birds were as agitated as the residents and the lovebird let loose a tiny stream of white poop that flew down, hitting behind the empty reception desk.

"Eww!" Wendy had been hunkered behind the desk. She jumped up, wiping her hair with a tissue, and ran to the director's office, where Nancy had locked herself inside. Wendy rattled the door. "Let me in! The birds are pooping on me!"

Nancy's response was muffled, but apparently negative because Wendy ran into the dining room shielding her head. Carmen, a high-school student working as a part-time receptionist, peeked over the reception desk and giggled as she watched Wendy racing for cover.

Jack Randall zipped past on his scooter waving a huge kitchen colander and whooping like a cowboy at a roundup.

Jenny looked at me with pleading eyes. "I've locked up the meds to keep them uncontaminated, and my aides are in the medical office with the door barricaded. The kitchen doors are blocked. We need to clear the dining room, then lock it down, and clean it."

I took a step toward the dining room, then saw Bingle, our janitor, walking down the hallway carrying a ladder. He seemed as calm and collected as ever.

"What's your plan?" I asked as a canary flew past. I took a swing at it with the net but missed. The rapid arm motion gave me a jolt of rib pain and I decided we needed a different plan to catch the birds.

He set the ladder under the stuffed moose head. "Well, I thought I'd get the moose down so there's one less high perch for the birds."

The lovebirds flew off the moose antlers as Bingle set up the ladder. Carmen scooted out from behind the reception desk, fearing that the moose might land on her. Bingle, well into his seventies, wrestled the moose off its mounting screws and slung it over his shoulder. The red ornaments adorning the antlers swung precariously. He climbed down the ladder one-handed and set the moose head, resting it on its antlers and nose, on the reception desk. I noticed that the birds had left several white puddles on the antlers. Bingle pulled a rag out of his back pocket and wiped them off.

Carmen ran to me and cringed behind me as another canary zipped past my ear. Rather than being scared, she was laughing. I waved Bingle into the dining room and followed with Carmen and Jenny close behind. Wendy was hunkered down behind the salad bar, with only the top of her head visible.

I handed Carmen, who seemed unfazed by the swooping birds, a landing net. "Let's go to the windows and spread out. Then start waving your arms and walk toward the door. Maybe we can herd all the birds out." I looked at Wendy, who was watching us. "C'mon. You've already been pooped on. It's not going to get any worse than that."

Wendy reluctantly joined us. There were only a couple birds in the dining room, and they reacted to our waving arms and shouts by immediately flying out the open door. Carmen ran after them, empowered by the net in her hands. Three women were standing near the entryway post office boxes and they ducked as one of the birds swooped close. Carmen was hooting and bouncing as she raced around, swinging the net wildly whenever she got near a bird.

She held up her net triumphantly. "I got one!" A canary struggled against the netting as Carmen rushed to the aviary. She pulled at the net and released the bird into the enclosure, smiling like she'd accomplished the impossible

"Wendy, close the dining room doors and don't let anyone in!" She shut the doors and pushed a chair against them.

Carmen raced off after a lovebird that was circling the reception desk. It flew away before she got close. Another landed on the guest register and Carmen swung the net. She missed the bird, but the guest book flew down the desk and hit the stuffed moose head which teetered on the edge for a second, then toppled to the floor garnering a collective gasp.

Bingle shook his head and picked up the moose head. "I think his nose cracked." He cocked his head as Carmen bounded off after another bird. "Maybe some duct tape and shoe polish will fix him up."

Jeri Westfall was collecting her mail and heard Bingle's comment. "You can't patch a moose's nose with duct tape and shoe polish!"

Bingle pointed up. "He's way up there. Who's going to see the duct tape anyway?"

There was a crash followed by Carmen's, "Oops."

The women at the mailboxes gasped. "That was the Crystal Award from the Society of Senior Residences!"

I chose not to look. Carmen, oblivious to the mayhem as only a teen could be, raced past after another bird flying toward the stone fireplace. I heard another crash and clenched my teeth.

I was shocked to see Howard Johnson and Lee Westfall sitting in the commons area playing cribbage, ignoring the chaos around them. "You guys didn't run to your rooms?"

Lee looked at me and shook his head. He ran his hand over his bald head. "What are the birds going to do, poop in my hair?"

Howard smiled. "They're only little tweety birds. It's not like they going to carry us away and eat us."

I swiped my net at a lovebird as she zipped past. Her ability to zig was quicker than my ability to adjust my swing, and she escaped. "Give us a hand. We're going to scare the birds back to the aviary."

Lee put his cards down and pulled the crib, a small stack of four cards, in front of him. He wagged a finger at Howard. "It's my crib when we get back."

Howard smiled. "It doesn't make any difference. I'm going to skunk you."

"Don't be so sure of yourself. I might get a twenty-nine hand."

Howard laughed as they walked over to us. "That's impossible, the cut card is a three."

Lee's eyes twinkled. "It might be a five if you have to pee again."

Howard, who was known for always being neatly dressed, with spit-polished shoes, sauntered over to us shaking his head. He'd been an Army officer, never revealing just what his rank or battle experience had been. He had military bearing and a sharp mind.

"What's your plan, Peter?" Howard asked.

"I assume the birds are all over the building by now. I thought we would go to the end of every hallway and herd them down here." I nodded toward the small aviary at the end of the large, open common area.

Howard looked around the atrium in the common area, then at the small aviary. A pair of lovebirds flitted high above us after evading Carmen's net. They took a perch on the molding above a two-story window.

Howard looked skeptical. "I don't see that solving the problem. You may get them down here, but how are you going to get them into the aviary?"

Bingle, who was in charge of aviary maintenance, cocked his head. He turned toward the dining room, where Wendy was sitting in a chair blocking the entrance. "The same way we get the residents together, with food."

As if punctuating Bingle's comments, a canary flew through the open aviary door and perched on the edge of a pan of bird seed and pecked at the millet.

"They'll all want to eat and get a drink pretty quick."

Howard nodded. "I've watched them when I've needed a quiet place to think. Their metabolism is really high and they seem to eat every hour." He turned to Bingle. "Can you spread some bird seed on the floor of the aviary? They've been flying around for nearly an hour. They're probably famished."

"Sure! It's in a cabinet." He ambled past the aviary and unlocked a wooden door under the counter.

I nodded. "But we still need to make a sweep of the hallways to herd them down to the food."

Howard nodded. "I agree. Their brains aren't any bigger than a pea, so we need to help them remember where the food is."

We split up, two people to a hallway, starting on the third floor. There were only a couple of the birds that made it into the residential areas, but they were happy to fly ahead of us into the commons. In half an hour we'd cleared the halls and the birds were in the commons. They flew around, but went to the aviary, then perched inside after pecking at the food.

Bingle closed the aviary door. Carmen looked disappointed that the excitement was over.

"Are they all in there?" I asked.

He glanced at the aviary and shrugged. "I don't exactly know. I've never counted them."

I closed my eyes.

Nancy peeked out of her office. "Is it over."

Howard waved her over. "Pretty much. Come on Lee, let's finish our game. It's my crib."

Lee's eyes sparkled. "It's not your crib!"

"Well, it doesn't make any difference, I'm going to skunk you before you get to count."

"I don't think so. I'm a whole street ahead."

"No, you're a street behind."

Lee smiled at me and wiggled his eyebrows.

I watched their good-hearted squabbling as a canary swooped down and landed on Jenny's shoulder. I lifted one of the long-handled nets. "Hold still."

"Peter! You're not going to net a bird on my shoulder!"

Jenny walked slowly toward the aviary and Bingle opened the door wide enough for the bird to fly in.

Jenny glared at me. "You weren't really going to try and net him off my shoulder, were you?"

I tried to look innocent. "Oh, no. I wouldn't do that."

Wendy, who had a clump of white bird poop in her hair, gave me an evil smirk. "You would, wouldn't you?"

I waved everyone to the dining room. "We've got to let the kitchen know it's safe to open the doors. They're going to need help disinfecting the dining room before supper."

Jenny left to dispense meds and the rest of the staff put on aprons and gloves, then got rags and spray bottles of disinfectant. Our cleanup squad worked for two hours, supervised by Helen, the nutritionist, and got everything wiped clean before we opened the doors for the residents to eat supper.

I was tired, smelled like chemical disinfectant, and hadn't thought about anything but the birds and cleaning since leaving Judy's restaurant. I flopped into my office chair causing a sharp rib pain. I eased back and closed my eyes.

"What do you call a pretty woman on a tuba player's arm?"

I looked at Brian, who was leaning on my doorframe.

"A tattoo!" He sat in my guest chair. "I've got some information on your murder."

"It's been a long day. Can we talk tomorrow?"

Brian beamed. "Sure, I'd love to talk with you tomorrow, too. But you need to hear this today."

"What?" I asked, a little too sharply.

"Ole Lundquist probably had a love child."

"Are you passing along a rumor, or is this a fact?"

240

"If a girl got pregnant back in the forties and fifties her family would 'send her off' to live with an unnamed aunt and uncle for six or eight months. She'd come back to school but be very vague about her stay with her relatives, what school she'd attended, and where exactly they lived. Her school records were usually hand-written notes with okay grades, but they didn't have anything more than a scribbled teacher's signature."

"How do you know this?"

"Our neighbor was the school secretary and she told my mother about the sketchy school records these girls brought when they returned. The school accepted them, turning a blind eye to the reality that the girl had probably been in a home for unwed mothers."

"Do you actually know who went away with Ole's love child?"

"Mom couldn't remember the girls' first names." He closed my office door. "Their family names were Steel and Post."

"Are they still local or did they move away?"

Brian whispered, "They both came back here to graduate, but Mom doesn't remember if they're still in the area."

I ran through the residents, trying to recall if any residents had shied away from the speculation and rumormongering about the revelations in the time capsule. I thought of three men, four women who'd been local people, but weren't in the social cliques. The

241

men were either socially inept bachelors, introverts, or were poor and wore tattered clothes. The women who came to mind avoided or were shunned by the cliques. The toughest cliques to crack, for men or women, were the people who'd been the athletes, cheerleaders, and the other children of successful businessmen. The others were the outcasts, the nerds, and kids who came to school with patches on their clothes, or maybe they were pariahs because they'd been pregnant and "gone away" for a few months?

It could fit. I thought

"Brian, please don't…"

He put up his hand. "There's no reason for me to say a word to anyone and I'll deny I ever told you if anyone asks."

"How did you?"

"Mom remembered the family names when I was having coffee with her. The school secretary…"

"Is the school secretary still around?"

Brian shook his head. "She died twenty years ago. Mom was her confidant and claims she's never told anyone until this story about Ole and the time capsule came up. It sparked her memories about those days."

"How sharp is your mother?"

Brian paused. "She can't remember breakfast, but she tells me details about driving a truck for the grocery store during the war. She

242

remembers every stop and who the contacts were."

"I don't know what to do with this. It's not like I can start asking women if they'd had Ole's child."

Brian stood up and opened the door. "I'll leave that up to you, but it may be a piece of the puzzle that's missing."

I shut down my computer, put on my coat, turned off the lights, and walked to my car. Jenny walked out behind me.

"You look like someone ran over your dog."

I turned and gave her a weak smile. "Bad day."

"Something besides the attack of the birds?"

I nodded.

Jenny slipped her arm inside mine, and we walked to her car. "Want to talk about it?"

We stood by her bumper and I kissed her. "I can't. It's something more volatile than violating the HIPAA laws."

"Oh, oh."

I let go of Jenny's arm. "Yeah. And I'm not sure how to deal with it."

"Something related to the time capsule murder?"

"Maybe. It's a bombshell that could mess up someone's life…if it's true."

Jenny stared at me. "You're going to tell Len?"

"I honestly don't know."

"It's that bad."

I ran my hand over my face. "Yeah, it's that bad."

* * *

I reminded Jeremy to do his homework.

"It's done. The teachers aren't giving us much homework this close to Christmas."

I surveyed the freezer for supper options and spotted chicken pot pies. I turned on the oven and changed clothes. I popped the pot pies in the oven and asked Jeremy to set the table. I got an "Oh, Dad," but he put plates and silverware out before rushing back to the television.

The oven timer went off just as Jenny walked in. "Where've you been since we left work?"

She hung up her coat and smiled, "It's a little close to Christmas to be so nosy."

"I'm going to pull the pot pies out of the oven. They should be cool enough to eat by the time you get changed."

We were halfway through supper when Jeremy stopped eating and looked at Jenny. "Mom, is Santa coming here or to Grandma's house?"

"Your stocking is here."

"How will he know we moved?"

244

Jenny smiled and put her hand on Jeremy's hand. "He knows. He's pretty smart about things like that."

Jeremy nodded and went back to eating his pot pie.

We carried dishes to the kitchen. Jeremy usually dried, but he leaned on the counter. "'Frosty's Christmas' is on. Can Mom dry dishes tonight?"

I tousled his hair. "Sure. Go watch Frosty."

Jenny and I did dishes and listened to the songs and narrative. "Part of Santa's team of elves is new to this Christmas stuff. Does Jeremy know you're Santa?"

Jenny grinned. "I'm pretty sure he does, but he doesn't want to admit it."

"This elf isn't prepared to deal with Santa's arrival. Does his other elf have it covered?"

Jenny checked the living room to make sure Jeremy was occupied. "What do you think?"

Jenny and I snuggled on the couch and watched Jeremy be enthralled with the Christmas specials. All the usual television shows were either reruns or had been pre-empted by the specials. We let Jeremy choose what he wanted to watch, which meant I saw Christmas cartoons forgotten since my childhood.

"How long has Burl Ives been dead?" I whispered to Jenny as we listened to him singing, "Have a Holly Jolly Christmas."

"Who's Burl Ives?" I was about to explain when I saw her grin.

Jeremy brushed his teeth, put on his pajamas, and we tucked him into bed.

Jenny and I went into the bedroom and she changed into a flannel nightgown.

"I suppose the long flannel nightgown means we're not consummating our marriage tonight."

"Your ribs still hurt, I'm tired, Jeremy's probably not asleep yet, and the ghost hasn't visited today."

I locked the bedroom door and smiled at her as she climbed under the covers. "My ribs don't hurt as much as yesterday." I slipped under the covers and pressed against her.

"I don't believe you, and there's still the issue of Jeremy not being asleep."

"I'll be quiet, I promise."

Jenny rolled over, facing me and kissed me. "I think we'd better hold off on bedroom gymnastics a while longer."

I pressed my hips against her and kissed her deeply. She resisted briefly, then relaxed.

The sound of the accordion came up through the floor. The notes were random, as were the chords. Jenny planted her hand on my chest and pushed. "The ghost!"

I jumped out of bed, bounded across the bedroom, twisted the doorknob, and planted my face against the locked door. Jenny twisted the lock, opened the door and held it while I rushed past her. Jeremy's door was open and I was surprised that he'd check on the ghostly

246

accordion playing without me. The atonal music continued as I raced down the stairs with Jenny close behind. We burst into the dining room where Jeremy sat with the accordion on his lap.

Jenny went from scared to laughing out loud in two steps.

"Why are you up?" I asked, trying to act stern, but unable to keep the smile off my face while Jenny laughed.

"I couldn't sleep, and you made the accordion look easy."

I took the accordion and put it back in the case. "We can find an accordion teacher if you're interested in learning to play."

Jeremy shook his head as I guided him to the stairs. "I hope it'd be as easy for me as it was for you, but it's hard."

"We could find a concertina, a little accordion, and you could start with that."

I tucked Jeremy back in bed. Jenny gently pushed his hair away from his forehead. I watched and realized the move had nothing to do with Jeremy's hair and everything to do with a mother's touch. With that one touch, Jenny had communicated that things were okay and that she loved him. I wiped a non-existent dab of toothpaste from the corner of his mouth and he smiled. Whether he was conscious of the meaning of those acts or not, they comforted him, and he relaxed.

Jenny took my hand as we walked to the bedroom and I realized I was getting the same subliminal communication. I squeezed her hand and left the bedroom door open.

I crawled into bed and pushed a stray lock of Jenny's hair aside and kissed her. "Did they teach you about touch in nursing school?"

She smiled. "That's why I take everyone's pulse. That's why a doctor listens to everyone's lungs with a stethoscope. It puts us in direct, personal contact with our patients. Their pulse rate and blood pressure drop. They know we're connected, and they're more willing to talk about concerns beyond whatever medical condition brought them in."

"You're wise beyond your years."

She snuggled into my shoulder and we fell asleep.

Chapter 15

I got a cup of coffee without being accosted by Wendy, then checked my emails. After deleting most of the messages I responded to a request from the director to set up a Christmas Eve get together with songs, hot cider, and cookies. I forwarded the request to Wendy and asked her to join me for the music. I could do it alone, but Wendy had the voice of an angel and the residents had complimented both of us on our duets. With that sent, I checked my watch and realized I was meeting Len and Kerry in a few minutes.

* * *

Kerry was sipping coffee in the back of Judy's straightening a sheaf of paper. I signaled for coffee and sat down. "It looks like you've been busy. I hope we're not keeping you from other things."

"Peter, I've been as happy as a pig in slop. I got out of the house and used my brain."

Karla brought me a mug of coffee. "I've got a couple caramel rolls left from breakfast."

"I think we'll wait until Len gets here. I wouldn't want to order until he's offered to buy."

Karla laughed out loud. "Peter, you are so devious. Should I pour a cup of coffee for him?"

I shook my head. "Not until he orders it. That way he won't think that Kerry or I are picking up the bill."

Karla shifted the coffee carafe to her left hand and put her hand out to Kerry. "I'm Karla. I saw you here with Len and Peter yesterday, but I don't think we've ever met."

Kerry stood up and shook her hand. "Kerry Stone, ma'am. I'm pleased to meet you."

"Ma'am is way too formal for Judy's. Please call me Karla, and please sit down."

Kerry watched Karla walk away. "She reminds me of my mother."

"I've seen Karla dig money out of her own pocket when someone's been down on their luck and is counting out pennies to pay their bill."

"My mother's done that. I suppose it's a small-town thing."

Len came in the door looking haggard. He waved at Karla and made a pouring gesture.

"Looks like you've been busy, Kerry," Len said as he shed his coat and hung it on the back of his chair.

Karla was pouring coffee for him and topping off Kerry's coffee before Len sat. "Peter said he was looking forward to the caramel roll you were going to buy him."

Len glanced at me and shook his head. "Sure, whatever Peter and Kerry want is on me."

Karla looked at Kerry, who was visibly uncomfortable with the prospect of managing a caramel roll with his scarred hand. I glanced at the red curled fingers of his left hand. Karla caught my look and nodded almost imperceptibly. "Today's cherry pie will be cool enough to cut in the time it'll take me to warm up the caramel rolls. Would you prefer a piece of pie, Kerry?"

"That'd be great, ma'am."

Karla put her hand on her hip and tried to look angry. "Listen, you keep calling me ma'am and I'm going to start calling you sir. Are we clear on that?"

Kerry smiled. "Yes, Karla."

"Thank you. I'll be back with your rolls and pie in a minute."

Kerry shook his head. "My mom waits tables in Flandreau, South Dakota. I can almost hear her voice when Karla speaks."

Len pointed to the stack of papers Kerry had under his elbow. "What did you find out at the assessor's office?"

Kerry separated his stack into three piles and handed one each to Len and me. "First of all, Peter's rumor mill was wrong about Ole Lundquist's house. It didn't burn down. Here's a copy of the abstract and you can see Ole owned it until it was sold after his death. Look down and you can see the four families who've lived there since that sale."

Len smiled and waved the paper at me. "Imagine that, Peter, the rumor mill was wrong."

Kerry passed us a few more sheets. "Here's the abstract from Simpsons' house. They lived there until 1954, then it was sold."

He passed us more papers. "Here's a plat map of the block and I've written in names of the owners from the late forties and early fifties in case any of those names are significant."

Len ran his finger down the neatly written names Kerry had written in when Karla arrived with caramel rolls and cherry pie. We pushed the papers aside for make room for the plates. She set the pie in front of Kerry. "No ice cream, right?"

Kerry smiled. "Right."

Len continued to look at the plat map as he pulled his caramel roll apart. "None of these names mean anything special to me."

I shook my head. "I'm not from Two Harbors, so they're meaning less to me unless we've got something else to cross reference them with."

Kerry nodded. "They all pre-date my arrival here, too. I showed this to my in-laws and they connected a number of the names to people they knew from school."

I looked again when Kerry said school, and stopped when I saw the name, Steel. The corner of their lot touched Ole's lot. I wondered if that was Genevieve's family home or if it was a different Steel family. I tore apart my caramel roll and pondered sharing Brian's story about the unwed mothers with Len and Kerry. I decided it'd be better to speak with Genevieve discreetly and see if that house was where she grew up.

Len waved a piece of roll at Kerry. "You did a lot yesterday afternoon."

"The assessor's office bent over backwards to help after your call, Len."

"This is interesting information, but like Peter said, it doesn't tell me much without being able to connect it to something else."

Kerry pushed around the last piece of pie crust with his fork, unable to scoop it up. He finally pushed the plate aside. "Well, my in-laws helped us out. They know Larimores, the current owners of Ole's house and if you're interested, we have permission to look around. I spoke to them and they're not really interested in having anyone 'search' the house, but we can 'take a look around'. As Peter said, we can poke into the dark nooks and crannies and look in the attic."

Len smiled and shook his head. "Kerry, you've earned your pie, unlike Peter who's just feasting on my good graces."

I wiped caramel onto a paper napkin. "Hey, I was the one who invited Kerry. That counts for something."

Len signaled Karla for the check. "Only because it's nearly Christmas and I'm feeling charitable."

"I spoke with Mrs. Larimore before I left home. She'll be around until noon if you're available to go over there now. Otherwise, she'll be back around two, after her hair appointment."

Len looked at me. "I've got nothing going on. How about you, Peter?"

I closed my eyes. "Yesterday I returned to a zoo. Someone had left the aviary door open and there were birds flying all over Whistling Pines. The maintenance man had to take down the moose head because they were perching and pooping on the antlers."

Kerry's eyes lit up. "I had no idea your job was so diverse."

"Diverse hardly describes what I do."

Len started laughing. "Tell him about the fat woman who got stuck on the toilet when she flushed before she stood up."

Kerry smiled and looked at me. "Let's go look at Lundquist's house. I've got nothing to rush back to other than planning the music for a Christmas party."

"Wow," Kerry said as he stood. "Everything from helping women stuck to their toilets, to chasing birds, and planning music. You're certainly versatile."

254

Len handed Karla a twenty-dollar bill, then hesitated and handed her another. "Merry Christmas, Karla."

She smiled and kissed his cheek. "Merry Christmas to you, too, chief."

Len spoke over his shoulder as we walked to our cars. "Not only does Peter plan the music, but he performs the music."

"I heard that," Kerry said.

"He plays guitar, piano…let's see, piccolo, flute. What else, Peter?"

I waved my hand, trying to change the subject. "Who's driving?"

Len pointed to his car. "Let's burn the city's gas. Hop in and hope I don't get an emergency call or you'll get a high-speed joy ride and be stuck with whatever I get dragged into."

Kerry got in the backseat. "That would be the most exciting thing I've done since I got to Two Harbors."

Len pulled out of the parking lot. "What's at the top of the list now?"

"Coffee with you two."

I laughed. "The bar is very low."

I looked over the seatback at Kerry who was grinning. "The bar is on the floor."

Len looked at Kerry in the rearview mirror. "As an Army investigator, did you carry a firearm and have arrest powers?"

"I wore a badge, carried a sidearm, and yes, I arrested people. I also filled out mountains of paperwork—in triplicate, slept on a cot in a tent without air conditioning, ate Army slop, and rode around in a Humvee wearing a helmet and body armor."

The conversation died until we got to the street with the Lundquist house. "Ole lived in the green two-story with the dormer on the side."

Len parked on the street. and we followed Kerry to the door. He knocked and an elderly woman with bluish-gray hair answered. She'd apparently never met Kerry because she blanched at the site of his scarred face.

"Mrs. Larimore, I'm Kerry Stone. I asked about checking for anything left in your house by the previous owners."

"Oh, yes. You're Marty's son-in-law. Please come in."

"You may know Chief Rentz. The other gentleman is Peter Rogers."

"Please call me Eve," she said as she shook our hands. "Please come in and tell me what you're looking for."

We sat in overstuffed chairs that reminded me of the furniture Dolores left for us. Eve's living room had plaster walls, hinting that the construction was probably early in the twentieth century. Everything was neat, decorated tastefully, and freshly painted.

Len leaned forward. "We hope to find something that'll tie in with the materials found in the band shell time capsule. Ole Lundquist, the man mentioned in the newspaper article

256

enclosed in the time capsule, lived here at the time of his death. We're really grasping at straws, but we thought there might be a box stuffed in a cubbyhole or something in the dark recesses of the attic that might give us a clue to solve his murder."

Eve nodded. "Well, you're certainly welcome to look around. Kerry promised me you wouldn't tear the place apart or anything like that."

Len shook his head. "We just want to peek into the rafters and poke around in the attic. I promise we'll put anything we move back in its place before we leave."

Eve stood. "The stairway to the attic is this way."

She led us to the second floor and showed us a narrow door. "It's cold up there."

I paused by an open door looking into a bedroom. It had lace curtains pulled back revealing a view of the neighboring house. "Eve, may I look out your bedroom window?"

She cocked her head and frowned. "I suppose so, but all you'll see is the house next door."

Indeed, the view was of the house next door. To be exact, I was looking through the window of the house next door. I saw an unmade bed and was staring at a distant reflection of myself in the mirror mounted on the back of the door. I thought of the Sarah Simpson poem and the line about the bedroom mirror and felt slightly sick to my stomach.

Len and Kerry steeped behind me. "What do you see?"

"Sarah Simpson's bedroom."

Kerry looked confused. "I'll explain later," I whispered.

We climbed up the stairs into a space that looked remarkably like my own attic. The floorboards were dusty pine planks covering the rafters. There were water stains in a few spots hinting at previous leaks. A single lightbulb hung from a wire and barely lit the center of the space. Len took out a flashlight and walked the length of the house, shining the light into the dark recesses that sloped down to the eaves. Spiderwebs hung overhead and I saw a hibernating bat jammed into a narrow recess between two boards. The wind sighed and moved the spiderwebs.

Kerry hung back, looking uneasy. "Eve should rent this attic out on Halloween."

Len's flashlight went farther toward the eaves as he crawled, ducking under the steep rafters. "I've got a box."

He came back and handed me a small cardboard box covered with dust. "I'll check the other direction."

The tape was yellowed, but still intact. I was about to pick at the edge when Kerry pulled out a pocketknife and slit the tape down the center and on the edges. "That'll make it easier."

258

Len returned empty-handed and shone his flashlight on the box as I opened the flaps. I pulled aside some newspaper and Len held up the corner. "It's from 1948. Ole might've packed this away."

Inside were a dozen metal candleholders.

Kerry held one up. "What are these for?"

Len ran his finger under the drip pan. "They've got clips to go on a Christmas tree."

"You're joking," Kerry said, studying Len's face. "People put lit candles on their Christmas trees?"

Len shrugged. "It was before my time, but my mother talked about cutting a tree on Christmas eve, putting candles on it, lighting them, singing a carol, then blowing out the flames."

"I imagine a few Christmas celebrations were interrupted by fires."

"She said something about having a bucket of water handy."

I carried the box down and handed it to Eve. "Merry Christmas." I took out one of the candle holders and held it up. "I imagine you could get a pretty penny for these at the antique store."

"They were in the attic?"

Len nodded. "The box was tucked under the eaves. The newspaper packing is from the late forties." He paused. "Let's take a look in the basement."

Eve led us to the kitchen and another narrow door. She flipped a switch on the wall

259

and stepped back. "The basement's warmer than the attic, but not a lot. Please forgive me if I don't go down with you."

Like the attic ascent, the stairway was narrow, the steps short, and the headspace limited. I heard Kerry bump his head behind me. "What's with these houses with the narrow stairs? Were people short with little feet?"

Len turned his head. "I think building materials were expensive and stairs to unused spaces were wasteful."

The basement was only five feet high. Floor joists were almost black, hinting at an earlier time when the house had an oil or coal boiler that created soot. The lighting was better than in the attic, but the dark joists and walls made the lighting insufficient for searching.

Unlike the attic, the basement was full of stuff. The walls were lined with dusty wooden shelves. There were hundreds of empty canning jars, wicker clothes baskets, crocks, kerosene lanterns, and more.

Kerry bumped his head again, this time cursing the midget who built the house. "She should hire an antique dealer to come in here. Hell, someone could start an antique shop with all the stuff that's down here."

I moved jars and crocks, looking behind them for a hidden box or nook, but seeing nothing but the stone walls. Kerry searched between the floor joists onto the top of the rock walls.

Len crawled along the floor, shining his flashlight under the bottom selves. "Anybody finding anything?"

"No," Kerry and I echoed.

Len got up and dusted off his knees. "Are we ready to call it a day?"

"Hello," Kerry said, reaching over the top of some dusty Easter baskets.

Len shone his flashlight where Kerry's hand was reaching. "What do you have?"

Kerry pulled his hand back and wiped dust off the top of a flat box, revealing a picture of six men dressed in eighteen-hundreds clothing. A banner above them read "Dutch Masters".

"Dutch Masters cigars," Len said. "My dad used to store nuts and bolts in old cigar boxes like that."

Kerry ran his fingernail around the edge until he found a spot to lift the lid. He carried it over to an overhead light and looked inside. "Sheets of paper."

I lifted one of the yellowed sheets out of the box and carefully unfolded it.

I'm so sorry to send you this news, but I couldn't bear to see your face when you heard I wasn't coming back. We were never meant to be together, you and I. Our time together was lovely, but I ~~won't~~ can't be there anymore.

261

I'll soon be through with school and am waiting for a calling. Some of the girls have already accepted contracts, but not I. Mine will come, but most likely I'll be in a little school somewhere far from you.

You'll find someone else, but my heart will ache for you.

G

I pulled the next sheet aside, looking for an envelope or any indication of a return address. "I don't know who this is written to or who 'G' is."

Kerry and Len each silently read a page and I picked up another. "This one is signed, Charlotte."

Kerry flipped his around and shook his head. "Just initials, P.T."

Len put the note he'd read back in the box. "There are more. Let's take them somewhere where there's reading light. The faded ink and scrawling handwriting make my eyes ache."

Kerry dusted off the box and tucked it under his arm.

Eve was waiting for us at the top of the stairs. "Did you find any treasures?"

262

Len smiled. "Your basement is full of antiques. You might want to invite a dealer in and have them make you an offer."

Eve flapped her hand. "It's all dusty old scrap. They wouldn't buy it unless I cleaned it all up and I'm not carrying up all that dusty stuff and dragging it into my kitchen."

"I think a dealer might be willing to box it up and carry it away."

Eve dismissed the thought with a shake of her head. She looked at the cigar box. "What did you find?"

Kerry opened the lid. "They appear to be love letters and poems."

Eve smiled. "That's sweet. Old love letters?"

Len lifted one out and showed Eve the faded ink on the yellowed paper. "May we take these and examine them?"

Eve smiled. "Take them away. They're not to me and I'd have never seen them if you hadn't found them."

We thanked Eve and she let us out the front door. We stood on her front sidewalk and flipped through the box. There were about a dozen notes, each on different paper. Some in black ink, others in faded blue ink. A couple had been written in pencil.

I found a poem:

Just now
Every evening bird
Sings so
Sweetly that
I find the reality
Crushing,
Amazingly alive.
Maybe, just maybe, we
Are here to
Rejoice
In witnessing
Each exquisite outburst.
"Jessica Marie."

Kerry looked at me. "What?"

I explained acrostic poetry to him. Len took out a pen and wrote over the first letter of each line and shook his head. "I can't believe these girls...women would all succumb to him."

Vibrant smile
Inviting my lips
Vamping teases
Stroking your face
Touching your body
Emerging womanhood
Erupting like fire, then
Lingering beside you

I handed the poem to Kerry. "Viv Steel. That's one of the names from the band roster and the Steel name is also on the plat map." I tipped my head back and reflected on the names the school secretary shared with Eleanor Johnson. "I don't know if any records still exist from the fifties, but I heard second hand that two girls went on extended stays with obscure relatives. Their last names were Steel and Post. You don't suppose…"

Len scratched his head. "Well, this is interesting. Let's read through these and see if we can find an envelope or at least another name written on one of the letters."

Something was nagging at me. The poetic styles were so different. "Len, let me look at those poems again." I read the poems, then held them side-by-side. "These were written by a different person than the rhyming odes in the time capsule. They're all descriptive odes, but the odes to Viv Steel and Jessica Marie are free verse."

Len took the poems back and reread them. "I'm not much of a poet, but these aren't what I think of as poetry. There's no rhythm or rhyme to them."

I thought back to the poems in the time capsule. "I think the poems to Sarah Simpson and Joanne Post were written by someone else. The murderer knew Joanne Post had a child when she was 'visiting relatives' and hoped we'd see that as a motive for killing Ole. Do you have copies of the time capsule poems? I'd like to compare the handwriting."

"They're back at my office. What are you thinking?"

"I wonder if someone threw a red herring into the time capsule to mislead whoever investigated the murder. I suspect the murderer wanted us to think Ole had a thing for Sarah Simpson and Joanne Post to divert attention away from something else."

Kerry was looking skyward and frowning.

"What's up?" I asked.

"There's an extra chimney over the kitchen."

Len looked and shrugged. "Some of these old houses were built when people were still cooking on woodstoves. I imagine that's a remnant from that era that never got removed."

Kerry put his hand on Len's shoulder. "There's something else. Most of the basement walls were rock. The one supporting this box was cinder blocks." He looked at Len like he was looking through him. "Do you have a measuring tape in your car?"

"I have a fifty-foot one I use for accident reconstruction. Why?"

"Get it. The basement seemed smaller than the footprint of the house."

Kerry ran up the steps and knocked on the door while Len pulled a yellow measuring tape out of his trunk. Kerry was waving us up the steps as Len closed the trunk. "Come on!"

Kerry led us downstairs and we measured the basement, then verified that indeed one wall was cement blocks. We went outside and measured the foundation. All four outside basement walls were stone.

"The basement is six feet shorter."

We walked to the end over the kitchen and under the spare chimney pipe. There was a dirty window in the basement stones.

Kerry put out his hand. "Len, loan me your flashlight. This outside wall is stones. I'm certain the inside wall facing this side is blocks."

Kerry got on his hands and knees, shining the flashlight into the window. "I can't see anything. I think the glass is covered with soot." He set the flashlight down and took a penknife out of his pocket. He inserted the blade under the edge of the window and gently lifted. It wasn't latched and it opened. He got on his hands and knees, shone the flashlight inside, then straightened up. The unscarred side of his face was smiling. "Ole was a bootlegger. There's a still down here and boxes of bottles."

I looked at Len and raised my eyebrows. "There's more to Ole than we thought."

Len smiled as Kerry closed the window and got up. Based on his stiff movements, I thought his burns probably covered a lot of the skin under his clothing. Then I thought about some of the guys I'd treated in Iraq after IED explosions and fires. The smell of burning flesh filled my nose and I started to shake. I tried to take a deep breath and that caused my ribs to hurt.

Len put his hand on my bicep. "Are you okay?"

I put up my hand and nodded but didn't trust my voice.

Kerry read my situation. Not knowing what triggered it but recognizing the symptoms of the flashback and PTSD. He gripped my other bicep firmly. "Stand down, sailor."

I nodded and stared at my shoes while I tried to get my head under control. It took a couple minutes to clear the visions from my mind, then I felt emotionally drained and put my arms around their shoulders.

Len put his arm around me. "Are you going to be okay?"

I nodded. Kerry looked at me and shook his head. "It takes more than two minutes to get your feet under you after a flashback. Doesn't it, Peter?"

"Yeah," I said shakily.

Len looked at Kerry, as the understanding hit. "Would you guys like to get a cup of coffee?"

I tried to focus. "No, let's look inside the basement."

Len shook his head. "I don't see how we're going to do that. Kerry promised Eve we wouldn't mess up her pretty house. I'm not willing to tell her we'd learn anything by breaking down a cement block wall. Hell, that room could've been there since Prohibition! There's no time stamp on it or engraved nameplate that says Ole Lundquist. I'm willing to bet that room used to be the coal bin for an old coal-fired boiler and the window is where the delivery chute was located. I'll bet no one's burned coal in this town since the thirties or forties."

I sized up the window. "Let me crawl down there."

"How in hell are you going to do that? I'll bet there's no ladder under the window."

Kerry got down on his stomach and pried the window open. He stuck his head inside and shined the flashlight around. He pushed himself back, shaking his head.

"No ladder, and there are shelves full of bottles under the window."

I pulled off my jacket and handed it to Len. "I'll use the shelves as a ladder."

Kerry's headshaking made me a little uneasy, but I lay down and stuck my feet through the window and pushed myself backwards. I was rewarded with a jabbing pain.

Kerry stepped away. "I'm going to warn Eve there may be some noise."

He wasn't out of sight when my foot hit a bottle and it fell to the floor and broke. I looked at Len who gave me an *I told you not to do this* look.

Bottles crashed to the floor as I tried to get a foothold on the shelf. As soon as I got a spot cleared I realized I had to step down to the next shelf, which caused another bunch of bottles to fall to the floor.

Len squatted down. "You do realize once you get to the floor you're going to be walking on all those broken bottles."

"Do you have anything positive to say, Len?"

Len considered that while I worked my way farther through the window. I paused as pain shot into my ribs as I rested on them while trying to get a purchase with my feet.

Len smiled, apparently finding something positive. "You'll probably live through this."

Kerry flew around the corner just as the shelf broke and I fell into darkness with bottles falling around me.

After shining the flashlight around the room, Kerry's head came through the window. "Are you okay?"

I'd fallen backward and landed on a wooden case rather than the broken glass that littered the floor. The impact sent searing pain into my ribs, causing me to see stars, and taking my breath away. I sat for a full minute before catching my breath and standing up. "I'm bruised but not broken. Hand me the flashlight."

There was a large dusty moonshiner's copper still in the corner with a cone-shaped top that fed a spiral of copper tubing. There were bottles on shelves, bottles in wooden cases, burlap sacks hung from hooks in the wall and rusty rectangular gallon cans labeled as molasses lined one wall. I noticed a desk made from rough-hewn wood in the corner and picked

270

up a pile of receipts. I set aside the top sheet, too dusty to read, and leafed through receipts for corn, molasses, malted barley, yeast, bottles and corks. They were hand-written and made out to O. Lundquist.

"Have you found anything?" Len yelled.

"Ole was making moonshine. There's a still, bottles, and piles of receipts for malt, molasses and corn."

I heard Len sigh. "It's a little late to prosecute him for making moonshine."

Kerry was back on his hands and knees peering through the window. "I don't know. It seems like the government never lets off tax prosecution." He stuck his head in the window. "How are you going to get out of there without the shelves?"

There was no way the broken shelving would support me. "I haven't thought that far ahead." I looked for a ladder or step stool. Ole was obviously using this room when he could walk out through the basement. Shining the flashlight on the block wall, I looked for a door hidden from the other side of the basement or a seam in the blocks. There was a crack along the floor and I pulled back some burlap sacks hanging on the wall. Behind the sacks was a narrow wooden door that swung in. Pulling on the handle caused a billowing cloud of dust. The hinges screeched in protest, but the door opened. The side toward the rest of the basement had been textured and painted to look like cement blocks. Pushing on the back of a wooden cabinet made it slide away into the other portion of the basement. Ole, or whoever built the low-ceilinged hidden room, had done a superb job of engineering the hidden access to the still. In the dim basement light the access door was virtually invisible.

I went back to Ole's desk and pulled a wooden chair back so I could open the drawer. It was also full of receipts. I flipped through the dates and they got older as I dug deeper. They were loose and poorly organized. I suppose you only had to be organized if you planned to pay taxes. I dug to the bottom but saw nothing but more slips of paper receipts. I pushed the chair back and it stopped short of going fully under the desk. I pulled it out again and pointed the flashlight under the desk, illuminating a small wooden workman's chest.

My first thought was that I'd found Ole's cash box, but then reasoned that whoever shot Ole probably took any money lying around. That thought froze me for a second as I tried to reason through the timeline of Ole distilling moonshine, Ole getting killed, and the block wall going up. Someone wanted to hide the still. Was it Ole or did the construction date back to Prohibition? Nothing I saw gave me a date.

"What's going on?" Len asked.

"I found a little chest."

"How little?"

"Two feet long. Eighteen inches high and deep."

"Is it full of Ole's plumbing tools?"

I lifted one end of the box. "It's too light for pipe wrenches and such."

I pulled the black wooden box out from under the desk and flipped the latches. The hinges groaned but opened exposing a tray of plumbing fixtures: Elbows. Tees. Reducers. Solder. Flux.

"What was the noise? It sounded like you were groaning."

"Rusty hinges. The trunk looks like it's full of plumbing stuff." Lifting the tray, I expected to find wrenches, hacksaws, and pipe fittings. Instead I found a stained rag. I unfolded it gently, shining the flashlight into the dark recess. I closed my eyes for a second, then wrapped the rag back over the contents.

"Uh, Len."

"What?"

"I'm going to hand you something. Be careful with it."

I lifted the bundle out of the box and held it up to the window where hands in blue nitrile gloves reached in and took it from me. I stood next to the opening, waiting for some reaction from Len and Kerry.

Kerry's head popped in the window. "Do you need me to find a ladder?"

"There's a hidden door down here. I'll go out through the basement."

I found Len and Kerry standing behind Len's car, staring at the dirty rag on the trunk lid.

I joined them. "Well?"

Len looked up. "Well, shit. We've got a nice unsolved cold case and you have to mess it up by finding evidence." Len lit his pipe, taking time to consider the find.

I walked over. "What do you make of it?"

Len looked at me and drew on the pipe again. "You got out okay?"

"Yeah. There's a door hidden behind the basement shelves."

Deep in thought, Len said, "Good."

Kerry looked at me and mouthed *good?*

"Len."

He turned again. "What?"

"Talk to us."

Len sucked on his pipe, but it was dead. He made a ceremony of taking out the lighter and puffing on the pipe as he relit it. He glanced at the trunk lid and shook his head.

"I don't know what to say." He peeled the rag back so we could see the mummified infant.

"Shit." Len hit his pipe on the heel of his shoe, knocking out the tobacco and sending hot embers onto the pavement.

I covered the body. "Do you think the child was Ole's?"

Len threw up his hands. "How the hell do I know? How can anyone know? Ole's been dead for sixty or seventy years. The baby maybe longer than that."

Kerry closed the rag and tied it. "You can test the DNA and determine who the parents are. The Army is testing bodies they're recovering from Italy and the South Pacific who died in WWII and identifying them."

Len looked at Ole's house and grimaced. "Army families want to identify their lost relatives and they offer DNA samples for comparison. I suspect whoever was this child's mother isn't interested in being linked to her."

"It might be one of Ole's children with his wife."

Len shook his head. "Ole's kids left with his wife, or so the rumor mill says. I'd bet a month's pay that all his children can be accounted for. No, this isn't anyone's legitimate child."

"What if someone put that child in the box long after Ole's death?"

Kerry had been silent as Len and I went back and forth. I looked at him and he glanced at the house. "Do you think there are bodies buried under the basement floor?"

Len started packing his pipe with vigor. "Damn it, did you need to bring that up?"

Kerry put up his right hand. "It was just a question."

Len stabbed the air with his pipe stem. "It was a damned good question. I just didn't want to hear it." He skipped his metal tamping tool, pressing the tobacco into the pipe bowl with his thumb, then sucked on the pipe stem vigorously as he lit it.

"I know a doctor in Eveleth. We could discreetly take our bundle to her."

Len looked like he was ignoring my suggestion while puffing on the pipe. "Do you have time to do that?"

"Not really."

I looked at Kerry. "If I called her, could you make the delivery?"

"I've got nothing else going on. How far is Eveleth?"

* * *

I drove back to Whistling Pines and looked up Roberta's cellphone number. She answered on the second ring. "Hey, Peter. Are you ready for Christmas?"

"We're getting there." I paused. "I've got a problem, Bobbie."

"You've only been married a few days and you're having problems already?" she said, laughing.

I explained the discovery of the mummified baby and my suspicions about its ties to Ole Lundquist's murder.

"That's interesting history. Why are you calling me? I'm an emergency room doctor and this person is way past getting benefit from my services."

"I hoped you could look at the body and give me some idea of the cause of death."

"You understand that I'm neither a medical examiner nor forensic pathologist. I can give you the name…"

276

"Roberta, this is way off the books and I'm sure the police are more interested in general impressions from someone who's seen a lot of trauma than paying for an autopsy on a seventy-year-old murder."

"Wow, you sure know how to sweet talk a girl. 'Take a look at my dead body. I'd rather have your free opinion than paying for someone who's actually qualified to do a post-mortem examination.'"

"Bobbie, I'm not a cop, I'm just helping the police try to find answers to old questions. No one is ever going to be prosecuted for whatever is involved. It's unlikely the people are even alive anymore."

"It's Roberta, or Dr. Carlton professionally."

"I know, that's why I called you Bobbie."

She let out a sigh. "What the hell. Have the mortuary send the body over. I may have a pathologist consult. She's a friend and gets off solving medical mysteries."

"There's no mortuary involved. I have a friend on his way to Eveleth with the body in his car."

"You friend is a cop?"

"No, he's a wounded veteran who's helping with the investigation."

"This just keeps getting better and better."

"Could you look at the body as soon as he gets there?"

"Peter, you do know that I'm not sitting on my hands waiting for you to ask for my help.

An ambulance could show up with someone in cardiac arrest or there could be an accident on the highway."

"Bobbie..."

"I'm Dr. Carlton."

I let out a breath. "Bobbie, this is personal. I'm invested in finding an answer."

"What's your friend's name and when will he be here?"

"His name is Kerry Stone. He left Two Harbors half an hour ago."

Roberta let out a sigh. "You are a pain in the butt. If you weren't such a nice guy, I'd tell you to take a flying leap." Then she paused. "I'll tell the front desk to send him to the ER when he arrives."

"One other thing."

"You're going to leave the pretty blonde and sweep me off my feet?"

Her kidding told me she wasn't going to hold a grudge for taking advantage of our friendship. "Will you put me on speakerphone when you do your examination?"

"If I'm interpreting this correctly, your friend isn't dropping off the package. You want me to set everything else aside and examine it as soon as he arrives?"

"Please."

"Jeez, who knew having you as a high school lab partner would mean I was handing you a lifetime 'get out of jail free' card."

I didn't know how to respond, but my witty response would've been wasted—I was listening to a dial tone.

I walked to the dining room for a cup of coffee. The lunch rush was gone, and the tables were empty. The clatter of pot washing came from the kitchen as I stared out the windows at Lake Superior. An ore boat pushed through the cold water, probably one of the last of the season. The harbors would soon be covered with ice and the Sault Ste. Marie locks would be closed, breaking the link between the Minnesota iron pellets and the steel mills on the other Great Lakes.

I heard the whisper of footsteps on the carpeting and turned. Jenny was carrying a container of medications, on her way to dispense them to residents. "You look lost again. Are you going to tell me what's eating you?"

I directed her to the table farthest from the kitchen and sat down. "Kerry Stone found Ole Lundquist's house. There was a hidden room in the basement, and I found a mummified infant in a trunk."

Jenny put her hand on my arm and I immediately thought of the value of touch. "You think it has something to do with Ole's murder."

"I don't know." I spilled the rest of the story, the still, the room being blocked up, the cigar box of poems and love letters, the acrostic names, and Kerry's trip to Eveleth to deliver the remains to the pathologist.

"Wow. There are a lot of dots there that haven't been connected."

"Yes. And there's one more. Brian Johnson stopped off yesterday with another dot. During Ole's years here there were several girls who 'visited relatives' for a few months and returned with sketchy school records. Brian's mother and the school secretary were best friends, so his mother heard names of the girls who probably spent a few months in homes for unwed mothers and came back as pariahs."

"That's what was eating you last night."

I nodded. "My fear is that one, or more, may be residents here, and are still pariahs excluded from the Whistling Pines cliques."

"Did Brian tell you who they were?"

"His mother could only remember last names, which are meaningless to me because all the women here have married names."

I could see the information was overwhelming Jenny, too. I regretted spreading the burden.

Jenny continued to stare at the lake. "More unconnected dots." She looked at me. "You're not going to…"

"No, I'm not going to ask our residents if they had children they gave up for adoption."

Jenny nodded. "I knew I had to keep Jeremy, but it was a different time, and it was never easy. My friends drifted away once he was born. If not for Mom and Dad…"

"Like you said, times are different now. Lots of women without husbands keep their babies. There was no way to do that back in the forties and fifties."

Jenny shook her head. "Not easily. Every man wanted to marry a virgin and marrying a woman who had a child…"

"It tainted both of them."

My phone buzzed and I recognized Roberta's number. "I'm in the morgue with Mary Olson the pathologist. Do you want to listen in?"

Jenny glanced at her pill caddy, then nodded. I pointed to the door and we walked to my office as I took the call. "Hi, Dr. Olson. I'm walking to my office so I can close the door."

"Hi, Peter, this is Mary. Your friend Kerry showed up a couple minutes ago with the package. We're in the pathology lab with Dr. Carlton and I just unwrapped the rags. Let me know when you're ready for me to go on."

I closed my office door and Jenny sat in my guest chair. I turned on the speaker. "Okay, I've got the door closed."

"My first impression is that this child was born prematurely, at about thirty weeks. The umbilical cord is still attached, so the child wasn't born in a hospital, and it may have been stillborn. Your friend, Kerry, guessed that the body is from about 1950. A delivery at thirty weeks was pretty iffy back then and certainly not survivable without intensive medical intervention."

I looked at Jenny, who looked very sad, but was nodding her head. "It sounds like the baby may have been a home birth if the umbilical cord is still attached."

"That's likely. I'm doing a superficial exam. The child was female. There aren't any external signs of trauma. What I find most surprising is that the body seems mummified, with little or no decomposition. I've read about cases like this in the desert, but it's unheard of in Minnesota because our climate is so moist and rife with bacteria that decomposition starts almost immediately."

Jenny leaned forward. "What would happen if the body had been immersed in high proof ethanol?"

The pathologist paused. "Well, that would effectively embalm the corpse. That's how pathologists used to preserve specimens. I've seen all kinds of tissue samples preserved in alcohol, some taken in the 1800s, that are bleached, but certainly identifiable and not degraded. What makes you think this child might've been preserved in alcohol?"

Kerry's voice came over the phone. "Peter recovered the remains from a hidden home distillery."

"Why would someone…pickle a baby rather than bringing it to a mortuary for burial."

I looked at Jenny. "I believe she was born to a teenaged unwed mother."

I heard murmuring. "Are you still there?"

282

Kerry answered. "Yeah, we're still here. The doctors are talking."

Dr. Olson came on. "I'm legally obligated to report this."

"Perfect," I replied. "Please send your report to Len Rentz, the Two Harbors police chief. The body was recovered from a house here. Len was on the scene when it was recovered."

"Damn it, Rogers, why didn't you tell me that to start with?" Roberta asked. "I thought this was some sort of under the radar…whatever! I was afraid you expected me to cover your…"

"Easy, Bobbie. Kerry and I are assisting the Two Harbors Police with a cold case investigation."

"You could've opened with that statement."

"Well, I'm a little rattled right now."

Jenny leaned forward. "Dr. Carlton, this is Jenny Rogers. We met at Hugo's."

"Hi, Jenny. I didn't realize that was you on the call."

"We suspect this might be related to the newspaper clipping about an old murder. The article was in the time capsule recovered from our band shell."

"Ahh. I watched a replay of that on the news."

Jenny continued. "The baby's body was found in the basement where Ole Lundquist was murdered. We suspect he was the father, but the identity of the mother is unknown."

283

"Okay, Peter," Roberta said. "You've always been a little awkward, so I'm going to give you a pass on this."

Dr. Olson came on. "For future reference, my role as a pathologist is to examine the victim, but I need the context of the discovery to complete my investigation. The key word there is *context*, and you skipped that part of your request. Got it?"

I leaned forward, "Sorry."

"Okay, so I'm looking at a premature birth of a child, probably born out of wedlock. The body was preserved in high proof moonshine, then wrapped in rags and stored in a basement for seventy years. Who do you think the parents are?"

"We suspect the father is Ole Lundquist, who was murdered in his basement in 1951. We found the baby in a tool trunk in a hidden room with his moonshine still. The mother may have been one of his neighbors, possibly a married woman who was having an affair with him, or one of his teenaged neighbors."

"There are a lot of weasel words in that statement. I deal with facts and data."

I looked at Jenny, who was shaking her head. "We're lacking facts. All we have are a bunch of rumors and unrelated bits that aren't connected or time stamped."

"Here's what I'm going to do," Dr. Olson said. "I'm going to back up and start over. I'll log this as an unidentified body found in Two

284

Harbors and delivered to me by a Two Harbors police representative. I'll start a file, including the background information you've provided, and I'll schedule a post-mortem exam. If someone from the police department or the Lake County Sheriff's Department wants to attend, they're welcome. I'll do a full exam and write a comprehensive report. I'll hold the body until either a family member or the police pick it up."

"Thank you."

"You'd better warn the police chief that he'll get a bill."

"I'll warn Len. Thank you."

"Hang on Peter," Roberta said. "Kerry and I are walking to my office."

We heard footsteps on the tile floor.

"Jenny, are you still on the line?" Roberta asked.

"Yes, I'm here."

"Congratulations on your marriage. I hope it's long and happy."

"Thank you."

"I rescind all previous comments I've made about future claims on Peter if you throw him back into the dating pool. I'd forgotten what a goofy nerd he was. My judgement at Hugo's was obviously clouded by alcohol and his brilliant musical talent."

I heard Kerry laughing in the background.

"Thanks, Bobbie."

"You'd damned well better thank me. There's no balance owed in our account, not that there ever was, and now you owe me big time."

"I thought Dr. Olson was going to bill Len."

"She'll bill the police department for the post-mortem. I'm talking about who owes whom a favor. If I ever need a band for a party or event, I expect you to be there with a guitar case and a few friends."

"Uh, Bobbie, I don't have a band."

"I didn't say you did. I told you what I expect. Got it?"

Kerry was laughing hard in the background and Jenny was grinning and shaking her head.

"Yeah, I got it." I paused. "Bobbie."

"I told you to call me Roberta. Or, Doctor Carlton."

"Bobbie, thanks."

"You're welcome," she said softly.

I disconnected the call and looked at Jenny. "I have no idea what to do with this information."

Jenny stood up and kissed the top of my head. "You and Len will figure it out."

Jenny walked away and I stared at the open door, pondering my next move. I thought about the cigar box, the band shell, the poems, the gun. The pieces flew around in my brain like balls on a billiard table, colliding, then caroming off in different directions. Two pieces came together, the plat map Kerry had given me and the band member ledger.

I dialed Brian Johnson and pulled out the plat map with the names written in by Kerry.

"Hi, Peter. What's up."

"Is your book of band members handy?"

"It's in the other room. What do you need?"

"Please get it and put your phone on speaker."

I heard Brian's footsteps and I set my cellphone on my desk and grabbed a pen and paper.

"Okay, I've got the book. What do you need?"

"Go back to 1948 and start reading me names."

Brian read down the names for 1948 as I compared his list with Ole's neighbors. In 1949 he read Robert Steel.

"Hang on a second while I write that down." I made a note. "Okay, keep going."

He got to Inga Lange and I stopped him again, noting her name and that the Lange lot touched Ole's lot.

"Keep reading."

"I'm in 1950 now."

He read four entries. "Stop! I'm writing down Viv Steel." I noted that their house was two away from Ole's. "Okay. How about 1951."

Brian read the seven names from 1951, but none corresponded with Ole's neighbors.

"Try 1952."

None of the three names were Ole's neighbors or were any of the 1953 entries.

"Thanks, Brian. That's enough. Does your list show the age of the members?"

"Not their age. Only which instrument they played." He paused. "What are you up to?"

"I'm trying to pull the pieces together with the other things I've heard. I was comparing your list with Ole's neighbors."

I disconnected Brian and called Len. I warned him about the superficial examination of the baby's remains, the upcoming pathologist bill and my efforts to connect Ole's neighbors with band members.

"Why connect with band members?"

"I thought we might find someone who was familiar with the band shell and connect them with Ole's rumored philandering. Have you read through the poems and letters in the cigar box?"

"Yes and no. Yes, I've read them. No, I didn't find any names, addresses, or smoking guns. My eyes ache from trying to decipher the faded ink and poor handwriting. I think there were at least four different authors. I also compared the handwriting on the poems in the cigar box to the ones in the time capsule. They were written by different people."

I disconnected from Len and stared at the open door again. I needed someone who knew the local people, who might know what someone's maiden name was, but who would be discreet. I flew out the door and went to the commons where Howard Johnson and Lee Westfall were playing cribbage.

"Excuse me, can I interrupt the game? I'd like to talk with Howard for a moment."

Lee smiled. "It's over. I'm crushing Howard like a bug."

Howard gathered his cards and looked at the board. "I'll concede the game if you'll concede the skunk."

Lee pretended to weigh the offer. "Okay, but you've got to pay up before you leave and forget the debt. You owe me for three games."

Howard took out a leather coin purse and set three pennies on the table. "There. We're square."

Lee scooped up the pennies. "Ha! I've taken seven cents from him this week!"

Howard shook his head. "I was four cents ahead last week." He smiled at me and nodded toward the hallway.

I led him to my office and closed the door. He sat in my guest chair and carefully crossed his legs, pulling at the fabric so it didn't wrinkle. "What's up, Peter?"

"I don't need to tell you this, but I have something that requires your utmost discretion."

Howard smiled. "Okay, as long as it doesn't require me to divulge something else that I'm holding in confidence, we're fine."

"We discovered a baby's body hidden in the coal bin at Ole Lundquist's house." I handed him the plat drawing of Ole's block. "I have the names of some of the band members from that era and a couple of them were Ole's neighbors. I hope you can tell me if any of these family names are the maiden names of any residents.

Howard studied the plat drawing for a moment, then looked at me. He drew a deep breath and blew it out. "If I connect these names to someone here, am I 'outing' them in some way?"

"Howard, I honestly don't know. Maybe. But they may be unconnected."

He handed me the plat drawing. "What are you going to do with the information?"

"I hope to have a private conversation with the women who were neighbors."

Howard nodded. "And you hope one of them will admit they were the child's mother and killed Ole Lundquist."

He put it so succinctly, but bluntly that I questioned my own plan. "It sounds pretty heartless when you say it out loud."

Howard stood, opened the door, then stopped. "You're not accusing anyone of Ole's murder." He waited for me to nod my agreement. "You're only trying to identify the mother of a premature baby who died outside a hospital."

"Agreed."

Howard nodded. "I was in Korea at the time of Ole's murder, so I don't have any direct knowledge of his killer, or of anyone he may have impregnated." He took a deep breath and blew it out, then stepped into the office and closed the door. "Genevieve Lang's maiden name was Steel." He opened the door and walked away.

I flashed back to the one love letter I'd read. It had been signed simply with the letter "G." Then I thought about the poem to Viv Steel in the cigar box and her name on the band roster.

I looked at the resident list and found Genevieve's room number, then walked to her apartment. I paused before knocking, questioning my own plan and motives, and weighing them against the impact it might have on someone's life.

My knock was answered by a quiet, "Come in."

Genevieve's apartment was spartan, with worn furniture and a few ceramic knickknacks on the shelves. Although spartan, the whole apartment was clean and neat.

She smiled, a look I feared would quickly fade.

"Peter, how nice of you to stop by. Do you have a moment to sit down?"

I sat on a threadbare couch across from the chair Genevieve sat in.

"I need help solving a mystery."

"Certainly. Has someone been stealing candy from the dish by the receptionist again?"

"I'm afraid this one is much older and darker."

"Oh, dear. What is it?"

"I've been helping Len Rentz investigate the Lundquist murder."

"It's been the talk of the town. Everyone in the dining room was talking about it until you put an end to the gossip."

"We searched Ole's house yesterday and found an old coal bin where Ole used to make moonshine."

Genevieve nodded, but didn't comment.

"You knew he was making moonshine."

"It wasn't much of a secret. Half the men in Two Harbors lined up when Ole had a batch. The police chief was always the first one. I heard he got the first bottle of every batch and five dollars in protection money."

"We found a cigar box of poems and love letters. We also found the body of a premature baby hidden in a trunk."

She nodded but didn't comment.

"Did you happen to write Ole a letter when you were in college?"

Genevieve stared at me, apparently weighing her answer. "That was a long time ago, Peter."

"You dodged my question."

"And if I did?"

"I heard you went to college in St. Cloud. Weren't most graduates teachers back then."

"I had a one-room school down by Quamba until they merged with the Ogilvie school district and closed the school."

"Is that when you moved back to Two Harbors?"

"I was out of work and moved in with my father, who was living in Duluth. I didn't move back here until I married one of my high school classmates in 1956."

"Did you have an affair with Ole before you went to college?"

"Again, I'd ask you what difference it makes. That was a long time ago. Ole's dead and so is my husband."

"Then it doesn't make any difference if you tell me."

Tears formed in her eyes. "Peter, I'm already an outcast. I don't need to become a complete pariah."

"It makes little difference if you weren't the killer, and I assume you weren't."

Genevieve reached for a tissue and wiped her eyes. "No, I didn't kill Ole. I thought we were in love, but now I know it was just a stupid schoolgirl infatuation."

"Were you living at home when Ole was killed?"

She shook her head. "I was at St. Cloud Teacher's College then. I graduated in '52."

"Thank you." I said as I stood. "None of this will go any further." I stopped as two other tidbits came to mind.

"One of the Steel girls was gone from school for a while. The school secretary thought she might've gone away to have a baby and give it up for adoption. One of the poems we found was to Viv Steel."

Genevieve's eyes turned to ice. "You can leave now," she said in a voice I'm sure she used on unruly students.

"There's a Viv Steel who was also in the city band. Was your nickname Viv?"

"My father and sister were in the band. Dad played trombone and Viv played the flute."

"Your sister was Viv?"

"Yes, Vivian Steel."

To say a light went on in my head would be an understatement. I was struck by a lightning bolt.

"Your sister and Ole…"

Genevieve got up and took my elbow. "I asked you to leave."

"They're dead, and we can put a murder to rest," I said as she led me to the door.

"I don't intend to sully their memory." I stopped at the doorway. "Can the police take a DNA swab from you to compare to the baby?"

Genevieve nearly pushed me into the hallway. She glared at me, then looked down the hallway both directions. "I like it here. If you reveal…"

I put up my hand. "You'll always be welcome here."

"Not if I'm a pariah and no one will talk to me."

"You have nothing to do with any of this. It was your father."

Genevieve shook her head. "My father had nothing to do with..." She stopped short, realizing she'd been about to divulge the secret.

"Your mother knew about Vivian's pregnancy."

"It doesn't matter," she hissed. "You're not from here. You don't understand that the sins of the family taint everyone."

My mind buzzed with the possibilities but decided on the most likely scenario and threw it out. "I suppose your mother was a teacher too. Did she like poetry?"

"Yes, she taught in a one-room schoolhouse in Silver Bay. I don't know what that has to do with anything."

"Did she write as well as read poetry?"

"She read Louisa May Alcott and Longfellow to us as children."

"She wrote the poems in the time capsule intending to point the finger away from Vivian."

"I'm sure my mother thought..."

"Your mother brought the baby to Ole to confront him and expected him to bury the evidence. But he didn't. I suppose he blackmailed her."

"Can't you leave well enough alone? It's bad enough that the whole thing got dredged up again. Mom should've thrown the gun in the lake instead of trying to..."

"Instead of hiding the gun and clues in a time capsule she thought would expose Ole as the lecherous old man he was and have people think he was involved with someone other than your sister. Did you know the time capsule poems spelled out Sarah Simpson's and Joanne Post's names?"

Genevieve shook her head. "I didn't even know there was a time capsule box."

"The poems were acrostic. The first letter of each stanza spelled out a name. We found another poem in a cigar box that spelled out Viv Steel."

Genevieve nodded. "You know what Ole did after Mom confronted him? He didn't bury the stillborn baby, he embalmed it in moonshine! Then he taunted mother, threatening to leave the baby on the courthouse steps and expose Vivian as a whore."

She turned away from me without closing the door. I heard her sob as she collapsed into her chair.

I closed the door and sat on the couch. "Where's Vivian now?"

"She bled to death after the baby delivered. Mom couldn't take her to the hospital because she didn't want anyone to know Vivian was pregnant. Mom lied to Daddy and paid the mortician to cover it up."

"The mortician was the coroner too."

Genevieve nodded. "I don't know what the death certificate said, but it was a lie."

"How long did your mother endure Ole's blackmail?"

Genevieve shrugged. "I don't know. Weeks. A month. Maybe longer. Eventually she

296

ran out of pin money she'd been hiding from my father."

"Where'd she get the gun?"

"I don't know. It wasn't one my father had. I suppose she got it from one of my uncles."

"What happened to your mother?"

"She died of grief while I was teaching. She stopped eating and wasted away. Daddy sent me a telegram and I took the train home for the funeral. No one but the family attended."

"The baby deserves a proper burial."

Genevieve nodded, weighing my words.

"Do you have family I should call to help you now?"

She waved me off. "I'll let them know. Where is she, my...niece?"

"Her body is in the Eveleth morgue. Do you want me to call a funeral home?"

Genevieve glared at me. "I think you've done quite enough."

I closed the door as I left.

I called Len, who answered immediately. "I know who baby Jane Doe is and who killed Ole Lundquist."

"What? How? Who?"

"I'll call Kerry and meet him at your office."

* * *

I filled in the pieces for Len and Kerry, everything from Ole's moonshine operation, including bribing the police, hiding the body of the stillborn baby, and blackmailing Genevieve's mother until she killed him and planted the evidence in the time capsule. Then we brainstormed how to keep a lid on the information. Len agreed to close out the police report and bury it where it'd never be found. Len also called Eveleth and cancelled the post-mortem, then asked Dr. Olson to release the remains when she was contacted by the family.

I looked from Len to Kerry. "There's nothing but pain that'll come from this if the information gets beyond us." They both nodded.

Kerry and I got up to leave, but Len stopped us. "Kerry, Peter's my best investigator, but he won't take a job with the police department. Will you?"

Kerry glared at Len. "I don't need charity."

Len stood and stepped between Kerry and the office door. "Sit down, soldier."

Kerry ground his teeth but sat.

"Tell me about your role in Army CID."

"I already told you. I investigated major crimes on Army bases."

"You're weren't a lowly PFC."

Kerry shook his head. "No. Most investigators were long-time sergeants who got specialized training or came into the Army with criminology degrees."

"Which were you?"

"I had a degree and came in through ROTC."

"Should I be addressing you as Captain Stone?"

Kerry shook his head. "We mostly worked without rank designation."

"But you'd been in the Army for a decade. Your pay grade was O-3 or O-4, right?"

Kerry looked at me like I was the source of his pain. "I was an O-4. What difference does it make?"

Len leaned on his desk. "I've got an opening for a police officer and I'm having a hell of a time getting someone with experience to accept a job here in the frozen tundra. You live here, you're an experienced investigator with a criminology degree, and you've got military experience that makes people immediately respect and trust you."

Kerry tried to interrupt, but Len put up his hand. "I'm not offering you charity. I'm offering you a job that you're qualified for. You've earned my respect and I think you'll be a good addition to the police force. You might be in line for my job when I retire in a couple years if you impress the city council as much as you've impressed me."

Len pulled a badge out of his drawer and slid it across the desk. "You can walk out, and that's certainly your right, but I'd be pleased if you'd pin it on."

Kerry stared at the badge, then looked at me. "Did you set me up?"

"I had nothing to do with this."

Kerry picked up the badge and fingered it, then slipped it in his shirt pocket. "Can I show this to my wife and answer you tomorrow?"

Len stood. "Of course."

Chapter 16

We'd watched a couple shows, then told Jeremy to shut the TV off and get ready for bed. We were walking through the dining room toward the stairway. Jeremy was arguing that it was Christmas break and he should be able to stay up later.

The sound of rattling in the kitchen silenced all of us. I turned on the kitchen light and looked toward the counter where I'd set the Corelle butter dish before covering it. The cover was shaking with an otherworldly irregularity, as if some unseen force was trying to lift it. With my heart pounding, I walked across the room. Jeremy was hiding behind Jenny by the dining room door and peeking around her leg.

I lifted the cover, which was vibrating under my touch. A butter covered mouse ran out, scooted across the counter, then slid down the cabinets. He slid across the kitchen floor struggling to get friction with his buttery feet.

Jeremy took two steps, lunged and caught it. It squirmed and when he squeezed to get it under control the mouse squirted out of his hands like a buttered rocket. Jenny grabbed the broom and was trying to sweep it toward the back door when she stepped in the butter trail and her feet went out from under her. She struggled to get up, but every time she pushed, her hands hit butter and she fell on her stomach. Jeremy made another lunge for the mouse but slipped and slid across the floor as if on ice. The terrorized mouse made his escape under the basement door. I braced myself against the counter, trying not to laugh because every guffaw gave me stabbing rib pain.

Jenny pushed herself into the corner and got up, looking for something to wipe her hands on. I threw her a kitchen towel, not wanting to slip on the buttery floor and add to my rib pain. Jeremy rolled around the floor, then got up. For him, the slipping and sliding was fun.

Jenny wiped her hands and laughed when Jeremy, sliding like he was on ice, hit a dry spot in the floor and pitched forward.

I looked at Jeremy, trying to be stern. "How did a mouse get under the butter cover? I'm sure I covered it securely after I took it off the table."

We both looked at Jeremy who shrunk back. "I had a biscuit. I thought I set the cover on top." He hesitated. "It might not have been tight."

I took a deep breath and smiled at Jeremy and Jenny. "I think we've found the ghost. I'll go back to the hardware store and buy some mouse traps tomorrow." Jenny resumed shuffling across the floor, wiping up butter as she moved.

We put Jeremy in his bed with low expectations that he'd fall asleep soon. Back downstairs, we mopped the floor until it wasn't slippery.

Jenny locked the bedroom door behind us, and we climbed into bed. She snuggled against me and kissed me gently. "How are your ribs?"

"They only hurt a little now the adrenaline has worn off."

Jenny shook her head. "You may be the first husband to ever beg off consummating his marriage because of his ribs hurt too badly."

I pulled her close. "My ribs aren't that bad."

The bedroom doorknob rattled and I closed my eyes.

"What dear?" Jenny asked.

"I can't sleep. Can I crawl into bed with you guys?"

I was laughing, causing more rib pain, when Jenny unlocked the door and let him in.

Jeremy climbed in bed between us and snuggled in. "Dad, you were brave."

"When was that?"

"When you picked up the butter cover. I thought a ghost was going to fly out, like in the movies."

"I was pretty sure there wasn't a ghost under the cover."

Jeremy took my hand and intertwined his small fingers with mine. "I'm really glad you're my dad. I don't think anyone else's dad would've been as brave as you."

We lay quietly until the kicking started, then Jenny and I retreated to Jeremy's bed.

"You know, we could just swap bedrooms with him."

Jenny shook her head. "You know that wouldn't work."

I was just about asleep when I thought about the Christmas stocking hanging from the fireplace mantel.

I sat up. "I don't have anything for you."

"Santa is bringing me a beautiful watch."

"Really? Santa will be very surprised when you open it."

Chapter 17

After breakfast I climbed the attic stairs and carried Dolores' boxes of Christmas decorations down to the living room. Jenny dusted off the box tops while I got a second load. Jeremy was sitting next to Jenny on the floor. He was almost vibrating with excitement.

"What do you think is in the boxes?"

"It's a surprise for all of us."

She opened the first box as I set the final two on the floor. I sat next to Jeremy and Jenny pulled out a piece of cardboard wound with many loops of outdoor Christmas lights, with big incandescent bulbs. The box had three sets of lights, all neatly wound up and carefully placed in the box. She pulled out a final piece of cardboard, fresh from the hardware store, with six spare bulbs in factory cut outs. The price tag said they'd cost twenty-nine cents.

I took a deep breath. "As a kid, I remember spending hours replacing bulbs, trying to find the one burned out bulb in the string."

Jeremy took one board from Jenny. "What do you mean?"

"If one bulb is burned out, none of them light up."

I took the string of lights from Jenny and carried them to the outlet next to the fireplace. I plugged it in, the lights flickered, then went dark. Jeremy and I spent the next ten minutes exchanging bulbs until the string lit up.

Jeremy pumped his fist. "Yay! Where are we going to hang it?"

Jenny handed me the next string. "Let's get them all lit, then we can take them outside and decide which tree should be decorated."

There were two burned out bulbs in the next string, and Jeremy was getting bored with the process by the time we got them to light.

I took the third string from Jenny. "Maybe this string will go faster." I plugged it into the wall.

Sparks flew out of the socket and the room went dark. I got up, then saw an ember glowing in the Christmas tree. I threw myself on the tree, knocking it over and breaking ornaments. Jeremy jumped back and Jenny held her hands up. I lay there for a second, feeling the pain of my ribs, followed by the pain of hot pine embers against my stomach.

"Get water!"

Jenny raced to the kitchen. I heard cupboards slamming, then the sound of running water. She was next to me, pouring water on the smoldering pine embers.

I lay on my back, trying to catch my breath.

"Why'd you knock the tree over, Dad?"

Jenny knelt next to me and pulled up my t-shirt, examining the spot that had been against the embers. She grabbed the pitcher and poured the last of the water on my stomach.

"Get into the shower and let the water run over your skin for at least five minutes."

Jeremy looked lost. "What happened?"

Jenny pulled me to my feet. "Your dad got burned when he put out the fire on the Christmas tree."

"What fire on the Christmas tree?" Jeremy asked as he followed us upstairs.

I threw my cellphone and wallet on the bed, then stepped into the bathtub and turned on the cold water.

Jenny stood next to Jeremy and watched the water run down my chest and onto my jeans. "The sparks from the wire set the tree on fire. Dad laid on top of it to smother it."

"The tree caught fire?"

I shivered under the cold shower. "Just a little bit of it. We're lucky the band gave us a freshly cut tree. A dry tree would've gone up like a torch."

Jenny pulled Jeremy close. "We're lucky your dad acted so quickly. Otherwise we could've had a big fire."

"Like one with fire trucks and stuff?"

"With fire trucks, smoke, and a lot of damage to the house."

I turned off the water and dripped on the bathmat. Jenny handed me a towel and I dried myself off, then took off my shoes and jeans.

Standing in my sodden underwear, I let Jenny examine the quarter-sized burn on my abdomen.

"It's starting to blister. It's going to hurt, but it's not going to leave a scar."

Jeremy stared at the burn, then at my near naked body. I was chilled and had goose bumps on my arms and legs. Jenny scooted him out of the bathroom and got a dry t-shirt and underwear for me, then closed the bathroom door. I heard their muffled conversation while I dried off and changed my boxers. I pulled the belt out of my jeans and hung it over the shower rod, then threw the wet shirt, jeans, socks, and tennis shoes into the tub.

I was sitting on the bed, pulling on a dry pair of jeans when Jeremy stood next to me.

"Mom said the house might've burned down if you hadn't knocked the tree over and laid on it."

"I don't know that it would've been that bad."

Jeremy lifted my shirt, reached out and gently touched the blisters on my stomach. "Do they hurt?"

I nodded and pulled on dry socks.

"Why did you...did you know you were going to get burned?"

"I didn't think about it."

Jenny sat next to me and took Jeremy's hand. "Sometimes we do important things without thinking about the consequences. Your dad saw the sparks and reacted so the tree wouldn't burn."

Jeremy nodded his understanding and I pulled the t-shirt down.

Jenny got up and I heard her rustling around in the medicine cabinet. She came out with a roll of medical tape and a package of gauze pads. She lifted my shirt and told me to lie down. Jeremy crawled onto the bed and watched her tape gauze over my blisters.

I pulled my shirt down. "We should unplug the lights and change the fuse."

I heard Jenny put the lights in the waste basket as Jeremy and I went to the basement fuse box. I found the partial box of spare fuses, let Jeremy determine which fuse was burned out and replace the bad fuse.

"The lights are on!" Jenny called from upstairs. Jeremy beamed at having mastered fuse replacement.

Jenny had the tree upright and was sweeping up the broken ornaments when Jeremy and I got upstairs.

Jeremy picked up the strings of good lights. "Are we going to put up the outside lights?"

Jenny put the broom away. "Let's open the other boxes first."

We found tree ornaments and filled in the blank spaces on the tree. One box had strings of incandescent tree lights which I took to the wastebasket without testing. The final, smaller box was taped shut. Jenny got a scissors from the kitchen and cut the tape. Jeremy was busy hanging ornaments when we opened the box.

He looked back when Jenny gasped. "What, Mom?"

Jenny gently lifted a plastic angel with a golden cardboard cone base. The aura around her head was made from fiberglass strands that glowed in the light coming through the windows.

Jeremy looked at the angel "What is it?"

Jenny pushed herself up from the floor with the angel in one hand. "Jeremy, this is the finishing touch to our tree. Dolores left us a beautiful angel that goes on the top."

I reached out for the angel, planning to put it in place, but Jenny stopped me.

"Is there a step ladder in the garage?"

I caught her meaning and came back with the wooden step ladder I'd used to replace overhead lights for Dolores. I set it next to the tree.

Jenny led Jeremy to the base. "Climb up the ladder."

Jeremy climbed the steps while I steadied the ladder. "You get to put the angel on top."

Jenny put her arm around my waist and pulled herself close as Jeremy carefully set the angel on the treetop. He adjusted it, then looked down to see if it was okay. He saw the tears in Jenny's eyes.

"Why are you crying, Mom?" He asked as he climbed down.

310

Jenny pulled him close, into a family hug. "Because Dolores left us the nicest gift of all."

"The house?" He asked.

"Our first family Christmas with our own angel."

Chapter 18

Sunday was a blur of church, lunch with Barbara and Howard, then hanging the outside lights on the juniper tree. It had special meaning to me. It was the tree being eaten by the moose before it threw me onto the porch, breaking my ribs on the eve of our wedding.

We baked a frozen pizza for supper, setting off the smoke alarm again, and I considered taking a Percocet to counteract the pain induced by the stretching to decorate the juniper, but skipped it hoping for romance later. Jeremy watched two Christmas specials on television. Jenny and I wrote out a few more thank you notes, then we sent Jeremy upstairs to brush his teeth and change.

"He's sleeping in his own bed tonight, "I said, more hopeful than convinced that would actually happen.

Jenny smiled as we climbed the stairs. "We'll start with that plan but be prepared for the usual outcome."

We tucked Jeremy into bed and stood in the hallway. Jenny took my hand. "Are you going to need another pain pill to fall asleep tonight?"

"I'll try without it."

There was a knock on the front door and I could see a blue uniform through the frosted glass next to the door. It was late for a delivery, so I was very curious about who would be there. I was surprised by the Two Harbors policeman's uniform, and it took me a second to process that Kerry was wearing it. He was beaming. The unscarred half of his face was smiling. Jenny joined me at the door.

"You accepted Len's job offer."

"Deb and I talked it over and...I needed something and this is a nice fit. The bad news is I'm the low man on the totem pole, so I'm working the next four nights, including Christmas Eve.

"Congratulations."

"On a more somber note, we just heard from the BCA lab. The rapid DNA screen they did on the baby you found in Ole's basement is a close female relative of Genevieve's. It's probably her niece. That fits the puzzle and Len says he's closing the case and burying the file back in the archives."

I sighed. "Thanks for the closure. I'm happy and sad for Genevieve."

Kerry handed Jenny a wrapped box he'd tucked under his arm. "This is from Len and me. You should open it now."

Jenny ripped off the paper and opened the white box inside. Kerry grinned with anticipation as she pulled back the white tissue paper. Then she laughed.

I had to look over her shoulder. Inside was a ceramic chipmunk.

"Len checked all over town and came up empty. Deb found it on Amazon and requested express shipping to get it here before Christmas."

Jenny hugged Kerry and we wished him a Merry Christmas.

Jenny set the chipmunk on the fireplace mantle. "I think we'll put Chipper here every Christmas."

We wrote out two more thank you notes, addressed them, then went to bed.

Jenny quickly rebuffed my romantic hints as against medical advice, and I was trying to convince myself I could fall asleep without the Percocet but was lying awake, losing the argument. I heard the click of the front door latch along with shuffling noises.

I shook Jenny's shoulder. "Someone's downstairs."

I jumped out of bed and ran for the stairs. The front door slammed before I got to the bottom step, and I heard footsteps on the porch. I flipped on the living room lights. There were wet footprints across the wooden living room floor. I heard a car start and looked out the front window just in time to see brake lights flash down the street. The car turned the corner and accelerated away.

"Peter."

I turned around. Jenny was standing in front of the fireplace. At her feet were a stack of Christmas stockings and a plastic package of screw-in hooks. She picked up the stockings and counted them.

"There are five stockings here." She fingered the tags and cocked her head. "The price tags are from the hardware store."

I pulled her close. "I think Santa's hinting he'd like five more grandchildren."

"Grandchildren?" Revelation swept her. "You knew about this?"

"Santa and I discussed it when he was here."

"Why five?"

"That's how many holes there are for hooks under the mantel."

Jenny ran her fingers under the edge of the mantel, stopping at each hole. "How do you feel about five more kids?"

I kissed her deeply and pulled our hips together. "I think we should plan for one more stocking and see how it goes from there."

Jenny smiled but pushed me away. "We can have this discussion, but we're still not going to engage in 'bedroom gymnastics' until your ribs are healed."

We walked up the stairs holding hands. "They don't hurt that bad."

"It sounds like someone still thinks he's up to consummating the marriage tonight." We stopped at the side of the bed and Jenny held my hand. "Take a deep breath."

I hesitated but knew Jenny wouldn't let me dodge the test. I took a breath and let it out.

"Take a *deep* breath."

I inhaled and a sharp pain shot into my ribs. I tried to hide it but gasped in pain.

Jenny shook her head. "You're still under doctor's orders to avoid bedroom gymnastics."

She left the bedroom door open, went into the bathroom, and locked the door. I climbed into bed. She came out with her face freshly scrubbed, still wearing a long flannel nightshirt that ended at her ankles. She put the five Christmas stockings and hooks in the nightstand, climbed into bed, and snuggled into my arms.

I kissed her gently. "We could see if your Mom and Dad will have Jeremy over for New Year's Eve. We'll open a bottle of wine and you can model your honeymoon nightie."

Jenny smiled. "Broken ribs don't heal in a week. Maybe we should plan for Valentine's Day."

"Let's buy a couple wide Ace bandages and you can wrap me up like a mummy and I'll let you take advantage of me."

"Mmm. Sex with a mummy. Gee, that sounds so romantic."

"I'm not talking about my *whole* body. We'd leave the pertinent parts uncovered."

I tried to kiss her, but she pushed me away. "Go take a cold shower. It feels like the *pertinent part* is overly interested right now."

316

I felt breath on my neck and turned. Jeremy's face was inches from my nose. "Dad, do you think Chipper is okay?"

Jenny laughed and pushed my shoulder. "Yeah, Peter, do you think Chipper is okay?"

"Chipmunks live in brush piles all the time. I'm sure Chipper is snuggled up with his friends, sleeping the winter away."

"You're sure?"

"I'm sure."

Jeremy nodded and walked out of our bedroom. I heard his bed springs squeak and rolled back against Jenny's side. "I think we've turned a corner."

She pushed me away. "He may be sleeping in his room, but your *pertinent parts* aren't going anywhere near my *pertinent parts* until your ribs are healed."

"But dear, we can skip vigorous bedroom gymnastics. I'll let you…"

"You'll let me what? You're going to lay there quietly while I make you happy? I don't think so. I want to make love, not feel like I'm having 'bedroom gymnastics' with a mannequin. I think we should aim for Valentine's Day."

"But that's two months away!"

She rolled away from me. "Valentine's Day."

I tried to take a deep breath to let out a dramatic sigh but got another stabbing pain.

"See! Go take a pain pill and focus on Valentine's Day."

I was nearly asleep, my mind in a Percocet haze, when accordion music drifted upstairs.

Jenny sat up. "I wish Jeremy would leave that old accordion alone."

I grabbed her arm. "Listen. That's not Jeremy."

"O Holy Night," was quietly coming up the stairwell, played by an accomplished accordionist. Chills ran down my spine. I got out of bed and pulled on pants and slippers. A pipe organ joined the accordion as Jenny pulled on her bathrobe.

We stopped at the top of the stairs. The accordion was coming from downstairs, but the pipe organ seemed to be coming from down the hallway. I walked to the room overlooking the porch with Dolores's collections and put my ear to the door. The organ seemed to be playing inside the room. I looked at Jenny, who appeared terrorized. I opened the door, but the room was empty, although the organ continued to play.

Jenny whispered. "There's no organ in the room."

I grabbed her hand and led her downstairs and turned on the dining room light. The accordion case was unopened and the music seemed to be coming from the living room. I stood by the tree in the darkened room with Jenny gripping my hand.

I listened for a moment. "It's coming from the porch."

Jenny opened the front door. A gray-haired man was sitting on the top step playing with his eyes closed. He had one foot on the top step and the other foot a step down. He didn't acknowledge us as he continued with the song.

The organ music was coming from the end of the porch, under the window with Dolores' collections. I stepped onto the porch with Jenny against my back. A CD player sat on the end of the porch, the organ music playing loudly from its speaker. A tuba joined the song from the other end of the porch. I turned and saw Brian Johnson standing in the shadows. Then came a trumpet, a flute, a clarinet, a saxophone, and a baritone horn. Musicians stepped out of the shadows at the ends of the porch and walked to the sidewalk as they played. Our very own flash mob.

The organ stopped, and the accordion player opened his eyes and looked up at us. I recognized him from the wedding reception. He stood and offered his hand to me. "I'm Ron Peterson."

We shook hands as the CD player started playing "Deck the Halls."

Ron joined on the accordion and walked down the steps to the sidewalk with the other musicians. Porch lights came on next door and down the block. Neighbors stepped outside wrapped in coats and bathrobes. When the song ended the neighbors clapped.

Brian handed his tuba to the flute player. "We figured we owed you a couple more Christmas carols. Since we'll be with our families until Christmas Eve, we decided to serenade you now."

"Brian, you scared us half to death. We thought the ghosts were playing an accordion and organ."

Brian smiled and turned to Ron. "Mission accomplished!"

Jenny pushed past me and hugged Brian. "You're an angel."

Brian's eyes twinkled. "I've been called a lot of things, but angel isn't among them."

We shook hands with all the musicians and closed the door. Jenny snuggled in my arms, carefully avoiding my ribs.

"A new husband, a new haunted house, a new life, and a wedding no one will ever forget. It's going to be hard to top this December."

I looked at the crooked tree with its mix of old and new decorations, Jeremy's stocking hanging from the mantle, and the ceramic tree glowing next to the front window. "And a Christmas we'll never top."

"I'd hate to think this is the best Christmas we'll ever have."

"How could Christmas be better than this?"

Jenny got a flat box from under the tree and handed it to me. "Open this one now, while Jeremy isn't around."

I had visions of inappropriate underwear, then wondered what embarrassing thing my very proper wife wouldn't want our son to see. I pulled off the ribbon, tore off the wrapping paper and gently opened the box. I was looking at a family tree with Jenny and me linked, and Jeremy underneath.

"That's nice," I said.

"Look at the rest of the pages."

I flipped the page and read the signed final adoption decree, making Jeremy officially my son. The third page was Jeremy's revised birth certificate: Under father it said, "Peter Rogers."

I flipped through the pages again, then looked at Jenny through my tears.

"There's another page in the box."

I pulled out a sheet that looked like a printout of an x-ray. "What is it?"

"It's a sonogram of our baby. Merry Christmas, daddy."

The End

If you enjoyed this book, please leave a review.

2019 Bestselling Author
Dean L. Hovey

Dean Hovey is the bestselling and award-winning author of the Doug Fletcher mystery series, the Whistling Pines cozy series, and the Pine County mystery series. His travel and scientific background bring richness to his stories. One reviewer said, "His character development is outstanding, and the dialog reads like an afternoon over a couple of beers." Dean and his wife split their year between northern Minnesota and Arizona.

BWL Publishing

bwlpublishing.ca

Made in the USA
Monee, IL
21 April 2022